DEVIL'S GUARD
BLOOD & SNOW

First published in the United Kingdom in 2011 by Swordworks Books

ISBN 978-1-906512-78-1

Typeset by Swordworks Books
Printed and bound in the UK & US
A catalogue record of this book is available from the British Library

Cover design by Swordworks Books
www.swordworks.co.uk

DEVIL'S GUARD
BLOOD & SNOW

ERIC MEYER

FOREWORD

This is a story that for a number of reasons, was almost never told. The epic victory of the Soviet Armies at Stalingrad was an event as momentous to the Germans as it was to the Russians, though for different reasons. Five months later, the greatest tank battle in the history of armoured warfare took place at Kursk, resulting in the destruction of much of Germany's irreplaceable armour. Yet in between these two great events there were many bloody battles, much of them taking place in and around Kharkov where constant attack and counterattack took its toll of the warring armies. It was into this maelstrom that Jurgen Hoffman began his military career and this story has been compiled from notes taken during that time. Incomplete notes, to be sure, and much of the surrounding material had to be completed from a great deal of separate and sometimes unrelated research. Yet what has emerged is an account that is essentially correct in its treatment of the war on the Eastern Front, capturing the brutality, the futility and man's inhumanity to man. There is also the involvement of the Sicherheitsdienst and the Geheime Staatspolizei, the Gestapo, the omniscient organisation whose shadowy tentacles reached to the very borders of Germany's conquests, even to the battlefront.

This is the first posting for Untersturmfuhrer Jurgen Hoffman, a posting that almost never takes place when his train is attacked by Russian fighter-bombers. Yet he survives and goes on to find that he has all of the necessary skills to make a ruthless soldier. Suicidal bravery, a cool head under fire and the determination to press home a stalled attack if he feels it has a chance of success. There were soldiers like Hoffman in every army that participated in the Second World War and there have been in war from the dawn of history until the present time. Men who possess that uncanny, natural ability to be hard, skilled fighters yet manage to do so without losing their own humanity. In telling this story, perhaps it would not be overreaching to suggest that I am telling the story of many of them and many yet to come. Soldiers do not start wars, politicians do. Soldiers only fight them and let us hope that those who do may fight with honour and respect for the lives of those who are but innocent bystanders.

INTRODUCTION

After the fall of Stalingrad, the Soviet Armies fought with renewed vigour on the Eastern Front. Not only was their morale lifted by the defeat of von Paulus' Sixth Army, but they were constantly reinforced by new supplies of weapons, armour and even whole new armies. The T34 tank had made its debut on the battlefield for the first time and was seen to be the weapon that could compete on the battlefield with the largest of the German Panzers, especially after the new 75mm gun was fitted. Yet the Germans were far from beaten. They perceived, correctly, that a substantial part of the force that was bled dry at Stalingrad was composed of inferior foreign troops, Italians, Hungarians, Romanians and other non-German nationalities. To the battlefields of the Ukraine they brought fresh troops and armour, in particular the debut of the much-awaited Tiger tank that was prophesied to be the deciding factor in future armoured confrontations. These factors were the background to the conflict that took place around Kharkov and Kursk, both important transport hubs and railheads that the Russians and Germans alike viewed as essential strategic targets.

There were two other factors of course that made such a difference, the Soviet and German leaders, Stalin and Hitler. Stalin had wisely realised, somewhat belatedly, that the battlefield should be under the control of his generals rather than himself, major historical figures like Zhukov and Timoshenko. On the opposing side, Hitler was still very much in control of his armies seeing himself as the military genius that his sycophantic inner circle constantly assured him he was. German Army Group South was under the command of Field Marshal Erich von Manstein and included such charismatic leaders as Paul Hausser, commander of the First SS Panzer Corps. They were constantly hampered by Hitler's irrational orders to hold ground at all costs and several times were forced to risk debacles such as the one that occurred at Stalingrad, when Hitler refused to allow whole armies to withdraw to avoid encirclement. The resultant chaos could only benefit the Soviets, on the German side the commanders often risked demotion and even imprisonment for simply taking the correct military decisions to avoid their troops being wiped out.

The result was that the battle continually swirled

between attack and counter attack. Cities were taken, lost, and retaken and all the time the German forces were constantly being bled of vital men and equipment. The Soviets lost substantially more men and equipment, but were in a position to replace it, which the Germans were not. Into this potent and lethal mix the young Jurgen Hoffman arrives, a newly commissioned Waffen SS officer who has only one goal, to be a successful fighting soldier. In order to pursue his ambition he has more than just the Soviets to fight. He becomes embroiled in the machinations of the SD and the Gestapo as they follow their own dark agenda. The result is an epic struggle as he fights to defend himself, his friends and even the girl he falls in love with, from the dark forces of both sides that threaten to engulf the Eastern Front in a cauldron of agony and blood.

CHAPTER ONE

'Without consideration of "traditions" and prejudices, Germany must find the courage to gather our people and their strength for an advance along the road that will lead this people from its present restricted living space to new land and soil, and hence also free it from the danger of vanishing from the earth or of serving others as a slave nation.'

Adolf Hitler, Mein Kampf

I straightened my tunic as the train steamed into the station. I felt slightly nervous, it was my first assignment, to the Waffen SS Panzer Grenadier Regiment Deutschland, part of the famous Das Reich Division. The platform was crowded with men, all soldiers, like me, they were heading for the Eastern Front. Perhaps I should have been rather more nervous, if the stories coming from the numerous returning soldiers, many wounded, were to be believed. But at nineteen I was only keen to join my unit and get into the thick of the fighting. Untersturmfuhrer Jurgen Hoffman, the three pips of my new rank on my collar tab, the lighting runes of the Waffen SS on the other. I brushed a tiny piece of lint from my field grey tunic, checked that everything was in order. Jackboots gleaming, trousers correctly aligned, belt buckle adorned with our motto 'Meine Ehre heisst Treue', my honour is my loyalty, polished metal shining, black leather belt and holster containing my issued Walther PPK automatic pistol. I felt the rim of my officer's cap, it seemed correct, then the train shuddered to a stop. I picked up my bag and was about to board when a voice stopped me.

"Herr Untersturmfuhrer?"

I looked around, irritated at the intrusion and my spirits dropped a few notches. Damn. An officer was standing there, an SS-Sturmbannfuhrer, but no, not SS. I checked his badges, he was SD, the secret intelligence division of the SS, the Sicherheitsdienst. I clicked my heels and stood to attention.

"Herr Sturmbannfuhrer?"

He was older than me, much older, and held a cane. Wounded, perhaps?

"Could you assist me with my case?"

I looked down, there was a large, heavy-looking leather case next to him.

"Of course, Sir."

I struggled to drag his case onto the train and found a vacant compartment in the officers' section, he followed me in, limping. I pushed the case up to the luggage rack, put my bag up with it, and then sat down. It was rotten luck to have bumped into an SD Major, a policeman or maybe a spy with whom I would presumably have to spend the journey all the way to Russia. Unless he got off the train before, of course, with his limp he would not be going near the Front. Maybe the Fuhrer Headquarters in Eastern Prussia? That seemed a real possibility.

"Your first command?"

He was staring at me, I sat to attention, whatever that was. Anyway, I sat erect.

"Yes, Sir."

"And who will benefit from your undoubted fighting qualities, Untersturmfuhrer?"

Was he mocking me? He reminded me of the old police sergeant in my hometown, he used to speak to me like that when I was about eight years old.

"Second Battalion, SS Panzer Grenadier Regiment Deutschland, Das Reich Division, Sir."

"Ah yes, near Kharkov."

I was surprised, how would he know that? But of course, he was SD. "Yes, Sir."

As I studied him more closely, I saw that he was even older than I had thought, maybe in his fifties.

"Relax, I won't be joining the fighting."

How the hell did he know what I was thinking? Had the SD invented some kind of mind reading technique, perhaps one of the secret weapons the Fuhrer was always referring to?

"Sir, I don't understand what you mean."

"Untersturmfuhrer, I used to be a police inspector in Berlin before I was transferred to the SD. It's my job to understand what people are thinking, it's what I get paid for."

"Yes, Sir."

I felt like a dummy, constantly repeating the same 'Yes, Sir', but as a junior officer I didn't know what else to say, so I played safe. Fortunately, he put his head back and started to doze.

I looked around at my surroundings, at the compartment. It bore little resemblance to the railway carriages I'd travelled in since childhood, they had been smart, clean and in good repair. This one was shabby, ill maintained, a crack in one of the windows, torn upholstery and the floor hadn't been cleaned in a long time. There was a bloodstain on the panelling to the side of the window, I knew that these trains were used to bring casualties back from the Eastern Front. Was it as bad as some people said it was, a mincing machine that sucked in good German soldiers and spat out bleeding, broken men, and corpses? Surely not, any battlefront that was occupied by SS Regiments would certainly be an example of good efficient soldiering, enough to frighten off any enemy that came near. I had learned that much in basic training and before that during my service in the Hitler Youth. Our Waffen SS units were the finest soldiers in the world, our troopers were legendary in every theatre of war that they had fought in, heroes of the newsreels that we watched in the cinemas. As a new officer, I was determined not to let them down, to devote myself absolutely to the service of the Fuhrer, the Reich and the SS. But I glanced uneasily again at the bloodstain.

"Yes, it is as bad as that, young man. It's a very bloody business."

He had woken up and was speaking to me.

"Sir, I've heard the rumours and I don't believe them, there's no way the Russians could inflict those kinds of defeats on our armies."

He smiled. "I can see you believe the propaganda. Listen, ordinarily you would be right. A Russian division tangles with one of our divisions and gets defeated, most of its men killed or wounded, they're no match for us, are they? Agreed?"

I nodded.

"So then the Soviets bring up another division. They get beaten, then another and another. Until we run out of ammunition and suffer so many casualties that we have to pull back."

"So you are saying that they are winning?"

He thought for a moment. "I am saying that they are a hundred kilometres nearer Berlin than they were a week ago. Draw your own conclusions."

It could not be true! Yet I couldn't argue with an SD Sturmbannfuhrer, so I didn't reply.

"You are Untersturmfuhrer, what?"

"Hoffman, Sir, Jurgen Hoffman."

"Good, my name is SD-Sturmbannfuhrer Walter von Betternich. Strange we may be serving in the same area, I have been assigned to investigate a little matter in the Kharkov theatre of operations. A murder, in fact."

"A murder? That seems, well, unusual in a war zone, there must be more than enough killings."

"Crime is crime, my young friend, it is no respecter of geography. Even in theatres of war."

He lost interest then and dozed off again. I went to the door and looked out into the narrow passageway, it was lined with soldiers of all ranks, talking, drinking, some playing cards. Some were silent, contemplating their fate, no doubt. The train lurched to a stop at a wayside station and more soldiers climbed aboard. None came near my compartment, the uniform of an SD Sturmbannfuhrer was a powerful deterrent. I could see troops loading boxes and crates onto the train, there must have been two hundred men passing them from hand to hand in a long chain. I had some time to spare so I got out onto the platform to stretch my legs. At the front of the train, the engine was letting out a small amount of steam as they kept up the boiler pressure. There was a four-barrelled Flak gun behind the coal tender, another at the back of the train manned by steel helmeted Flak gunners, anxiously scanning the sky for signs of a sudden attack. As I watched, they swung the barrels around constantly, searching for a target. There was a sudden flurry of alarm when three aircraft appeared, flying quite low, but they were ours, a Junkers JU52 accompanied by two Messerschmitt 109s. It could have been the Fuhrer, of course, he flew in a JU52 and always with an escort of 109s. I could imagine the gunners hurriedly taking their fingers off the triggers. An accident of that kind, to fire at the Fuhrer's personal aircraft, would be unthinkable. However, maybe it was just another Nazi bigwig, it was impossible to tell.

I got back on the train and walked back to my compartment, the SD Sturmbannfuhrer was still alone. I was about to sit down when there was another flurry of excitement in the corridor, a hubbub of excited shouting and noise erupted. I went out to see what the fuss was about, a young SS private approached me excitedly.

"It's Stalingrad, Sir."

The epic siege on the Volga, the talk of all Germany, von Rundstedt's heroic but encircled Sixth Army fighting off several Soviet armies, supplied only by the Luftwaffe flying around the clock missions to take them food and ammunition.

"Yes, what is it? Have they broken out, is it a victory?"

"They've surrendered, Stalingrad has fallen!"

It was as if I suddenly stood in an icy rainstorm. It was impossible, surely, the largest army that our German armed forces had ever put into the field.

"Are you sure?"

"Certain, yes. They are marching off into captivity, it's on the news from Berlin. They're playing those Wagner tunes with the announcements, you know, the funeral marches. It's terrible."

I shook him off and went into my compartment. Von Betternich looked up.

"Stalingrad?"

I nodded. "Yes, Sir, apparently they've surrendered."

"Of course they have, what else could they do?"

I looked at him astonished. "They could have fought on like German soldiers."

He raised an eyebrow. "Without food, without ammunition, in thirty degrees below zero with no warm clothing, how would they do that?"

"But Reichsminister Goering assured them that he would keep them supplied by air."

He smiled. "Then it would seem that the Reichsminister was not telling them the whole truth, would it not?"

I thought it wisest not to reply.

As the train rolled eastwards it started to get very cold,

the train was heated but it wasn't enough to cope with the plummeting temperatures. Even with my greatcoat on and inside the heated compartment I was shivering, I began to understand the kind of problem they had faced in Stalingrad. And in Kharkov, perhaps, the new post where I was taking up my first command. Three times the train had to stop and wait in a siding while westbound trains passed us, all of them carrying casualties, thousands, tens of thousands of casualties, a tidal wave of human misery that had been generated by the Russian steamroller. Von Betternich didn't look at me once while they rolled past, he didn't need to. Without seeing a single shot fired, I was getting a firsthand glimpse of the progress of the war on the Russian Front. Finally, the train stopped at a small wayside station that had been converted into a military transit camp, I got off the train and stepped into my first experience of the Russian snows. It was the SD officer's destination too, I took down his leather case for him. He followed me, treading carefully in the snow with his walking cane. A soldier was waiting for him with a staff car flying the pennants of an SS Gruppenfuhrer, a Major General, von Betternich climbed in and was driven away. I looked around, unsure of where to go. It was chaos everywhere, a squadron of Tiger tanks was parked nearby under clumps of trees. There was a group of tents, that housed the soldiers who guarded the station in the middle of this freezing waste, the poor devils. I was surrounded by a seething mass of soldiers, what the hell was I to do, where was I to go? But as I hunted around in confusion, I heard a voice calling. "Untersturmfuhrer Hoffman, Second Battalion, Deutschland Regiment, where are you, Sir?"

I looked around to see an SS NCO, an Oberschutze, calling my name.

"Here, over here," I waved desperately, trying to make myself seen over the roiling mass of uniformed soldiers. His eyes settled on me and he came over.

"Oberschutze Karl-Heinz Voss, Sir, I've brought you a lift to Regimental Headquarters."

There was no salute, no ceremony, he just grabbed my kitbag and walked off at a fast pace, I had to rush to catch up with him. He led the way to a Kubelwagen and threw my kitbag in the back.

"Jump in, Sir, HQ is about two kilometres away, you'll need to hold on tight, the track is pretty bumpy."

I climbed in and stared at him. He was one of Reichsfuhrer Himmler's elite troopers, a Waffen SS corporal. He was supposed to be the best of the best, the toughest, the fittest of our German racial elite. He didn't look it. He was very thin and he looked half-starved. He was also unshaven and wore wire-framed glasses, his hair was long and greasy, unkempt. His uniform tunic was ragged, ripped and repaired in several places and clipped to the windshield of the Kubi was a very non-standard

Soviet PPSh submachine gun. I recognised it from basic training, when we were shown a variety of captured enemy weapons. His uniform trousers were also non-standard, made of baggy, black leather tucked into what looked like paratroopers lace-up jump boots. In his belt, he carried no less than two pistols in open holsters, like a cowboy from one of those American films. He was like a creature from that Fritz Lang movie Metropolis. I was about to ask him about his appearance when all hell broke loose. He'd leaned forward to start the engine when a siren started to wail, voices shouted. The Flak cannons on the train started to fire, soldiers were running in fear and confusion, diving for cover, exhaust smoke appeared around the Tiger tanks in the nearby wood as they started their engines.

"Get out, get out!" Voss shouted. I was reaching for my kitbag when he dragged me out of the jeep and I followed him as he ran for the cover of some nearby heavy balks of railroad timber. As I threw myself down beside him, the first bomb exploded and I heard an aircraft engine revving hard to climb after its bombing run, I looked up and the next aircraft was already banking towards us to make its own attack.

"Sturmoviks," Voss told me. I nodded, understanding that he meant the Ilyushin Il-2 ground-attack aircraft that we'd learned about. The Il-2 was produced by the Soviets in vast quantities, it was certainly the single most common aircraft on the Russian Front, but we'd been told that they were no match for any of our fighters.

"Where are our aircraft, the Luftwaffe?"

He laughed. "Tied up somewhere else I expect, Sir. There are just too many of these Sturmoviks and we don't have enough fighters to deal with them."

Another bomb dropped nearby, then a third that hit one of the carriages of the train. Dozens of men were sheltering underneath it and when the sound of the aero engines had died away, I heard their screams distinctly.

"Corporal, we should go and help those men."

"You do that and you'll die," he snapped at me as if I was a stupid child. He held onto my tunic but I threw him off to run to help the wounded, just as all three of the Sturmoviks came back in for a strafing pass, bullets hammered all the way along the train and around the station. One of the Flak guns scored a hit and a Soviet aircraft blew up in mid-air, but the others finished their attack, raking the ground with machine gun and cannon fire, then they flew away. I could still hear one or two screams, but they were fainter. They died out completely.

"I think they've gone, we need to get to HQ, Sir."

"Yes."

I felt like a fool, if I'd run to the train I would have been killed. Voss understood what I was thinking.

"They do that, Sir, drop the bombs and then come back in to machine gun the rescuers."

I got in the Kubi and Voss started up and drove away

from the wreckage of the station. We bumped along country lanes, past two Field Police points where we both had to show our papers to grim faced Feldgendarmerie, resplendent in their silver gorgets. Both times we were waved on and soon we arrived at the chaos of SS Panzer Grenadier Regiment Deutschland. It was also the church and monastery of St Basil's, we were outside the town of Korenevo a few kilometres west of Kursk.

The commanding officer, Standartenfuhrer Werner Brandt had little time for me. His office was just inside the front door of the monastery, I clicked my heels and gave an immaculate salute, 'Heil Hitler', as regulations demanded, then stood waiting. He gave me a friendly wave. I'd been told he was thirty-five years old, he looked more like fifty, he was wearing field grey uniform trousers and a camouflage pattern jacket. The reversible kind that could be turned inside out to display the white surface on the outside for winter fighting. On his head he wore a Schiff, the side cap that all ranks of Army and SS troops sometimes wore as a more casual alternative to the regulation headgear. He carried an Erma, the MP38 machine pistol, slung over his chest and half a dozen spare ammunition pouches festooned on his belt. He displayed no visible rank insignia, which I thought strange.

"We're not big on formalities here, Hoffman. I'd cut that 'Heil Hitler' stuff if I were you, it's out of favour here, you see."

Did he mean the salute, or the Fuhrer? I thought it best not to ask.

"I've sent for your platoon senior NCO, Scharfuhrer Willy Mundt. I'm afraid your unit is detailed to carry out a reconnaissance mission, we're mounting a counterattack first thing in the morning and I need your men to do some scouting for us. Don't worry, Mundt will show you the ropes, can you handle it?"

"Yes, Sir."

He nodded. "Good, you jump off at two am. Dismissed."

I went to salute, then gave a more conventional army salute. It seemed strange, I had understood that joining SS Deutschland Regiment was an honour, I was to become part of an elite, crack unit of Panzer Grenadiers. I'd had visions of ranks of immaculately turned out troops, weapons, uniforms and equipment all smart and gleaming. Instead, I felt as if I had arrived in a partisans' camp. The mixture of weapons and clothing was incredible, much of it wouldn't have been out of place in a Russian unit. Scharfuhrer Willy Mundt nodded a greeting as I went outside, he was standing in the snow chatting to a trooper who glanced at me and then went on talking. Like Voss, he was anything but smartly turned out, an ill-fitting tunic with an old blanket wrapped around his shoulders, trousers patched with pieces of leather and jackboots covered with strips of some kind of animal fur. His face was hard, dark, etched with the experiences of a hard life, or maybe that was just too much time spent fighting on the Eastern Front. His eyes were squinted half-closed as if against the glare of the snow, when he looked at me they appeared to be empty of emotion, empty of soul. All at once I felt irritated, maybe he'd had some hard fighting here but it was time to get a grip on my first command.

"Scharfuhrer, don't you salute an officer when he approaches?" I said sharply.

He grinned. "Well, Sir, if that's what you want, of course."

He gave a lazy salute, the trooper stood smiling.

I returned the salute. "Look, we'll never beat the Russians without good discipline, it's important to remember that, the Fuhrer has said so himself."

They both roared with laughter.

"What are you laughing at?"

"The Fuhrer's plan to beat the Russians with salutes," Mundt replied. "Have you ever fought the Russians?" After an insolent pause. "Sir?"

Perhaps I'd deserved the put down and I felt embarrassed. These were veterans of the Winter War, I was just a newcomer, had yet to fire a shot in anger on the Eastern Front. I should have known better and held back. It was time to retrieve the situation.

"You're right, I have not seen any action yet, Scharfuhrer. Believe me, I do know the record of this regiment, I have a lot to learn, I trust that as my platoon NCO you will help me."

He nodded, mollified. "If you're to stay alive you'll need to learn mighty fast. Beating the Russians is not the first concern, Sir. Staying alive, that's all you need to concern yourself with on this Front, at least for now. I'll take you to meet the men, then you'll need to draw equipment and a weapon from the quartermaster."

He picked up my kitbag and led me across the snow-covered ground to the church, my platoon was camped inside, to the side of the main altar. There were ten men apart from Mundt.

"Ten? Where are the rest, Mundt?"

"Dead, Sir, for the most part, some were wounded and shipped back to the Reich, I doubt they'll be back. I'm afraid this is it."

I'd expected thirty men at least. Ten! I wondered how many Russians we were facing, but it wasn't something to dwell on. The men nodded a greeting, none stood up or saluted, they all looked exhausted, ragged, half starved. Were these the elite standard-bearers of the Fuhrer's shock troops? I could hardly believe it.

"I'll introduce you to them individually later, Sir. First, I'll get you kitted out. The platoon commander's bed is here."

He showed me an alcove separated from the main room by an old blanket.

"The previous platoon commander?"

"Dead, Sir. The Soviets were using a Maxim gun when we went in to attack, it took his head off, killed three of the men too, before we got it with a couple of grenades."

He put down my kitbag and I took out my steel helmet and put away my cap. Somehow the smart, officer's cap seemed out of place in this camp of scarecrows. Then we went to the quartermaster, an older SS Scharfuhrer who presided over the unit's stores.

"Right, Untersturmfuhrer, you'll need a weapon, most of the officers and men favour the Erma machine pistol, the CO wouldn't be seen dead without one. Of course, we've got plenty of the Soviet PPSh, if you fancy one of those, but there is a danger you'll be mistaken for the enemy carrying one of them."

"I'll take the MP38, Scharf."

"Good choice. I'll give you plenty of spare magazines, we've had so many casualties that weapons and ammunition are no problem."

If he was trying to reassure me, he was failing miserably. He dragged out a reversible camouflage tunic, the SS pattern with an attached hood there was also a pair of trousers to match. I picked up the tunic and noticed a bloodstain on the front, it had been washed but was still visible. Had this been worn by my unfortunate predecessor? If so, it hadn't done him any good. We went back to the church and I put on the white sided camouflage tunic and trousers. It was cold, bitingly cold and I was glad of the extra clothing. Feeling more like I belonged in this strange place, I went for a walk outside, my boots crunching in the snow. It was early evening and activity had slowed around the camp, most of the soldiers had disappeared inside their shelters.

Only the sentries were in view, stamping around to keep warm. They eyed me warily as I approached, but none offered salutes. I had no officer's insignia showing, they were hidden inside the winter camouflage, but perhaps in this dismal place it would have made no difference. Curiously, there was a small encampment off to one side of the HQ area, a group of monks sat around a blazing campfire. I approached one of the sentries.

"What's the story there?" I asked him, pointing to the monks.

"They own this place," he replied, "or at least they used to. When we took over, they refused to leave, even when the second in command, Sturmbannfuhrer Muller, threatened to have them shot."

I nodded and walked on, it was just one more oddity in this strange new world that I had arrived in. Monks in an SS camp! However, no doubt everything would become clearer as I got to know my way around, it was just a matter of time. I walked back to the church, overhead I could hear the droning of aircraft, the sentries looked up nervously but the planes didn't come near. I went to my billet and Mundt introduced me to the men who were sitting around sharing a bottle of brandy. Sturmmann Josef Beidenberg, Oberschutze Karl-Heinz Voss, the driver who had collected me from the station. Schutze Stefan Bauer and Schutze Dieter Merkel, then I lost track of the names. They seemed friendly enough and there was no standing on ceremony, little if any deferring to me as an officer. We were all Waffen SS, if there was to be any respect it would obviously have to be earned in combat. I remembered we were due to go out at two in the morning to scout the ground prior to the attack, it would be my first test in front of the men, I determined not to mess it up. I went behind the blanket screen and settled down to try and get a little rest, it had been a long and strange journey.

Someone was shaking me, for a moment I thought I was back at home in Germany, then I sat up and felt the biting cold.

"It's time, Sir. We need to go very soon."

Scharfuhrer Mundt was staring down at me, he let go of my sleeve and stood up. "There's a mug of coffee for you and some bread, we're leaving in ten minutes."

I swallowed my embarrassment. I was in command of this platoon yet he was up and awake and I had been sound asleep. I was still fully dressed so I just got up and pushed the blanket aside. The men were clattering around, talking nervously, strapping on their webbing and checking their weapons.

"I thought you'd like a lie in, Sir, you had a long journey," Mundt smiled. I checked my watch, it was one thirty in the morning. He didn't seem to be making a joke. I guess I had enjoyed more sleep than the others before I was woken up, it had indeed been a tiring journey from Germany. I picked up my MP38 and strapped on my belt with the Walther in the holster. Mundt handed me a white webbing set.

"For the spare clips, you'll find them easier to carry."

I thanked him and strapped it on. Then he gave me a white pack. "This was Untersturmfuhrer Fieseler's, he won't need it now."

"Do officers normally carry a pack in this unit?"

"Yes."

He offered no other explanation and I pulled it over my shoulders. Mundt showed me the map.

"This is our objective, all we need to do is scout out the opposition and get back here and report. If we can bring back a prisoner, so much the better. No heroics, no shooting, ok, Sir?"

"Yes."

"I'd better lead, just follow me, you'll be fine."

I didn't feel fine, I felt like a lamb being led to the slaughter. Why the hell was I here? They didn't need me, I was just a passenger. But I was determined to learn so I kept quiet and followed the lead of the laconic Scharfuhrer. We went out past the sentries, Mundt leading, me behind him, then the rest of 'my' platoon. We walked quietly through the snow, no one talked, no one smoked, all I could hear was the crunch of our footsteps in the crisp white crust that covered the ground. We entered a wood and Mundt kept up the pace, only stopping every five minutes or so to listen for sounds of the enemy. Then we came out of the wood and I saw we were at the base of a low rise. Mundt pointed to two of the men and they went swiftly out to the flanks, then we went forward again. We reached the top of the rise, there was no sign of the enemy. Or so I thought. He pointed to a clump of bushes about a hundred metres in front of us. I looked closely, nothing. I looked again and saw a tiny movement, it was the wisp of steam from warm breath meeting cold air. Mundt dropped to the ground and started crawling forward, it was a long, slow crawl. The two flankers were still invisible to me, I just followed his lead and crawled on towards, what? A machine gun nest, an observation post, maybe one or two shivering Soviet riflemen? Or the first in a formation of Soviet T34 tanks? Oh God, no, not on my first mission. We crawled nearer and I heard a muttered conversation, it sounded like Russian. We were within ten metres of the bushes when I saw two shadowy white shapes leap up, one from either side and descend on the enemy. There was the distinct sound of a struggle, a grunt as someone was struck, then silence.

"Come on, we're clear," Mundt whispered. He got up

and ran forward and I joined him with the rest of the men. Two Soviets were in the foxhole, one of them dead with his throat slit, the other apparently unhurt but shaking with terror. He looked to be about my age, what struck me as odd was that he was wearing warm, padded winter clothing, much more suited to the conditions than we had been issued with. That was unexpected, I thought the Soviets were supposed to be more primitive than us, less well equipped.

"Look!" Mundt murmured, he was looking further ahead. I made out irregular shapes, slightly darker objects that stood out from the distant horizon. Tanks. They were about two kilometres away.

"Do you have any idea of how many?" I whispered to him.

"About forty, almost certainly T34s, that's our best guess."

"Shouldn't we get closer and make sure?"

"No. Unless you'd like to go and get yourself killed, Herr Untersturmfuhrer."

I realised I was making a fool of myself in my enthusiasm. But what if there were more tanks, wouldn't we also want to know how many infantry they had in support?

"We need to know, Scharfuhrer. I'll go forward and check it out, I'll need a volunteer to go with me, the rest of you can wait here."

There was silence for a moment, I could imagine their thoughts. A gung-ho new officer, fresh from training school, determined to get them all killed. I didn't care, I felt that it was important to bring back the intelligence.

"I'll go with you."

Sturmmann Josef Beidenberg, I remembered. "Thank you, Beidenberg. Let's go."

I didn't wait for an answer, just climbed out of the foxhole and started creeping forward. Beidenberg was right behind me, I could hear his footsteps crunching in the snow. We were both going slowly, both nervous of hearing a sudden challenge from an unseen sentry, then the burst of gunfire that would scythe through us, but it didn't come. We veered to the south of the line of tanks and worked our way around them, finding a path that led through some trees to give us cover. When we were behind the tanks we saw the Russian encampment, looming suddenly out of the night as the cloud drifted past and moonlight shone down on the steppe. There was at least a division of infantry camped in front of us with their vehicles, motor-rifle troops by the look of them, with towed mobile artillery and rocket launchers.

"I think that's enough, Josef, we'll get back and report what we've seen."

"Sir."

We retraced our steps, after fifty metres we almost ran into two Soviet soldiers. They were walking into the woods hand in hand, their intention obvious. Homosexuality was punished as severely in the Soviet armies as in ours. Both of the men were keeping watch on their own lines and didn't notice us as we waited. We stood behind a tree and when they came abreast of us, I stepped out and simultaneously cocked my machine pistol, Beidenberg had a combat knife ready to use. Both put up their hands, even in the dark I could see that their faces had gone as white at the snow they were walking on.

"Do either of you speak German?"

One of them nodded. "I do," he said shakily.

"Good. You are now our prisoners, if you make a sound you'll both be killed. Clear?"

He nodded and explained it to his comrade who nodded eagerly.

"Let's go, we need to get back as quickly as possible," I said to Beidenberg. "Our people will need to question these two prisoners urgently."

We walked quietly back the way we came to the south of the lines of T34s, each of us with a gun barrel pressed to the backs of the Russians. When we approached the foxhole, I called out softly to the platoon.

"This is Hoffman and Beidenberg coming in with two prisoners."

"Very well."

We joined the platoon and I at least had the satisfaction of seeing the men's awed faces as we displayed our two new prisoners, we now had three in all to take back for interrogation. Despite the cold, the misery and the uncertain start to my new command, I felt I had acquitted myself quite well. I wondered if I'd stay alive for long enough to build on it.

The CO, Standartenfuhrer Brandt was impressed, one of the prisoners turned out to be a Russian major, the other two were private soldiers and they were all led away for interrogation. He turned to me.

"Well done, Hoffman, a good start. Pity there are so many Russians in front of us, we'll have our work cut out. Muller, what's the word on the Panzers?"

Sturmbannfuhrer Muller, the second in command, answered immediately.

"HQ reports we have eleven Tigers operational. We also have a StuGIII that will be deployed as soon as we start the attack."

The StuGIII assault gun mounted a 75mm StuK37 gun and was a formidable tank killer, built on a Panzer chassis it was effective in a number of infantry and armour support roles. It was also known to be much more reliable than the sophisticated and heavily armoured Tiger tank, which could dominate the battlefield but had proved to be prone to breakdowns.

"Anything else?"

"A few mobile artillery pieces, that's about it. We're still waiting for the half-tracks to be delivered, so the Panzer

Grenadiers will have to go in on foot."

Brandt grunted. "Again! It's not enough, Otto, not enough. What if those T34s break through our armour?"

"We've issued Panzerfausts to all units," Muller said hesitantly.

"Panzerfausts! What the hell next, do we start throwing rocks at them, we might as well?" But he nodded. "Forget I said that, Otto. If it comes to it, we'll use the Panzerfausts and hope for the best. Very well, get the men to their jump off points and we'll follow the Panzers in."

I joined my platoon waiting outside the church. We'd had a sleepless night after being assigned to the scouting mission and it looked as if the coming day was going to be an even harder one. No one had said joining the SS was going to be a picnic, though, so I'd have to get used to it. The men had brewed some coffee and I was given a steaming mug of the hot, rich mixture that bore little resemblance to any coffee I'd ever tasted before. There were also a couple of slices of thick, black bread coated with dripping or some kind of animal fat, for breakfast.

"Breakfast or dinner it all looks the same, you'll have to get used to it, Sir," Mundt smiled.

"But look on the bright side, we may not be alive by tonight so we won't have to eat this muck again."

"Isn't that kind of comment bad for morale?" I asked him firmly. It didn't seem a good idea to suggest to the men that we were short of food. But he laughed out loud and the men around him smiled with him, obviously I had a lot to learn. We finished the food, it was indeed foul, then the regiment moved up to the jump off point and I made sure I had everything, MP38, two stick grenades that Mundt had given me and my pack. "You never know when you may need an advantage, Sir," he said as he handed me the grenades.

Water and food in my pack, just bread of course, spare ammunition and a rudimentary first aid kit. Two of the men carried Panzerfausts.

"Schutze Bauer, have you used one of those before?" I asked the private. I'd used one at the training school and I was genuinely interested, it seemed such a tiny weapon with which to stop and destroy a tank.

"You're not serious? I'm still alive, aren't I?" he replied brusquely.

I was puzzled, I was about to ask him what he meant when Mundt put his hand on my shoulder. "Untersturmfuhrer, if the battle comes down to using one of those, you're normally as good as dead already. If you ever score a hit with a Panzerfaust you get awarded a Tank Destroyer Badge. Posthumously!"

"I see."

We marched through the wood, retracing the route our patrol had taken during the night. When we came out the other side, we waited. At first the night was quiet, there was no noise at all. Then in the distance I heard a clanking, mechanical noise. It resolved itself into the roar of powerful engines and the clatter of iron tracks. Suddenly, the Tigers broke out of the wood, eleven of them deployed in a wide line with plenty of space between them. The leading tanks fired, star shells lit up the battlefield, the T34s were now stark, bright targets on the horizon. Even at this distance, I could see the crews scrambling to dive through the turret hatches and prepare to defend themselves. Our Tigers were all firing now, armour-piercing rounds that exploded all around the Russian tank positions. Already three of them were on fire, their ammunition starting to explode, fuel catching fire and crews running for cover. Then five more exploded as our accurate gunfire kept hitting them, but they still outnumbered us by a large margin. Now it was the Russian's turn and they opened fire, high explosive shells landed and lit up the onrushing Tigers. One was hit and started to blaze, the others rushed on. Out of the corner of my eye I saw the STuGIII assault gun clank out of the wood already firing anti-tank rounds at the T34s and more of them exploded as the combined fire of our Tigers and the STuGIII wreaked deadly havoc.

"Let's go, let's go!" I heard the shout along our lines. Whistles blew and we were up and running, I led my men straight towards the enemy positions, we were going to have our work cut out this morning, especially if the Tigers failed to deal fully with all of the T34s. We ran like demons towards the Russian lines, the Soviet infantrymen had advanced and set up firing positions, rifles cracked along their lines, a machine gun started to fire, then another. We had to go more carefully now, dodging from cover to cover, foxhole to foxhole. Fortunately this ground had been fought over before and it was littered with shell holes and trenches in the ground where we could shelter from the continuous gunfire and explosions that swept the battlefield. Two T34s started towards us firing their coaxial machine guns but the STuGIII continuously fired at them and they both exploded, hit by the armour-piercing rounds. Some of our men set up machine gun positions and soon we had four MG34s hammering away at the enemy.

Mundt shouted a warning, as I turned to clarify what he'd said a hand grabbed hold of my tunic and yanked me down into a shell hole. I was about to protest when a T34 swept past us, heading for the STuGIII. Then the T34 was itself hit by one of our Panzers, but when I looked up another Russian tank was bearing down on us heading for the STuGIII tank destroyer.

"Panzerfaust," I shouted.

Bauer was crouched down in the shell hole, looking at me with terrified eyes. I didn't blame him, the Soviet armour was awesome to a soldier on foot but there was no time to be overly worried, I needed to act.

"Give it to me, man."

I ripped the weapon out of his hands and primed it

ready to fire. I squinted over the rim, the T34 was almost on us. As it went past I leapt up, I'd done this in training though never very successfully, but that day the gods of war smiled at me, and my rocket flew true, straight into the vulnerable rear of the tank and I had the satisfaction of seeing it explode.

CHAPTER TWO

"For centuries Russia drew nourishment from this Germanic nucleus of its upper leading strata. Today it can be regarded as almost totally exterminated and extinguished. It has been replaced by the Jew. Impossible as it is for the Russian by himself to shake off the yoke of the Jew by his own resources, it is equally impossible for the Jew to maintain the mighty empire forever. He himself is no element of organization, but a ferment of decomposition. The Persian empire in the east is ripe for collapse. And the end of Jewish rule in Russia will also be the end of Russia as a state."

Adolf Hitler, Mein Kampf

The two officers disappeared into the regimental office and I went into our quarters in the church with the rest of the men. We had no casualties in my platoon, for that at least I was thankful.

"Sir, I've sent Voss to drum up some food, we all need a meal after this morning's work."

I nodded, "Thank you, Scharfuhrer."

Damn, I should have thought of that first, feeding the men, but I was tired, so tired, all I wanted to do was crawl into a hole and sleep for a week. But first things first, I checked my weapons and cleaned and reloaded my MP38. I made sure my water bottle was full, then lay down for a short rest. It was to be very short, Voss brought back some loaves of bread and a container of beef dripping and we sat to enjoy our feast. Mundt brought out a bottle of schnapps, I should have disapproved but I needed it as much as they did. I realised that, to my shame, I was shaking after the action. The food and drink revived me and we sat talking about the action. I tried to underline how well we had done, after all it was my task to maintain morale.

"I know we had to pull back but we seemed to give them a real beating," I said to Mundt.

He smiled. "Look, Sir, think of it this way. They've got two hundred T34s, we've got ten Tigers. That means that every one of our tanks has to knock out twenty of theirs. And even then they'll just bring up another two hundred when they're all gone, we can't replace our losses at anything like that rate."

"What about the Stukas?" I reminded him.

"Yes, the Ju87s are good and they got away with it today. Normally the Russians send up fighters by the dozen and just shoot the Stukas out of the sky, they can't defend themselves against fighters."

I pondered the enormous implications of what he was saying. "So you don't think we can beat them?"

"Of course we can, Sir. We're all waiting for the secret weapons that the Fuhrer promised us, then we'll knock them down like skittles. Until then our half-tracks would be helpful, at least we could travel over the battlefield without being totally exposed."

He had a straight face when he mentioned the secret weapons, was he being serious or sarcastic? But I knew that our High Command had vastly more resources than Scharfuhrer Mundt realised and I explained that we'd soon have much more equipment than the men knew about, and that not every aspect of high-level strategy was obvious to the troops on the ground. I was certain that a couple of good victories would convince them. I didn't elaborate on the Fuhrer's secret weapons, it was a subject best avoided. I made a mental note to enquire about the half-tracks.

"Believe me, men, we'll be back knocking on the front door of the Kremlin before too long."

I'm not sure I believed it myself. I was certain that the men didn't, but I had to try. A messenger came up to me. No salute, as usual.

"Untersturmfuhrer Hoffman, you are to report to the

regimental adjutant immediately."

As I walked across the camp, an officer stopped me, a Hauptsturmfuhrer, a captain.

"Are you that bloody fool that nearly got us all killed, the one that stood up and fired the Panzerfaust?"

I was utterly bewildered, there was a huge contradiction in what he was saying. How could my destruction of a Soviet tank be foolish, wasn't that what we were here for?

"Well, yes, Sir, that was me. I did destroy a T34."

"And what about the other two hundred T34s bearing down on us, Untersturmfuhrer? When they saw you shoot at their tank several of them swung around and headed towards your position. We were slightly to the side and in front of you, when they fired at you their shells went wide and came close to our position. It was only sheer luck that prevented us being hit. You nearly got us killed, you idiot! Next time, keep your fucking head down and mind your own business, clear?"

"Yes, Sir."

I saluted and he stormed off. What the hell was that? Were we fighting the enemy or not? I hurried on to the regimental office, a flag hung outside next to a sign, 'HQ, SS Standarte Deutschland'. A corporal was standing outside smoking a cigarette. He glanced up, "Untersturmfuhrer Hoffman? You're to go right in." Then he turned away and lost interest in me. I knocked and went through the door into the CO's office. Sturmbannfuhrer Otto Muller sat behind the desk, temporarily in command of course, after the death of Standartenfuhrer Brandt. Another officer sat in an old armchair beside the stove at the side of the office. I felt a moment of trepidation. SD Sturmbannfuhrer von Betternich. Whatever the reason for the Intelligence Officer being here, it was not likely to be anything good. Was it about that Russian tank? I saluted and waited for them to speak.

"Yes, Hoffman, I need to speak to you. You know the Sturmbannfuhrer?" he indicated the SD man.

"We met on the train, Sir."

"Of course. Before I go on, I have had a complaint that you deliberately put the life of one of my officers and his men in danger by drawing the fire of enemy armour. Is that true?"

I was still utterly bewildered. "Er, well, Sir, I did destroy a Soviet tank, a T34 with a Panzerfaust. It seemed an opportunity to me, it came close and there was a weapon to hand. I'm sorry about that, Sir, it just seemed the right thing to do."

"Next time, wait for orders and don't do anything stupid, do you understand me?"

I felt annoyed, I thought I'd joined an elite regiment, one that would stop at nothing to destroy the enemy, not a band of cowards.

"Yes, Sir, you want me to avoid firing on the enemy in the middle of a battle unless so ordered, I see, Sir."

He gave me a hard glance. "Don't fuck with me, Hoffman. Just do as I say."

"Yes, Sir."

"I'm leaving you with this officer. You will consider yourself under his orders." He got up and left the office.

"Hoffman, pull up a chair and sit down by the stove," von Betternich said cheerfully. "I imagine you're a little confused."

I pulled up an old bentwood chair that looked to be in imminent danger of collapse and sat down. "Yes, I confess I am rather puzzled as to what you might want me for, Sir."

"Very well, I will do my best to enlighten you. Firstly, my congratulations on killing that tank, that was a brave action. The officer who made the complaint is the nephew of a Party Gauleiter, an old friend of the Fuhrer's. Muller is under orders not to put him in too much danger, do I make myself clear?"

I nodded.

"However, I am certain that the Fuhrer would not approve of such an arrangement, neither would Reichsfuhrer Himmler. Be a little patient, I assure you this little matter will be cleared up shortly."

"Yes, Sir." I wasn't quite sure what he meant, I seemed to have walked into a political shit storm, but he'd said to be patient so I resolved to forget about it.

"You recall I told you I was here to investigate a

murder? Well, now there is at least one more murder to investigate."

"A murder?" It was so strange, murder in the middle of so much killing. "Who was murdered?"

"Your Commanding Officer, Standartenfuhrer Werner Brandt."

I guess I looked dumb for a few moments. "The Standartenfuhrer, impossible, he was killed in battle."

"Indeed he was, Hoffman, at least, he was killed during the battle. The regimental surgeon is conducting an autopsy at this moment and I confidently expect him to find a German bullet inside him. Perhaps we can go and see how much progress the good doctor has made."

He noticed my hesitation. "Hoffman, your CO explained that you've been fully assigned to me, that means you and your men are to escort and assist me in this investigation. I suggest we go."

He stood up. He looked terribly out of condition, flabby and overweight, apart from being too old to be in a theatre of war. Then there was his wounded leg, I got up quickly and followed him out of the door as he limped across the snow to a tent bearing the red cross of the medics. Inside, a body was on the table, the trunk cut open and much of its contents removed to lie on the enamel tray next to the body. I felt like puking but I kept it down. The surgeon, a tired looking man, thin and arrogant, his apron bloody and filthy, looked up angrily.

"Really, I haven't got time for this, Sturmbannfuhrer. I've got wounded men waiting for treatment, this could have waited."

The SD man totally ignored his protest. "Do you have the bullet, Doctor?"

The medic sighed and picked up a white enamel bowl and handed it to von Betternich.

"Here, take it. Lodged in one of the ventricles of the heart, death was almost instantaneous."

"Thank you, Doctor."

I followed him out of the tent and we stood in the snow to inspect the bullet. I didn't need to look too hard, it was a German 7.92 mm round. The ammunition we used in both rifles and machine guns.

"Well?" von Betternich asked me.

"It's one of ours, of course, but it proves nothing," I said.

He nodded. "Maybe, maybe not."

"Look, Sir, accidents involving friendly fire are nothing new, it's by no means unusual in the heat of battle for bullets to fly everywhere, it's the risk we all have to take."

"Yes, that's true. It seems that our senior officers are taking more of this risk than usual, though."

"Sir?"

"Brandt is the fourth senior SS officer to be killed by a German bullet in less than three weeks and all in the same Division, SS-Das Reich."

"Four killed? That's impossible!"

He drew me away from the main body of the camp. "Keep your voice down, Hoffman. Impossible or not, that is exactly what has happened. It is why I was called from my nice warm office in Berlin. Someone is killing our commanders and the Reichsfuhrer wishes to know who and why."

So it was a direct order from Himmler. Possibly I could have had a worse start to my military career, but it was not likely. Nobody in Germany wanted to be under the direct scrutiny of the Reichsfuhrer, his fearful reputation was an incentive to steer well clear of him.

"But why do you need me? I've only just arrived, I don't know anything about this, I've got no experience of the Eastern Front."

"Exactly! You have only just arrived and so you can't possibly be involved, that's why I want you, Hoffman. I'll need three of your men for now, you can leave the rest under the command of one of your NCOs. I may need more men later, of course, when I know what we're dealing with. We'd better get back to the monastery, Major Muller is organising an office for me. Then you can bring your men over and we'll get started."

An hour later I reported to the temporary office that von Betternich had been assigned, it had formerly been a monk's cell. I had three of my troopers with me, Scharfuhrer Mundt, Schutze Stefan Bauer and Schutze Dieter Merkel.

DEVIL'S GUARD BLOOD & SNOW

The two privates, Bauer and Merkel stood guard outside the office, both wearing their steel helmets and carrying their MP38s ready for use. Mundt stood inside the door like a respectful butler, if a somewhat warlike one. I sat on the old wooden chair next to von Betternich's desk, actually a repaired table that had been brought in for him to use. I smiled when I saw that his chair was in fact the deceased Standartenfuhrer's comfortable old leather chair from the regimental office. Clearly the SD could throw their weight around.

"I have a list of officers who were near to the Standartenfuhrer when he was hit, I want you to bring them here one by one for interview. We'll start with Sturmbannfuhrer Muller who I believe was standing right next to him."

I went with Mundt to find Muller, who was not in the mood to waste time.

"Untersturmfuhrer, I need to make preparations, we're expecting the Russians to counterattack again very soon. Unless we shore up our defences they'll come right through us."

I politely persisted and took him grumbling into the office to speak to von Betternich.

"Yes, yes, I was standing right next to Brandt, the situation was very fluid, some of the Soviets were threatening to outflank us, there were bullets and shells flying everywhere. One moment the Standartenfuhrer was shouting orders, the next he was laying on the ground covered in blood. I took command and sent him to the surgeon, that's all there is to it."

"Did you see any of our men in the direction of where the bullet came from?"

Muller smiled grimly. "Yes, about five hundred of them."

"Thank you, Sturmbannfuhrer, that will be all for now." He handed Muller a piece of paper. "That is a list of the men who I understand were also nearby when the bullet struck the Standartenfuhrer, would you send them to me one by one?"

"Really, von Betternich, this is ridiculous, I have a battle to prepare for, we all have work to do."

"Perhaps you would prefer a direct order from the Reichsfuhrer himself? I can arrange that?"

Muller gave him a vicious glance and stormed out of the office.

"I think that went well," the SD officer said quietly.

Mundt and I exchanged glances.

Throughout the day we interviewed officers, NCOs and troopers, each time von Betternich made meticulous notes on a pad. We went on late into the evening, the next morning after a hurried breakfast we rejoined von Betternich, rounding up interviewees for further interrogation. By mid-afternoon he said he was satisfied and we could rejoin the regiment while he collated the various statements that he had already taken. It seemed pointless to us, officers and men saying the same things again and again, it was just bureaucracy gone mad. We managed to get some food from the cookhouse and sat inside the old church to eat it. There were several platoons billeted in there and they had found an old iron stove that they had rigged up, we clustered around it to enjoy some of its warmth. I could have asked to eat in the officers' mess, such as it was, but in the SS it was encouraged for officers, especially junior officers, to fraternise with the men. After all, we were all equal in the service of the Fuhrer and Reich and eating with the men was supposed to support that viewpoint. I was listening to an old Scharfuhrer from another platoon extolling the merits of our Erma MP38 over the Soviet PPSh.

"Of course, it doesn't have the capacity for a drum magazine, but it's more reliable, packs a heavier punch, a much better all round weapon."

One veteran of the old stormtroopers, the SA, muttered that the Bergman MP-28 was a much superior weapon and later models had got progressively worse. The others laughed, it was obviously an old argument.

"Untersturmfuhrer Hoffman to report to Sturmbannfuhrer Muller."

I looked up, a Hauptsturmfuhrer, a captain, was looking directly at me.

"At once, Sir!"

I got up and reluctantly left the warmth of the stove to go out into the cold and over to the Regimental Office.

"Ah, Hoffman. You did well on that first reconnaissance mission, those prisoners have been more than useful," Sturmbannfuhrer Muller said. "I want you to go out again, tonight, in fact. You're new here, you need the experience. I need to find out more of the enemy's intentions, make sure you bring back more prisoners. Ideally, we need another officer if you can find one. Our intelligence suggests that the Russians are planning another counterattack."

I was astonished at the sudden change of mission. "Sir, I thought I was assigned to..."

"I've spoken to your SD friend, Hoffman. I told him that SS operational requirements come before everything, he knows he must accept that. I suggest you rejoin your men and prepare to move out as soon as it gets dark."

So it was my SD friend now, von Betternich. It was a friendship I'd neither sought nor wanted. If it continued, it could drive a wedge between me and the other officers. Damn, of all the luck, to have run into the SD officer on the train. I determined to get out of the SD escort assignment after I got back from tonight's mission. I went back to the church and found Mundt and the rest of the platoon still huddled around the stove.

"Men, we're going out again, another mission. Get yourselves ready, they want us to bring in another prisoner, a Soviet officer."

I heard someone mutter something about sending over one of ours for one of theirs, a straight swap, I wasn't sure if they meant me. I ignored them, they were a good platoon. Within minutes they were lining up with their weapons and equipment, all wearing snow camouflage and carrying white packs. Even their machine pistols were covered in strips of white material. While Mundt checked them over, I buttoned up my own camouflage uniform, put on my steel helmet and pack, and picked up my MP38. As I was getting ready, a thought struck me. Why would anyone kill several of our senior SS officers? It was strange, a conspiracy, perhaps, it sounded as if it could be. I'd need to ask von Betternich, perhaps when I requested him to get someone else to escort him would be a good time.

"Ready, Sir."

I nodded at Mundt. "Let's go."

I knew that this time it would be more difficult, the Soviets were fully alerted to the likelihood that we were planning our own counterattack on this front. I pondered the problem as we walked towards the lines. We headed to the north of where we'd crossed the lines before, at least a different starting point may help us a little.

"Mundt, we need to rethink this, I don't want to walk straight into a Soviet trap."

"Nor me, Sir. What did you have in mind?"

I told him I didn't have a clue, and was rather hoping he would.

"Sorry, no, nothing. Whatever we do they'll be waiting for a German raiding party to walk straight into their laps."

He struck a chord in my mind and I had an idea. "Mundt, does anyone in of our platoon speak Russian?"

"Well, yes, Merkel's mother was Russian, I believe he's fluent."

Schutze Merkel was brought to the front to speak to Mundt and me.

"Merkel, I want you to become an officer, a captain."

"Sir?"

"In the Soviet army, Merkel. If we get near any Russian troops, start giving us orders in Russian, can you manage that?"

"Well, yes, I guess."

Our winter uniforms were almost identical to the Soviets, they would certainly pass muster during the night. I had the men take a quick lesson in Russian.

"Da, Nyet, Comrade, that should be enough, pull your white camouflage hoods over your helmets, their silhouette would give us away. Da, Comrades?"

There was a chorus of 'Da' and 'Comrade' from the men, one wag said 'Nyet'. The plan was all I could think of on the spur of the moment, short of an artillery barrage or Stuka attack to divert the Soviets, so we pressed forward. One of the men had a captured Soviet PPSh, I directed him to give it to Merkel, at least we would have one soldier that may convince the Russians that he was authentic. After the first kilometre, we began to see the lights of enemy campfires about another kilometre further on. I directed the men to drop to a crawl and we edged cautiously forward. We were within half a kilometre of the Soviet perimeter when the challenge came.

"Halt!"

Merkel was in the lead, he walked slowly forward speaking in Russian. We'd come upon a hidden sentry, the man got up and went forward to speak to him. They exchanged a few words and the Russian looked at me and barked out a question.

"Da," I replied.

It was the wrong answer, his expression changed to alarm and he started to swing up his rifle but Merkel swung his PPSh and hit him hard on the skull. Fortunately for us, he wasn't wearing a steel helmet. The man hit the ground and Mundt ran up to him, his combat knife flashed and the man's blood started to pour out onto the snow. They'd obviously done this many times before, they threw the body into the foxhole where he'd been hiding and scooped snow over the evidence.

"What did he say to me?" I asked Merkel.

"He said 'Yob tvoyu mat', Sir. He was swearing at you for getting him out of his warm foxhole, it means 'Fuck your Mother'. You replied da, yes, which no Russian would ever do of course."

I smiled inwardly. We moved carefully on and dropped

to the ground when we heard voices. I saw a chink of light show as a canvas shelter flap moved to one side and the figure of a man climbed out, still talking to the occupants. Merkel whispered to me.

"Soviet Commissar, he's doing the rounds of the troops, giving them pep talks."

"He'll do nicely, Merkel. Perhaps he can give a pep talk to our intelligence people. Challenge him, as if you were a sentry."

Merkel called out to him and the Russian looked around. We were lying flat in the snow, he didn't see us in our white uniforms, only Merkel standing there with his PPSh. His voice sounded irritated when he replied, but Merkel persisted, obviously demanding some kind of identification. He finally came over to us. Merkel simply put the barrel of the PPSh against his nose and told him to shut up. Simultaneously, the rest of us jumped up and Mundt put the blade of his combat knife against the man's throat. It was enough, he froze without protest.

"Merkel, tell him he's our prisoner, he won't be harmed if he comes quietly but if he makes a sound Mundt will cut his throat."

"I speak German, there is no need to translate."

"Very well, you are a Commissar?"

"Yes, Commissar Captain Valentin Tereschova."

I told him who I was. "Are we going to do this the hard way, Captain, or the easy way?"

"I have no wish to die, SS man, I will come quietly."

We walked slowly from the area, I judged that if we crawled away it would look suspicious. When we got near the point where we had killed the sentry I ordered them to drop to a crawl. I went in the lead, the Russian behind me, then Mundt and the others. Merkel brought up the rear, as a Russian speaker he'd be able to answer any challenge that came from behind us. In the event, it came from in front of us.

"Halt!"

We all froze. To his credit, Merkel crawled forward and spoke in Russian, but I could tell from the cold voice that the man didn't believe we were genuine. As the cloud drifted across the sky I was able to make them out, two men standing up, one armed with a rifle, the other with a PPSh, both pointed at us. I silently took off the safety of my machine pistol and felt the trigger. Merkel was arguing with them when I took up the final pressure and let loose a long burst that took the pair of them. Both men spun to the ground, I could feel my platoon's incredulous eyes on me. A voice called out from the Russian lines, then a burst of machine gun fire, tracer bullets, spat across the snow-covered ground about thirty metres from us. We had one option left.

"Run!" I shouted to them.

I dragged the Commissar to his feet and began to sprint for our lines, the others scrambled after me. The machine gunner shifted his aim and a hail of tracer flew over our heads, then we were over the lip of the low hill and racing through the snow towards the shelter of the trees. We had about a hundred metres to go when all hell broke loose, a flare burst in the sky, then another machine gun opened up and several sub-machine guns and rifles fired. All around us bullets buzzed and zinged past our heads, fortunately their aim was high and our camouflage made us difficult targets in the night.

"Down, get down, take cover!" I shouted. It was rotten luck, we'd encountered a large Soviet patrol, they were sheltering in a foxhole and we had run right past them without noticing. Now they were shooting at us and we were out in the open. I pressed the Commissar's head into the snow, and then looked around my command.

"Is anyone hit?"

"We're fine," Mundt replied, "but we're not going any further until those Russkis are dealt with."

"Unless they deal with us first," a sullen voice murmured.

"Shut up, Bauer," Mundt told him.

"Mundt, keep an eye on the Russian prisoner, I'll see if I can't lob a grenade to take that machine gun out."

"It's too far, you won't get them from this distance."

"No, I'll crawl nearer. Can you give me covering fire? I just need a minute to get myself ready."

Voices were calling out from both the Russian and

our own lines now. We'd stirred up our own mini battle, exchanges of gunfire all along the front. I unclipped a stick grenade from my webbing and pulled out the pin. When I let go it would explode in four seconds.

"Now, Mundt."

They started to fire, I saw Mundt out of the corner of my eye as I ran. He had one hand holding down the prisoner, the other firing his MP38. Merkel still had the PPSh he'd borrowed, he was emptying the drum towards the enemy, the rest of them were firing furiously. I got halfway toward the observation post when one of the soldiers popped his head up, saw me and loosed off a burst. I dived to one side and rolled, but I was near enough, I threw the grenade as accurately as I could and pressed my head down into the snow. The soldier saw me throw the grenade and ducked down for cover, it exploded on the edge of their hole. Quickly, I unclipped a second grenade and crawled forward while they were still stunned from the first explosion. I could hear voices shouting in Russian, I pulled the pin and threw my second grenade neatly into their shelter. There was a scream of fear, then the explosion and they were silent. I ran back to my men.

"Let's go!"

We had a worrying moment when we reached our lines, the whole front was alerted and they nearly mistook us for Russians, but we managed to persuade them to let us through with our hands held high. Once we were safe,

I hurried back to HQ and we handed over the prisoner. Muller came out to see what the fuss was all about.

He nodded with approval. "Well done, men. I'm sure we'll milk this one for everything he knows."

"He speaks German, Sir, and I believe he's anxious to cooperate to save his skin."

"Is that so?" He looked at Tereschova.

"And why are you so keen so rat on your comrades, Comrade Commissar? I thought you people were all dedicated communists."

The Russian looked Muller over. "Yes, so we are, Sturmbannfuhrer." He spat out the rank 'Sturmbannfuhrer' as if it was a swear word. Muller raised his eyes.

"So you know our SS ranks, do you?"

"Of course, it is my job to know the enemy we face. Do you know what we call you people?"

Muller shook his head.

"You take the orders of the devil in Berlin, Hitler. You are his guard, are you not, the Schutzstaffel? We call you the Devil's Guard. What I say makes no difference, you and the devil Hitler you guard are beaten. All of you Germans will regret the day you ever set foot on our soil!"

Muller's expression darkened. "What the hell are you talking about, beaten? You are a prisoner of the SS, we have a whole Panzer army here, my friend, more than enough to smash anything you send against us, so how are we beaten?"

"For every Panzer division you put in the field, Sturmbannfuhrer, we can mount three tank armies to oppose you. For every soldier you send forward with a rifle we can send forward twenty, with twenty more waiting to take their place when they fall. For every aircraft you send over, we will put ten aircraft up to shoot it down. You are finished, SS man, you and every other German that has invaded my country!"

There was silence in our group for several seconds. I'd heard the same defeatist talk from my own men, perhaps the Soviet propaganda machine was very effective. But the Commissar was clearly wrong. I knew, beyond a shadow of a doubt, that the German armies were the most powerful fighting force in the world. And our SS Divisions were the elite of that fighting force.

"Take him away," snapped Muller. "Get our intelligence people to talk to him, they'll soon find out what's in front of us. Well done, Hoffman."

"Thank you, Sir."

"You and your men had better get something to eat and get some rest, we may be in action very soon."

We managed to locate some foul tasting stew from the cookhouse with thick slices of black bread. I couldn't face the ersatz coffee again, so I washed the meal down with fresh water, probably melted snow, but it tasted fine. We spent the rest of the day repairing and maintaining our weapons and equipment and then we went into the church and I flung myself down behind the blanket and fell straight to sleep, praying that neither army, German or Soviet, would disturb me this time. They didn't and I slept the whole night, in the morning I was awoken by Mundt, who said it was time for stand to. I was still fully dressed to keep out the cold, I even still wore my winter camouflage. It was a simple matter of pulling on my jackboots and rushing outside with my men for the assembly. There was no alarm, no emergency, so we were able to get a leisured breakfast. I even thought about a shave, except that the prospect of trimming my beard in ice-cold water was distinctly unappealing. We sat around the camp, cleaning and checking our weapons.

"What did you think about what the Russian said, Sir?" Merkel asked me.

"What do you mean?"

"About them outnumbering us so massively, do you think it's true?"

"They outnumbered us at the start of Barbarossa, it didn't make any difference then and it won't now."

"So why are we constantly retreating, Herr Untersturmfuhrer?"

I noticed the other men were looking at me intently. I knew I had to be careful with my answer. The trouble was, I honestly didn't know, I was newly commissioned and had only just arrived at the Front.

A new voice answered him. "It's part of the Fuhrer's

strategy to pull the Russians onto our guns so that we can slaughter them in even larger numbers, then outflank them and mount a joint drive on both Moscow and the southern oilfields."

I looked around, it was SD Sturmbannfuhrer von Betternich, leaning on his cane. The older man managed to look fresh and clean shaven, his uniform immaculate in regulation field grey, he had a wide lapelled black leather greatcoat over his tunic and wore a smart peaked cap. We all stood up to attention.

"No, no," he waved us back down. "Hoffman, would you report to my office in, shall we say, half an hour?"

"Yes, Sir."

He walked away and we relaxed.

"So that's it, is it?" Bauer asked me. "We're pulling the Russians onto our guns to kill more of them?"

"I imagine so, Bauer. Why else would we be constantly pulling back?"

After half an hour I got up to leave.

"I thought we'd finished helping him out," Mundt said, "he makes me uneasy, that SD man. I never did like policemen much."

I smiled. "Had problems in the past, Scharfuhrer?"

"Well, yes, one or two. I remember when the Party first started, I joined the SA, damn, we had some fun. Fistfights, battles with the communists, always made a profit too, of course, if you kept your eyes open. The police were

ERIC MEYER

always two faced, mind, let you do anything you wanted one minute, throw you in jail the next."

"Well, you've got plenty of fighting to do here, so I trust you'll stay out of prison."

He laughed. "As long as they don't catch me, or the Russians shoot me before it's all over."

The other members of the platoon cheered him as he said it. He was a likeable rogue and a good man to have as my senior NCO.

"Don't ever steal anything from the SS, Mundt, they'll have you shot."

They all laughed again. I went over to find von Betternich, he was sat behind his desk.

"How is everything going, Hoffman, I gather you had a successful night?"

"Yes, Sir, no problems. Look, I thought that my work with you was over, you've finished investigating the Regimental officers, I'd prefer to stay on duty."

"Had enough of police work, have you?"

"It's not that, Sir. I just want to fight the Russians, I feel that's what I'm here for, not investigating my fellow officers."

He looked thoughtful. "Come with me, Hoffman."

We walked outside and strolled around the camp in the fresh air.

"I see the monks are still here," he said abruptly.

I had forgotten about them, they were part of the

scenery of the camp, but yes, they were still there, sitting outside their makeshift, ragged camp, just outside our perimeter. One of them had erected a crude, wooden cross on a pole.

"Yes, I expect they're waiting to regain possession of the monastery and church when we leave," I replied.

"Is that what they're doing?"

I looked at him sharply. "What else would they be doing, Sir?"

"No, no, I think you're probably right, they're just trying to get back what is rightfully theirs. That's the trouble with war, property gets, shall we say, re-assigned. Churches, monasteries, buildings, artworks."

I was mystified, where was this conversation heading.

"You know of Reichsmarschall Goering's art collection in his home at Karinhall, of course, Hoffman?"

I'd heard rumours but I decided to say I'd never heard of it. Von Betternich smiled.

"Is that right? Well, well. The Reichsmarschall is of course holding it all in trust for the nation, very noble of him, don't you think?"

"Yes, of course, Sir."

"But war, you see, confuses things. Loyalties, for example, people forget who they owe allegiance to."

I was horrified. "You mean there is some kind of a conspiracy against the Reich?"

"Who knows? I am merely a policeman investigating

the murder of those senior officers, it leaves their regiments leaderless, rudderless. That's what happens, you see, you chop off the head and people run around without orders, without knowing who to trust."

We walked on, I was enjoying the chill and fresh spring air, but not the company, not the ominous way this conversation was heading. Or was the chill coming from the very dangerous SD officer next to me? I laughed inside at that melodramatic thought. Von Betternich, of course, was a policeman, he could almost read minds as he'd mentioned before.

"I am not your enemy, Hoffman. Quite the opposite."

"No, Sir."

"Are you a Christian?"

What kind of a question was that? "Er, not really, Sir, no. Not for a long time."

"No, of course not. I imagine your loyalties are clear?"

"Absolutely, Sir, to the Fuhrer, to the SS, to my regiment."

"Good. I need you to continue, Hoffman. I need someone I can trust to assist me. This investigation could have a serious effect on the course of the war on the Eastern Front. At the very least, it may uncover a serious conspiracy to undermine the discipline and loyalty of the Das Reich Division of the Waffen SS. That kind of thing can lose battles if it is left to grow and fester, do you understand how easily it can happen?"

I thought for a few moments, but lying to this man would not be a good idea.

"No, not really, Sir, I don't understand at all."

I didn't want to understand either, it was politics. The further I drifted into this murky world, the further I would get from the glorious career I'd dreamed about in the Waffen SS.

I left him and walked back towards my billet in the church. Overhead, a bunch of aircraft flew past causing the alarms to sound, men running to don steel helmets, Flak guns sighting on the planes, there were perhaps thirty of them, a strong force. They were heading west, quite low, more Ilyushin Il-2s, the infamous Sturmovik. No match for our Messerschmitts and Focke-Wulfs, of course. Except that the Luftwaffe wasn't anywhere to be seen.

"Going to give our Panzers some problems, I imagine," a voice said behind me, Sturmbannfuhrer Muller, now acting commander of the Standarte 'Deutschland'.

I heard the distant sound of anti-aircraft fire, the whine of the aero engines as they dove in for the attack, the whistle of bombs as they hurtled earthwards, then the explosions as they struck.

"Where are our aircraft, Sir? It seems crazy to let the Soviets have free rein to attack our Panzers."

"Where are they indeed? That's a good question. A question we often ask ourselves, Hoffman, and we never seem to get a satisfactory reply."

We both stared into the distance at the smoke and explosions. Our own Flak guns were on standby, the whole camp buttoned up tight, but other than being able to take a shot at the enemy as they returned after their mission it was doubtful we'd be able to help the Panzers.

"I'm not happy about you cooperating with the Sicherheitsdienst, Hoffman. I don't trust that officer, von Betternich. The last thing I need is a policeman running around upsetting morale."

"I don't like it either, Sir. I'd sooner just be with my platoon."

"Of course you would. You can help me out you know, keep me informed of the investigation. I'll do what I can to get you relieved from this SD matter as soon as possible, I don't want one of my officers tied up with policemen."

So it was to be quid-pro-quo. Somehow, I felt even more uneasy about being asked to spy on the SD. In effect, to spy on the spies.

CHAPTER THREE

*"We are determined, as leaders of the nation, to fulfill as
a national government the task which has been given to us,
swearing fidelity only to God, our conscience, and our Volk...
This the national government will regard its first and foremost
duty to restore the unity of spirit and purpose of our Volk.
It will preserve and defend the foundations upon*

*which the power of our nation rests. It will take Christianity,
as the basis of our collective morality, and the family as the
nucleus of our Volk and state, under its firm protection...
May God Almighty take our work into his grace, give true
form to our will, bless our insight, and endow us with the trust
of our Volk."*

Adolf Hitler February 1933

There was no time for me to think any more about my loyalties concerning either the SS or the SD. My regiment, Deutschland, was part of SS Division Das Reich, itself part of the newly reformed SS Panzer Corps under the command of one of our SS heroes, Obergruppenfuhrer Paul Hausser who the men had nicknamed 'Papa'. One of our regiments, Der Fuhrer, had been pushed back from their advance positions on the River Oskol, had to regroup and dig into new positions. During the day, we were amused to see streams of our allied Italian troops fleeing from the Soviets. Yet our morale was good, our Army Group South Commander, von Manstein, made it clear that the Russians had run out of steam and shortly we would be going back on the offensive, one that this time would sweep the enemy away and put us firmly back on the road to Moscow. I joined my platoon and we marched away to join the Panzers of our Division ready to mount our new attack. We would be riding in style as we'd been assigned a new delivery of armoured half-tracked vehicles with which to go into battle. Clearly, our commanders were anticipating a lightning thrust against the Russians that would carry everything before them. We assembled in a wood outside the village of Valki, line after line of our heavy tanks, artillery pieces, troop carriers and more, a formidable force. It was snowing heavily, a blizzard started to obliterate the countryside and it was difficult to see more than fifty metres in any direction.

Muller, our regimental commander, came back from Division and started giving orders. For my platoon, out task was simple, we were to follow the Panzers and suppress any pockets of resistance that threatened us in the rear of the advance and of course clear enemy mines.

"It's quite straightforward, stay with the tanks and watch out for any enemy that they miss, we're going in fast and hard. You will all be riding in the new armoured personnel carriers, so you shouldn't have problems keeping up. Any questions?"

I put up my hand.

"Hoffman?"

"Sir, what about radio communications?"

"No, most of our vehicles don't have radios, they're in short supply. I shall be in contact with Division, so keep your eyes on me for any changes in orders."

It didn't sound satisfactory, more like a Great War army, but I acknowledged the order. Kretschmer, an Obersturmfuhrer asked him about mine detectors.

"We're still waiting for replacement batteries, Kretschmer."

"Sir, we don't have a single working mine detector and we know the Soviets will have planted plenty of them, how do we clear them?"

Muller thought for a moment, he looked a little embarrassed.

"Look, we're waiting for fresh batteries to come in

from Germany, at the moment we're all in the same boat. If you think there's a minefield, you'll have to go forward and use your bayonets to find them."

I had to be careful to keep a straight face, our mighty First SS Panzerkorps forced to go forward and dig out the mines by prodding for them with bayonets. And no radios in our vehicles either, should I ask Muller about carrier pigeons? Better not.

There was a clamour in the distance, Muller looked up with an irritated expression. "Damn fools, we haven't had the order to go yet."

We looked towards where the noise was coming from, suddenly the snowstorm cleared briefly and we could see men scrambling to climb into their tanks, artillery gunners working frantically to deploy guns. It was chaos, shouts, the roar of engines starting, whistles blowing. Then a siren started to wail and we heard distinctly a sentry shouting as he ran towards us.

"Alarm, alarm! They're attacking, sound the alarm!"

Behind him there was the explosion of a tank shell as it exploded, then they were coming down on our position.

"It seems that someone neglected to tell the Soviets that they were overextended," Kretschmer said drily. "They've decided to take the initiative and attack first."

But Muller overrode him, shouting "Mount up, mount up, stay with the tanks!"

I ran for my vehicle, a Sonderkraftfahrzeug 251 half-track, designed specifically for our Panzer Grenadiers to keep up with the tanks. Equipped with a 37mm Pak 36 anti-tank gun, as well as two mounted MG34s, we were confident that they would give us sufficient firepower and mobility to support our new advance. Except that the enemy had decided not to wait, they were coming straight towards us.

I leapt aboard, the men were already there waiting for me.

"Follow the Panzers," I shouted at the driver. I hadn't a clue where they were going, it seemed that neither did anyone else. Several of the tanks turned around and headed away from the action, but to their credit, most had the sense to go forward to engage the enemy. We bumped through the wood, trying to make sense of the confusion in front of us. Another half-track running parallel to us took a hit from a T34's main gun and disintegrated, several men were thrown screaming to the ground. The driver slowed, but I shouted at him to keep going. Mundt was manning the small Pak anti-tank gun fitted to our half-track.

"How are you with that gun, Scharfuhrer?" I asked him.

"Good enough," was the laconic reply.

Ahead of us our Panzers were shooting now, a furious exchange of fire had developed between the tanks of both sides. Then we were out of the snowstorm and running through a wide area of sparse scrubland dotted with low hills. The six-cylinder Maybach engine roared as the driver gunned it along to keep pace with the racing Panzers. The snowstorm worsened and we were running almost blind, then it cleared again and our tanks again opened fire as their targets came back into view. T34s, there seemed to be hundreds of them, incredibly the Russians seemed to have them in inexhaustible supply. I was trying to make out targets with my binoculars, but they were so close, so numerous that I put my field glasses to one side and leaned across to Mundt.

"Are you ready with that gun?"

But even as I spoke, there was a mighty roar as he pulled the trigger and I jumped away to avoid the breech as it slammed backwards on its mountings. I was deafened, I could see Mundt's loader slamming another round in the gun.

Ahead of us a Soviet tank went up in flames as it was hit, I'd no idea if Mundt's shell had struck it or someone else's. Then I saw troops, Soviet tank riders, leaping off the back of the tanks and jumping for cover, then beginning to fire at us. The butt of the MG34 was right next to me, I grabbed the weapon and aimed it towards the enemy, then shouted at the men behind me.

"Bauer, get here quickly, I need a loader to handle the belt."

While he was scrambling through the cockpit of the

vehicle, I opened fire. The gun vibrated in my hands, the belt rattled through the chamber at an alarming rate, empty cartridge cases spewing out around my feet, but the effect was deadly. The Soviets scattered but not before at least ten of them fell to the hail of lead I threw out at them. Just in time, Bauer attached a new belt to the end of the old one and I was able to keep firing. Mundt's gun boomed again and again as he fired at the Soviet armour.

"Sir, you'll have to stop, it'll overheat," Bauer shouted in my ear. Just as he did, so the gun stopped. He looked at me as if to say 'I told you so.' But he was right, I should have remembered my training. We had another gun, sitting uselessly at the rear of the vehicle in an anti-aircraft mount.

"You men," I shouted at Voss and Beidenberg, "unhitch that gun and bring it here!"

They jumped up to detach the second MG34. The roar of outgoing shells, the crash of incoming rounds and the chatter of machine gun bullets that whistled and whined all around us gave them plenty of incentive to hurry. Less than twenty seconds later they were slamming the replacement machine gun onto the mount and Bauer had removed the jammed weapon and placed it on the floor of the carrier. Five seconds later the gun was loaded with a full belt of ammunition.

"Take the jammed gun and fix it," I snapped at them. Then I started firing again. Targets were harder to find, the battlefield was covered in smoke, the noise was intense, constant crashes and explosions, engines, machine guns, rifles, it was the raucous music of the cauldron of hell. But our Regiment was inching forward. Bauer suddenly cried out as he was hit and spun away.

"Merkel, the gun, I need a loader."

He rushed forward as the men picked up Bauer, I heard someone say he wasn't hurt badly, a shoulder wound.

We were pressing ahead, defeating the enemy attack, the Soviets were clearly stunned at the intensity with which we hit them. The blizzard increased in intensity and with the smoke that hung everywhere we were almost blinded. A T34 appeared alongside us, fleeing towards his lines, I was astonished that he had got behind us, we were lucky he hadn't seen us and opened fire. The 76mm gun of the T34 would have made short work of our 251 half-track with its thin armour. He had only been three metres from us when he'd materialised out of the fog. As he surged past, I shouted to Mundt.

"Scharfuhrer, on your left!"

"Got it."

Another crash as he fired and the almost instantaneous explosion as the point blank target was hit. It burst into flames and slewed to one side, smoke pouring out of the large hole that Mundt's shell had blown into the side of the hull. There would be no survivors, that was obvious. The interior of the tank would have been a hell of flames and molten metal shredding human flesh to raw mincemeat.

There was no time for thinking of the dead, other than the fact that it could be us next. We were caught up in the blood lust of the charge, like the famous English 'Charge of the Light Brigade'. I prayed that on this occasion there wouldn't be lines of heavy guns waiting for us ahead. I saw another group of Russians, they were running back to their lines but I aimed the machine gun and sent burst after burst of machine gun fire after them, a few fell, the others dived for cover. I kept firing, the more we killed today, the less would come back to kill us tomorrow. Then we were hit.

An explosion on the side of our vehicle, a jet of flame spurted up in the air and our 251 made a half turn and came to a stop. Fire was licking all around us.

"Everybody out before it explodes!" I shouted. We carried a large tank of petrol and it was at least half-full, when the fire reached it the half-track would explode like a bomb. Men were jumping over the sides, I got out the fire extinguishers and threw them after the men and jumped out myself. We attacked the flames, another carrier stopped near us and the men leapt out with their own extinguishers to help. It was Kretschmer's platoon, I noticed. His eyes were bright, dilated with the excitement of the action.

"Bad luck, Hoffman," he grinned, "you'll have to walk next time."

"At least we're all alive. Thanks for the help."

We both looked around as a STuGIII mobile gun came

through the smoke, looking for targets. But the Russians had vanished, retreating to their original defensive positions. The STuGIII commander looked over the side at us.

"Any problems?"

We shook our heads. "It looks like the Soviets have run for it, there's no business for you guys today."

"I can live with that," he said. He was an Obersturmfuhrer, like Kretschmer, although a little older. Artillerymen tended to be older, their trade was one that required a good deal more technical ability and something less of the warrior determination that drove younger men on.

"Obersturmfuhrer, do you have a radio in there?" I asked him.

He nodded.

"I could do with a recovery crew to come out and pick up my half-track, I'd guess it could be repaired."

"I'll give Headquarters a call," he replied.

We waited by the half-tracks, the STuGIII seemed content to sit with its engine idling waiting for orders. Muller arrived in a Horch 801 Leichter Panzerspahwagen, a light armoured car that he used as his command vehicle. He climbed down from the cockpit and strutted up to us.

"What are you waiting here for, you men? We're pulling back to our own positions, the Russians have dug in a line of heavy artillery to the front of us, too much for us to break through."

I told him about the damage to our half-track and he walked over to inspect it.

"You say that you've put in a call for a recovery crew?"

"Yes, Sir."

"Very well. You'll need to stay by your vehicle until they can arrive to tow it away, the partisans operating in this area will destroy it completely if we give them half a chance. Or booby trap it. But if those guns start laying down a barrage get out of here fast."

"Right. How will we get back, Sir?"

I estimated we'd travelled about eight kilometres from our headquarters.

"You walk, Untersturmfuhrer Hoffman."

I could swear he had a slight smile on his face as he said that. He swung back into his armoured car and drove off.

"There's hot water in the radiator, Sir, we can brew up some coffee," Mundt said.

"Do it, Sergeant."

The recovery team were quick to arrive, we'd barely finished our coffee tasting of unnamed vegetable substances and rusty water, at least it was hot. They made a quick inspection and decided to recover our half-track. The Scharfuhrer in charge of the recovery crew, a cheerful looking old soldier, made light of the damage, they hooked it up to their towing equipment and were getting ready to leave.

"It's nothing very serious, we'll patch up the hole, put a new track on, a new pair of drive wheels, we'll have it back in action by tomorrow evening. How are you getting back, Sir?"

"I think we'll have to walk, Sergeant."

"We'll be towing the half-track, why not ride back in that?"

"I think we will, thanks. Men, mount up, we're going back in style."

They jumped up into the cockpit and soon we were bumping along the Russian steppe, the men grumbling because I wouldn't let them smoke. The threat of leaking petrol made that very unwise, but when I reminded them that the alternative was to walk they quickly quietened down and started to extol the virtues of motorised troops. Our unit had newly been issued with a variety of transport, from Kubelwagens to heavy lorries and armoured half-tracks. But the Russian terrain was very unforgiving and after fearful losses of vehicles and equipment they'd fought for some time purely as infantry, with nothing to carry them to and from the battlefield. Of course, our new half-track was damaged, but I vowed to keep a watchful eye on it and make certain it came back to my platoon when it was repaired.

It was early evening when we got into camp. We managed to get the cookhouse to ladle out hot stew and we sat eating in companionable silence.

"I see those monks are still here," Merkel said. "I'll bet they're praying to their God that we get a good hammering, so that we go away and they can have their home back."

"Wouldn't you?" a voice said.

Damn, von Betternich had come up on us quietly and was standing nearby, leaning on his cane.

"What do you mean, Sir?"

"If foreign troops came and took your home, wouldn't you want it back?"

"Er, Yes, Sir," Merkel replied. "I guess I would."

"Hoffman, would you join me in my office when you've finished your dinner?"

"Yes, Sir."

I took my time, I knew it was going to be a difficult conversation. I'd had enough of divided loyalties, I was going to ask him firmly to find another officer to assist him. I'd been in combat and felt that I'd acquitted myself well, the regiment needed me on the battlefield, not in a police station. I finished up and walked towards the monastery. Two officers stopped me.

"Untersturmfuhrer Hoffman, a word."

They were both SS Hauptsturmfuhrers, Captains.

"Of course, Sir."

"This business with the SD man, von Betternich. None of us are happy that an officer of our regiment is involved helping the police, Hoffman."

I smiled grimly. "I'm not happy either, believe me. I joined the SS to fight, not to be a police snoop."

"So tell him to go and mind his own business, Hoffman. If you refuse to help him maybe he'll go elsewhere to snoop around and we can get on with the business of fighting a war."

I was about to tell them that I was going in to see von Betternich now to give him exactly that message, but something stopped me. Ever since I could remember, I'd been suspicious of other people trying to influence the way I thought. I guess it went back to my father, he'd been an infantry officer with the Bavarian Infantry during the First War, had even spent some time in the same regiment as the Fuhrer, although he refused to ever discuss it. The lesson he always tried to teach me was to be my own man. When the whole country was going mad for the new Chancellor, Adolf Hitler, my father was cautious, saying that he'd need to see some evidence of his abilities as a politician before he ever voted for him. He certainly told me he disagreed with the Nazis' treatment of the Jews, insisting that they were just Germans, no different to the rest of us. Wisely, he instructed me to keep quiet on that issue, as well as other issues of politics in general, and the Fuhrer in particular. Hitler had brought many new things to the destroyed nation he'd inherited in 1933, some of them good, some of them not so good. Amongst the latter was the loss of free speech, we could disagree, but keep it inside our own heads.

My father had tried to dissuade me from joining the SS at first, saying they weren't proper soldiers, just a bunch of political thugs, but at least in that he was wrong. It was obvious to me that the unit I had joined was part of a military elite, one that I was proud to be a member of. It was all very confusing for a new officer, but I decided to err on the side of caution. Yes, he would certainly keep his own counsel on the business of the SD versus the good of the regiment, until he knew more about the political undercurrents that swirled around everything in our new Germany. Both my parents were dead now, killed in a massive American bombing raid, victims to the B-17s that flew daily missions over The Reich and bombed civilian homes with impunity. I remembered coming home and finding a heap of rubble surrounded by rope barriers to keep people away from unsafe buildings. Their bodies had been bulldozed into a mass grave alongside dozens of others of their neighbours. I'd been angry at first, a white hot anger that made me want to pick up a machine gun and go looking for the enemy to kill. But I remembered my father's words when we heard Dr Goebels shouting on the radio about the Luftwaffe bombing raids on London.

'Jurgen, you know that they will simply retaliate for this, soon their aircraft will be dropping bombs on towns and cities all over The Reich.'

He'd been only too accurate in his prediction. I lost my

passion for vengeance and instead put all of my energies into becoming a good soldier.

"I'll think seriously about what you've said."

"Very wise, Hoffman."

They walked away and I continued to von Betternich's office.

"Untersturmfuhrer, thank you for calling in to see me."

I raised my eyebrows, it was as sarcastic as I dared be, we both knew it was no invitation.

"I came as soon as I could, Sir."

"Quite so. Have you encountered the Langemarck Regiment on your travels? I am due to visit them in the morning. They're the motorcycle reconnaissance unit."

"I haven't, Sir, no. I'm not happy about continuing with this assignment."

He looked up, his expression blank.

"No?"

"Well, Sir, I feel that I should be serving the SS as a fighting soldier, after all, it's why we're here, isn't it?"

"Fighting who, Hoffman?"

"Well, the enemy, Sir, of course."

"And who are the enemy, Untersturmfuhrer?"

I nearly lost my temper with his bland, calm yet stupid questions.

"In case you hadn't noticed those people over there taking pot shots at us, Sir."

I put a strong emphasis on the 'Sir'.

"And what about the people taking pot shots at us on this side of the line, Hoffman?"

His manner was still calm and quiet but his words fell like hammer blows, I felt he would be a formidable chess player. He always seemed to think several moves ahead of me. I kept silent.

"You think about it, my friend. I will need a driver and escort to take me to talk to those Langemarck people. I'd like you with me, but not against your will and not if you plan on giving in to pressure from your brother officers. Decide in the morning. Let's hope no more regimental commanders get shot in the meantime. The Reichsfuhrer would be very distressed."

"Sir."

I saluted and left. His last words calculated to make me lose sleep overnight, as if it was my entire fault if some lunatic was killing our senior officers. Surely that's all it was, if it even was one of our own people. It could easily be partisans, though that would be something of a coincidence. In the morning there was no prospect of any action, providing that the Ivans left us alone, and I decided it would be churlish not to escort the old SD man on his visit to the reconnaissance regiment. Besides, he'd thrown the gauntlet down, suggesting I'd give in to pressure from the other officers. I detailed Mundt, Voss, Beidenberg and Merkel to come with us, Voss to drive. Bauer was apparently recovering at the unit hospital and due back with us in a couple of days. Voss brought the Kubi around to HQ and I escorted von Betternich out, and he sat down in the back seat. He made no comment about me accompanying him, merely wished us all a good morning. Voss drove us the five kilometres to where SS Langemarck were based. It was an old farm, the yard littered with the BMW motorcycle combinations that they used for high-speed mobility on the battlefield. Voss stopped the Kubi outside the farmhouse being used as the Regimental HQ. While we waited, von Betternich went inside and asked to see the acting commanding officer, a Sturmbannfuhrer Eicke. An NCO came out of the building with him and pointed out what looked like the old stables.

"The CO is in there, Sir, he's checking out our stores situation. It's a bitch to get spare parts for our machines, is that why you're here, to chase them up for us?"

"I'm afraid not, Scharfuhrer, but I'll pass your comments on."

The Sergeant smiled and nodded.

"To Reichsfuhrer Himmler when I return to Berlin."

The NCO's face fell, "I didn't mean..."

But von Betternich had already walked away, he was after all the master of the last word.

I followed him at a distance with Mundt, the other men stayed with the jeep. He reached the barn and turned to us. "I need to speak with Sturmbannfuhrer Eicke alone, would you wait for me here?"

Again, that polite request, that was no request. He opened the door and limped into the barn, the floor was covered in wooden crates, uniforms and coats hung from nails banged into the wooden walls. Eicke was shouting at a harassed NCO who was clutching a clipboard. Von Betternich went straight up to him. "Sturmbannfuhrer, a word with you, alone!"

Eicke stared at the officer approaching through the gloom. "Who the hell are you?"

"Von Betternich, Sturmbannfuhrer, Sicherheitsdienst. I'm here on the orders of Reichsfuhrer Himmler."

Eicke snapped at the NCO. "Get out, man. Out and close the door after you!"

He scuttled through the door and closed it. We waited outside. At first, we heard nothing, then the sound of a raised voice. It had to be Eicke, I knew that the SD man never raised his voice. Eicke shouted louder and louder, 'who the hell are you to ask me that kind of question' and so on. Then the door opened abruptly and Eicke came storming out, still shouting at von Betternich, who followed him out of the barn.

"You've no business coming here, the SD, we're trying to fight a war, people like you..."

He didn't get any further, the roar of aircraft engines drowned out his voice, together with the wail of the air raid alert, men shouting.

"Alarm!"

I looked up and saw the fighter coming in, a Yakovlev Yak-1, the description from my officer training etched in my mind. Our soldiers often mistook it for the British Spitfire, which was understandable, the British supplied their famous fighter to the Russian Front and they had become feared by the Luftwaffe after they began to appear in increasing numbers. But the Yak-1 was no slouch either, it had proved to be a match for many of our ME-109 Messerschmitts. As we scattered for cover, I looked around for other aircraft but it seemed to be a lone raider. Machine gun and cannon fire rained down on us as the pilot opened fire, we were sheltering underneath a Sonderkraftfahrzeug 251 armoured half-track, similar to the vehicle being repaired for us. The protection of the half-track was more for morale than reality, the fourteen-millimetre armour would not protect us from the 12.7mm machine gun bullets from the Yak, even less from its 20mm cannon. The Yak roared overhead and climbed away from the camp. Our anti-aircraft guns were slow to react, but now they started to fire in deadly earnest, sending streams of bullets after the Yak. I watched it turn in the sky less than a kilometre away from us, and then it came in again. A salvo of combined cannon and machine gun fire hammered into one of our machine gun positions, reducing it to a bloody pile of scrap and torn human tissue. The remaining gunner fired after him, but his shots went wide as the Yak swept past still shooting. A storm of fire enveloped an armoured half-track and left if a broken, shattered ruin, smoke and flames pouring out of it. The screams of the men sheltering underneath heard for several seconds until they went silent.

We ran over to try and pull out the casualties, but the flames kept us back. The men underneath would already have been dead anyway, burning fuel had saturated them and they had become human torches, hopefully dead through lack of oxygen before the worst of the flames started turning their bodies into charred meat. Firefighters ran up and started spraying the wreckage to put out the flames, but it was more for form's sake than anything else, there was nothing left to save, neither man nor machine. I looked around for my charge, the SD officer. Eicke was getting up from behind a pile of old engines parts, his uniform smeared with grease. Von Betternich had not moved, had just stood outside the barn in full view throughout the raid leaning on his cane. He looked at Eicke with a straight face.

"Sturmbannfuhrer, I imagine you'll be busy for some time dealing with the damage. I would like a full, written report on those matters I have mentioned, together with names and locations of the officers concerned. Would you send it over to SS Deutschland HQ, my office is located there. If you have any questions, I suggest you contact Berlin, Office of the Reichsfuhrer SS. Good day."

He came towards us. "Ah, Hoffman. Did our transport

survive undamaged?"

"I believe it did, Sir."

"Good, then let's get back to Headquarters. If we leave now we'll be in time for lunch."

We drove back along the bumpy track to Korenevo. Von Betternich kept checking through his notes and the journey was conducted in silence. The smell of roasted flesh was still in our nostrils, we'd come close in our own half-track to suffering the same fate as those poor devils at the Langemarck Regimental HQ. Voss stopped outside the monastery and I was about to walk away when the SD man stopped me.

"Hoffman, I'm going to speak to that Russian you captured, would you care to come with me?"

"Of course, Sir."

We found Commissar Captain Tereschova in his cell, von Betternich asked the guard to open it and we went in. Then he dismissed the guard. Tereschova looked nervous, I think I would have in his position. There was a standing order that all Political Commissars should be shot out of hand, he would be well aware of it and well aware of the author of that order, Adolf Hitler. Equally, I had been told that many unit commanders ignored the order, especially when the prisoner was a uniformed soldier, as was the case here.

"Captain, I wonder if you would answer some questions for me."

The Russian looked at the older man, his face was white. Did he think I was here to start pulling out his fingernails? Probably. The Russians deliberately spread myths about SS brutality to encourage their troops to fight on when they would otherwise surrender. Not all of them were myths, however.

"What do you want to know?" he asked suspiciously.

"Your Russian rifles, Captain, tell me about them. Are they better than ours, would you say?"

"Rifles? What the hell would I know about rifles?"

"Hoffman, ask the guard to bring us a pot of coffee, let's make it more comfortable in here. You do drink coffee, Captain?"

"Yes, I do."

"Good. Now, tell me what have you heard, do you form the impression that the German Kar 98 is better regarded than your Mosin–Nagant? What's the impression amongst the troops? Come, Captain, this isn't a military secret, I ask only out of curiosity."

The Russian shrugged. "Some of your rifles have fallen into our hands, it's true. There'll doubtless be large stocks of them after your defeat at Stalingrad."

He smirked as he said the name Stalingrad and I felt angry. A quarter of a million of our men were in the Sixth Army, the largest army in the German Order of Battle. All were dead or had surrendered to the Soviets in the ice-cold wastes on the banks of the River Volga.

"You weren't up against the Waffen SS in Stalingrad," I said hotly. I was proud of my place in an elite regiment, sure that we would not have allowed the surrender to the Russians.

"Wehrmacht, SS, it makes no difference, the result would have been the same," he said wearily. "An army cannot fight without food, fuel or weapons, Lieutenant."

I was about to snap back an angry retort when von Betternich told me to keep quiet.

"But, Sir, we lost a hundred thousand men killed at Stalingrad."

"And we lost three hundred thousand," Tereschova snapped back. "You shouldn't have come, SS man."

"Gentlemen, enough," the SD officer stopped us. "We are not here to discuss Stalingrad. Now, the rifles, Captain, is it true that some of your men prefer using captured Kar 98s?"

The guard returned carrying three steaming tin mugs of coffee. He brought them into the cell and left again. Von Betternich tasted it and pulled a face.

"Captain?"

"Well, yes, a few do prefer them, a very few, mainly partisans who have more access to captured German weapons and ammunition. But our regular troops, no, it is quite rare, I would imagine."

"What about your snipers, would they tend to prefer the Kar 98, especially the longer variants, over your own rifles?"

"Never!" the Captain snorted. "Our Mosin–Nagant is the finest sniper rifle in the world. Did you not hear of the record of Vasily Zaitsev in Stalingrad?"

We had all heard of Zaitsev through the unofficial grapevine at training school, where an appreciation of the tactics of Soviet snipers was part of the curriculum. The Soviets claimed that his career started in Stalingrad when Zaitsev's commanding officer pointed at one of our officers in a window eight hundred metres away. Vasily took aim from his standard issue Mosin-Nagant rifle and with one shot, our officer was down. A few moments later, two other German soldiers appeared in the window, checking their fallen comrade. He fired two more shots, and they were both killed. For this Zaitsev became a sniper and was awarded a medal. He became elevated to the status of virtual hero through the use of Soviet propaganda and established a snipers' training school in the Metiz factory in the ruined city of Stalingrad. Zaitsev's trained snipers were nicknamed leverets, or baby hares. They were extremely lethal hares too. Their toll on the morale of the Sixth Army was out of all proportion to their number of kills.

We chatted on for ten minutes more, but von Betternich had got what he wanted, the significance wasn't wasted on me. The person who was killing our senior officers wasn't likely to be a Soviet soldier. We left the cell and walked out through the camp.

"What are you thinking, Hoffman?" he asked me abruptly.

"It had to be the partisans, Sir."

He didn't reply as we walked on. Then Voss ran up to us.

"Sir, I need you to take a look at the Kubi, someone has interfered with it."

"Interfered, Oberschutze? In what way?"

"They planted a bomb, down in the engine compartment."

We hurried over to look at what they had found. A box, that seemed to be made of brass. Attached to the side was a pair of copper contacts, the whole thing wrapped in thick, rubberised insulating tape and coated with thick grease.

"Stand back, Sirs, Merkel is taking the top off to disarm it."

"Is that safe, Voss?"

"Safer than leaving it armed, Untersturmfuhrer, it could go off at any moment."

I didn't say anything, but we stood back ten metres from where Merkel was working with a box of tools. He finished unscrewing the lid and gently, very carefully prised off the lid. Then he snipped through the internal wires.

"It's safe now, I've disconnected the firing mechanism," he said, standing up and coming towards us to show us the bomb.

We inspected the device. It was filled with enough explosive to destroy the Kubi and all of its occupants.

"Why didn't it go off?" I asked him.

"Useless battery, look, they used a dud. Probably didn't realise it, else we would have gone up like Mount Vesuvius."

"The materials to make the bomb, do you recognise them?"

"Oh, yes, Sir. Before I transferred to the SS I was in an engineer regiment. It's all standard stuff. German, of course."

I went with von Betternich back to his office.

"Well, Hoffman, what do you think now of my investigation? More of your partisans?"

"Possibly not, Sir, but I'm not sure who could have done it."

Clearly the bomb could have been planted at any time recently, when we visited the Langemarck Regiment, even before then at the camp of Der Fuhrer Regiment. Or here, within Deutschland Regiment itself.

"So the questions we have to ask ourselves are who is doing it and why is it so vital to them that they stop my investigation?"

"Maybe it is a conspiracy, Sir, one to destroy the SS from within."

Even as I said it I realised how absurd that premise

97

was. I wasn't aware of the current strength of the Waffen SS on all fronts, but it had to be more than half a million men under arms.

"But surely it must be partisans behind it, what other explanation would there be?"

The SD officer looked at me steadily. "In my experience as a policeman there are only a limited number of motives for murder. There are crimes of passion, of course. Revenge, that's not uncommon. Then there are the psychotic killers, they do it purely for the thrill of it. Lastly, there is financial gain, by far the biggest motivator of men."

"Are you saying that these officers were robbed when they were killed?"

"It doesn't appear that way, no."

"So do we have a mad killer on the loose?"

"Probably not, no."

I was becoming exasperated with von Betternich. He was clearly not prepared to share his thoughts about the murders, which was his right, but if he wanted my cooperation it was making things much more difficult. It came as no surprise to me that he was almost reading my thoughts.

"You need patience, Hoffman. I have some ideas but nothing definite. Have you decided to assist me now that they've tried to kill you too?"

"Yes, of course, Sir." And when I found them I'd like

to hang them from the nearest tree.

"There you are, Untersturmfuhrer, you have a strong incentive to keep in mind while we look for the killer. Self preservation."

I was certain that he would always be one jump ahead of me. As for the murderer, or murderers, if there were such people and it wasn't just a succession of unfortunate coincidences perpetrated by partisans, it may even come down to whether they could kill von Betternich before he discovered who they were. I think I would have put my money on the wily old policeman, except that staying alive on the Eastern Front was as much a matter of luck as of skill. The more I thought about it, the angrier I got. My own side may have tried to kill me, fellow SS men. I was outraged, frightened and furious in equal measures. They would have to be stopped.

CHAPTER FOUR

"In the course of my life I have very often been a prophet, and have usually been ridiculed for it. During the time of my struggle for power, it was in the first instance only the Jewish race that received my prophecies with laughter when I said that I would one day take over the leadership of the state and with it that of the whole nation and that I would then among other things settle the Jewish problem...but I think that for some time now they have been laughing on the other side of their face. Today I will once more be a prophet: if the international Jewish financiers in and outside Europe should succeed in plunging the nations once more into a world war, then the result will not be the Bolshevising of the earth and thus the victory of Jewry, but the annihilation of the Jewish race in Europe."

Adolf Hitler January 1939

Later that evening Sturmbannfuhrer Muller again approached me.

"Hoffman, have you considered this business with the SD?"

"Sir, I have, I shall continue to assist Sturmbannfuhrer von Betternich."

His face went red with anger. "I thought I made it clear that I take a dim view of my officers helping this," he paused to think of a suitable word, "this policeman, he's poking his nose into the regiment's affairs when we're trying to fight a war. If the CO hadn't been killed he'd never have allowed it."

"But, Sir, the CO was almost certainly murdered by the same person, or persons."

"Rubbish. Colonel Brandt was killed by partisans."

I didn't answer, but I was beginning to agree with von Betternich. Partisans were not known to be that selective, they'd shoot officers only when targets of opportunity appeared, otherwise they'd just snipe at anyone. Muller wasn't done with me.

"Hoffman, I'm beginning to wonder if you're the right kind of officer for the SS, perhaps you should consider a transfer to the Wehrmacht."

I was stunned. It was almost like suggesting I desert to the Russians.

"I would prefer to say here, Sir, in the SS."

"Well, you'll need to learn to behave like an SS officer,

won't you?"

He stormed off and I wondered had I made the right decision. Yet they had tried to kill me. I was determined to find out who was behind it and ignore Muller's threats for the present, I know my father would have done exactly the same thing.

I went back inside the church where my platoon had clustered around the old iron stove, the temperature outside was well below freezing, as usual. I wondered about the monks, they sat around a small fire out in the open, close to the camp. Surely they would freeze to death in these conditions, they needed to be indoors. Some of them were old men, outdoors on the Russian steppe in winter was no place for them. I felt guilty as I warmed my hands on the stove, after all, this was their place before we came here. I was sitting in their church, warming myself on timber that had undoubtedly come from their church property.

"What do we do now, Sir?" Mundt asked.

"We carry on as before, I'm determined to find out who's behind this, Sergeant. You feel the same, one or more of our people are trying to kill our own men, to kill us, even. Doesn't that bother you?"

"Not as much as having a bomb hidden under my backside, Sir, no."

"So you think we should give up, Mundt?"

He squirmed, I'd spoken sharply to him. "Well, maybe,

yes, perhaps it's not a good idea to keep going, surely you can see that? That bomb was just a warning."

"No, I can't see it that way at all." The others were watching with interest, but I didn't care, I was sick of being pushed around. "It's quite simple, you see. I was brought up never to walk away from a fight, and I'm not walking away from this one. Goodnight, gentlemen."

I got up, pushed my blanket screen aside, and slumped down on my mattress. I'd joined the SS to fight the enemy, not our own soldiers. I knew exactly where my loyalties lay, it was just that not everyone else did.

The following morning I reported to von Betternich's office with Mundt and three of the men. He seemed more cheerful.

"Ah, Hoffman, we're going to see the surgeon, come along with me, perhaps you'll all learn something."

Inside the temporary morgue, Colonel Brandt's body was laid out as I'd seen it before. There was no need for refrigeration, the temperature never went above freezing even during the day. The surgeon looked irritated again maybe he had a hangover. Heavy drinking was by no means unusual on the Eastern Front, we'd all been warned about it.

"What now?" he snapped. "I told you everything I know."

"Yes, of course you did," von Betternich replied. "Since then, I had the other post mortem reports forwarded to you, the ones concerning the previous officers that were killed."

"And?" the surgeon said, his manner growing surlier by the minute. "You do realise that I still have many wounded men to attend to?"

"If you think I am impeding your duties, feel free to make a report and I will attach it in my next report to the Reichsfuhrer, Doctor. He has a personal interest in this affair. Perhaps you would prefer this to be a Gestapo investigation, you could of course suggest that to him."

The surgeon had tried to bluff it out, that was clear. Equally clear was that his mind had worked through the various possible outcomes of non-cooperation, he quickly backed down. The Gestapo was the trump card. Generalleutnant der Polizei Ernst Kaltenbrunner was both head of the Sicherheitsdienst and the Geheime Staatspolizei, as every member of the SS well knew. It was well within von Betternich's power to call in the Gestapo.

"What do you want to know, Major?"

"You have had time to look at those reports, my question is simple. Were they all killed in a similar manner, a bullet from a Kar 98?"

"Yes, as a matter of fact they were. It was partisans, of course. They are known to use our own weapons against us, it's nothing new."

"Yes. Doctor, describe for me how you believe the Colonel was shot."

"It's only guesswork of course."

Von Betternich nodded.

"I would say that he was shot from behind, probably at quite long range, none of his soldiers saw who shot him so the shooter must have been quite some distance away. The Colonel would have been going forward. The marksman was armed with a Kar 98, positioned in a slightly elevated position from Brandt, perhaps in a tree or on top of a vehicle. He fired, the bullet angled downwards and hit him from behind and went straight into his heart, where it lodged in the ventricle, as you already know. Had the shot been from closer range, the bullet would almost certainly have gone straight through him and we would never have recovered it."

"And the other senior officers who were killed?"

"Yes just the same, remarkable really, an amazing coincidence."

"That the shooter identified and killed all of the officers from a similar distance in a similar way with a similar gun?"

"Indeed, yes, well..." he tailed off.

"Thank you, Doctor. Write everything up you just told me and send it across to my office. Hoffman, we're leaving."

He limped away and we hurried after him. "Where to next, Sir?"

"Get the Kubelwagen and make sure it's clear of any

explosives. We're off to SS Der Fuhrer Headquarters to speak to Standartenfuhrer Stettner."

Voss and Mundt checked the Kubi over thoroughly, someone was obviously serious about us not finishing this investigation and their inspection was meticulous. Finally they said it was clear of any explosives or booby traps and we drove away to find the temporary HQ of Der Fuhrer Regiment. Like us, they were Panzer Grenadiers attached to the Das Reich Division of the First Panzer Army. The Regiment was settled in a small village about five kilometres from Deutschland HQ, if the Russian artillery barrage hadn't started we might have reached there in less than ten minutes. Instead, we had only driven a kilometre before we were pinned down as both sides exchanged artillery fire. About half a kilometre away I could make out the dark grey shapes of some of our tanks, the Second Panzer Regiment were laagered just inside the tree line of a nearby wood, clearly the Russians were aiming at what they assumed was their location. Instead, they found us.

Voss drove the Kubi off the road and into some trees. We scrambled out and dove into the nearest shell hole as more rounds whistled in and landed nearby. They fell all through the wood, trees splintered to matchwood as shell after shell destroyed the ancient trunks that gave us our shelter. Von Betternich was next to me, looking with interest towards the bright flashes that lit up the Russian positions as their guns fired.

"They don't know their business, do they?" he said to me.

"Sir?"

"They're hitting the wrong trees, Hoffman, obviously they wanted to hit the tanks in that wood over there."

I could see our Panzers, they had started up, smoke pouring from their exhausts and they moved off in formation towards the enemy.

"Perhaps someone saw our Kubi and mistook it for a staff car," Mundt said. "They watch out for things like that, the Russians are not all that stupid."

"Nor that clever, Mundt, they've missed the tanks altogether," I replied.

Our Panzers went into action, we could see the explosions as they fired their main guns at the Russians and the artillery barrage slackened as the gunners took shelter from the deadly barrage. Our own artillery stopped firing altogether to avoid hitting our tanks. We couldn't see anything now, just flashes of fire and smoke everywhere, a thick fog, deafening explosions and the chatter of machine guns. Then the first of our tanks came back, racing out of the far wood, heading straight towards us, swerving to avoid the Russian anti-tank fire.

"Let's go," Mundt shouted. Before I could protest, he and the men almost threw von Betternich and me bodily into the Kubi and Voss was driving away at speed.

"Scharfuhrer, what the hell is going on?" I asked,

when I finally had time to get over the shock of being manhandled by my own men.

"Russian counterattack, Sir, they're coming this way," Mundt gasped.

The Kubi rocked on its springs as Voss flung it along the track and then braked to a halt.

"Russian artillery, they're covering the road, we can't get past them."

We could see the guns, they'd rushed them up on the flank of their T34s, it was obviously an ambush. A shell whistled overhead.

"They've seen us!" Beidenberg shouted. "I can see one of their soldiers pointing at us."

Another shell whistled past and exploded in the trees.

"Voss, turn around man, hurry," I snapped.

He flung the Kubi around and hared back the way we had come. Ahead and to the side of us, our Panzers were still racing away from the enemy.

"Very clever, don't you think, Hoffman?"

"If you say so, Sir."

Von Betternich was watching the enemy action with keen interest. I wished that he would put his brain to work to find us a way out of this, we were in serious trouble and it wasn't even our fight.

"But I do say so, it's a clever trap, the Russians caught our Panzers with their pants down."

I didn't reply, up ahead a group of T34s had almost

reached the track, we were boxed in.

The Panzers just crashed into the trees in their headlong flight away from the Russians, their immense weight and power with the grip of their caterpillar tracks smashed a way through for them. Our Kubelwagen was a simple, two-wheel drive vehicle based on a Volkswagen saloon car. The off road performance was lamentable, but it was all we had.

"Into the trees, Voss, try and follow a trail that the Panzers have made."

He threw the wheel over and we began bumping through the deep wood. He twisted and turned to follow the path blazed by the tanks, I thought we'd got away with it until I was suddenly flying through the air. I landed heavily, the Kubi was upturned in a deep gully concealed by foliage. The dip was no barrier to a Tiger tank but impassable for our vehicle. Von Betternich was lying on the ground groaning, at least he was alive. The others seemed unhurt, Voss, Mundt, Beidenberg and Merkel picked up the SD officer and carried him away from the wrecked Kubi.

"Down into the gully, quickly, the Russians are nearly on us."

We scrambled down into the cover of the shallow ravine and hid in the foliage. The thundering of the T34s was awesome, diesel engines roaring, guns firing, machine guns chattering as they swept after our Panzers. One roared right over our position, its tracks carrying it like a portable bridge over the narrow ravine as it plunged on. Then another and another. Some had tank riders clinging grimly to their hulls, it seemed like a suicidal way to go into battle, probably it was. Then they were past in their frantic pursuit and the wood started to go quiet. I looked down at von Betternich.

"How are you, Sir? Have you been injured?"

He gave a tired smile. "I'm too old for this, Hoffman. No, I'm not injured, just a few bruises. Where are we?"

"Behind the Russian lines, Sir."

We kept down in the shelter of the gully for over an hour, waiting for the last of the Russians to go past. Several stragglers came by, bringing up supplies, one unit dragging along a Maxim machine gun on its two-wheeled carriage. Then we were on our own. They were all looking at me, von Betternich was the senior officer but he deftly passed the ball to me.

"I'm just a policeman, Hoffman, I wouldn't dream of interfering in military matters. I'm sure you'll find a way out for us back to our own lines."

I went a few metres away from them to clear my head and tried to think. In front of us, to the west, we had what had looked like a division of Soviet tanks. To the north, there were the Soviet anti-tank guns, dug into their position to support the tanks, behind us to the east was most of the Soviet army, several million men. The solution was obvious. I went back to them.

"We head south. The T34s were blocking us there but hopefully they've pushed on as part of the Russian advance. Voss, Mundt, can we get the Kubi operational again?"

They looked at me in shocked surprise. "But, Sir, it's smashed, besides, how would we get it out of the gully?"

"You must have ropes, Voss. Isn't there a winch attached to the front?"

"Well, yes, there is, but I doubt the engine will run."

"Why not?"

He scratched his head. "It may run, I suppose."

"We'll try it, get the ropes and let's try and get it out first."

Fortunately, it had slewed around so that the front was facing us, they were able to fasten the ropes to the winch and the other end to a strong tree. They began winching and within ten minutes the wheels started to show above the edge of the gully.

"Wouldn't it be better to walk back?" von Betternich asked me.

"We don't know how far the advance reached, Sir. Suppose it was fifty miles to our new headquarters?"

"I see what you mean."

The Kubi finally got onto level ground. It was bent and buckled in places but intact. We all heaved on one side of the bodywork and managed to right it. Voss pressed the starter and the engine fired immediately, they looked around with wide grins. Someone muttered something about Volkswagen engines, 'take you anywhere'.

"Well done, men," I told them. "Let's get in and head back to the track, then we'll turn south."

Voss drove carefully through the wood, back the way we had come until the track came into view. I asked him to stop before we got into open ground and I went forward on foot with Mundt. It was a no-go. The Soviets had established an encampment within full view of the track, not much more than a kilometre from where we stood. They had already begun to pitch mess tents and even from this distance, I could smell food cooking. I felt hungry, wondering when we'd get our next meal. Mundt was licking his lips.

"Do we have any food in the Kubi, Sergeant?" I asked him. It should have been a routine mission, we'd not been part of any planned attack and there'd been no obvious need to bring supplies. That was then, now we were stuck out on the frozen steppes, behind enemy lines and getting hungry. Mundt shook his head. Well, we'd have to be hungry, it was quite simple. We walked back to the Kubi and I explained the problem to them.

"So that way is blocked, we have to go forward through the wood, we'll follow another tank trail and keep away from any holes in the ground this time. Any questions?"

"Perhaps if we get the opportunity we should take a prisoner, Untersturmfuhrer? Find out where the front lines have moved on to?" von Betternich suggested.

"Yes, Sir, that's a good idea. In the meantime, we'll keep moving south west until we meet up with our own lines." Or until we run into a Russian division of tanks, I didn't add. We got into the Kubi and Voss drove away carefully, watching the forest ground for ditches and holes. We stopped once and Mundt cleared the bodywork from where it was fouling the rear wheel, it had been making a loud clanking noise. After that, it was quieter.

It took us an hour to reach the edge of the wood. In front of us, to the southwest was a small town, possibly a village, a regiment of Soviet tanks had stopped immediately outside. To the west was an area of unbroken steppes with no sign of movement, to the north were more low snow-covered hills and woods. There was no obvious sign of the enemy over there and we picked our way carefully in that direction. It was also the direction of Korenevo, our last regimental headquarters. We skirted the edge of the wood, several times Voss drove into the trees when aircraft flew over. Finally, I estimated that we were within three kilometres of Korenevo and still no sign of the enemy. It seemed incredible that the Soviets could have swept across the wide battlefield and swung away from our headquarters but I had to allow for the possibility that our HQ was still operational. While we were tucked inside the shelter of the trees, we all heard the sound of an engine coming towards us, I deployed the men out of sight. Von Betternich sheltered behind the Kubi while Voss stayed to guard the vehicle, Mundt sent Merkel and Beidenberg to our flank with the MG34 and then came with me to the edge of the wood. We saw the jeep moving slowly towards us, then it stopped, less than fifty metres away. It was an American Willys adorned with a red star, the Russians had been given hundreds of these by their American allies and when they fell into our hands they were highly prized. Unlike our Kubelwagen they were four-wheel drives and kept going in the snow and mud that was a constant hazard on the Eastern Front. The jeep had a driver and a single occupant, he looked to be a middle ranking officer but I couldn't see his rank badges from where we were.

"Why have they stopped?" Mundt asked.

"Maybe to take a leak, Sergeant?"

I got out my binoculars and focussed on the jeep. The officer had his own binoculars and was looking west. While he did so, the driver was setting up a radio aerial, a complicated affair with several poles and guy ropes. On the back seat of the Willys was the radio, bulky and complicated looking with many dials and knobs. It was all too good an opportunity to miss.

"We need to take them," I said to Mundt. "I'll watch them, tell Voss and the other two to leave the MG34, we'll start working our way through the trees until we're close, then we can just surprise them."

"No MG34? It could be useful if they see us coming."

"We may be able to use the radio, I don't want it shot full of holes."

"Right."

He crept away and was back minutes later with the men. I told them what I wanted and we started to creep through the trees towards the Russians. When we were abreast of them and no more than twenty metres away, we cocked our weapons.

"No shooting if you can avoid it, I want that radio."

They nodded and we crawled slowly across the forest floor. Voss was covering us with the rifle he'd brought from the Kubi, if they spotted us he would try and hit them with well-aimed shots that would avoid the radio. However, when we reached the edge of the wood it was very undramatic, we jumped up, Merkel spoke to them in Russian.

"You are now our prisoners, put your hands up!"

The officer, who was a captain, looked at us in shock. We were well behind their lines, the last place he had expected to find a contingent of SS. His driver simply put up his hands and waited in that resigned way we'd found was typical of both the Russian soldier and peasant, as if they'd seen so much misery, what was a little more? Merkel and Beidenberg swiftly checked them and removed their weapons. Fortunately, the officer spoke some German, apparently there'd been something of a scramble to learn the language ever since we'd first invaded back in 1941. I heard the snap of a twig as someone approached and we all whirled around, but it was only von Betternich, limping forward to take a look. I addressed the captain.

"I wish to know how far your advance has taken you, where are your armies?"

Not the hero this one, he pointed straight across the steppes. "We're camped about five kilometres in that direction, due west. Are you going to kill us?"

I couldn't see how we could possibly deal with taking them back, but neither could I kill unarmed prisoners out of hand. I shook my head. "No."

"What next, Hoffman?" von Betternich asked. "Is the radio useful to us?"

"I don't think so, Sir. If the lines are only five kilometres away we could give our position away by using it."

"And the prisoners? You know there is not enough room in our vehicle to bring both of them. We can hardly leave one of them here to raise the alarm. The officer could be useful, though."

It was a difficult position, I looked across the endless steppes, hoping to see a sign of our troops but there was nothing only the village to the southwest, where the Russian tanks had halted.

In the end, I pumped the Russians for as much information as I could get from them. We tried the radio but were unable to raise our own people, perhaps they were on a frequency that the Russian set did not cover. I got the men to smash the radio and disable the Willys, Voss found a hammer and knocked a hole in the engine block and ripped out the wiring.

"It seems a shame, Sir, we could have used this vehicle back in our unit."

"I'd sooner not re-enter our lines in a Soviet jeep covered in red stars, Voss. There have already been reports of our people firing on captured Willys jeeps that we've taken into service, we're running enough risks as it is."

"Yes, Sir."

I smiled as he continued grumbling, but finally I was satisfied that the vehicle and radio were useless. We took the Soviets' boots and weapons and the men tied the prisoners to the bodywork of the jeep with a length of fencing wire, I also got them to drain the petrol tank to give us extra fuel to get back. The prisoners would work loose eventually but I intended to be well clear of the area by that time. Von Betternich was sceptical.

"Your concern is touching, Untersturmfuhrer, I just hope it doesn't get us killed."

"Would you like to shoot them yourself, Sir?"

He smiled. "I'm just a policeman, Hoffman, why would I do that? That's a job for a soldier."

But he didn't argue very forcefully. I suspected that he was more policeman, than SD thug. The security services had a reputation for having both in its ranks, from the former SD leader Heydrich, an intellectual and sportsman, to Muller, the notorious head of the Gestapo department of the RSHA. Muller was the very personification of the Gestapo, murderous to anyone who fell foul of the Gestapo, he was known to be almost as vicious and ruthless with his own people. He had little allegiance to any political persuasion, other than the one that would give him career advancement. More than one party member had gone on record as stating that they could not understand how so odious an opponent of the movement could become head of the Gestapo. He had once referred to Hitler as 'an immigrant unemployed house painter' and 'an Austrian draft-dodger'. Hardly the way to ingratiate himself with the leaders of the Third Reich, yet his tireless brutality had taken him to the very top of his profession. Muller would of course have shot the prisoners, probably tortured them first for fun.

We returned to the Kubi and drove on, keeping close to the trees so that we could duck inside at any time. For several kilometres, we saw no sign of any soldiers, neither the enemy nor ours. Suddenly, an artillery barrage bellowed out from within the trees about a kilometre in front of us. The distant ground suddenly boiled with tanks and men, our own Panzers were attacking, I felt like cheering. We hid in the trees and watched the glorious sight of an SS Panzer Regiment charging across the plain. They were accompanied by STuGIII assault guns and behind them dozens of other self-propelled guns and Sonderkraftfahrzeug 251armoured half-tracks. Das Reich Division was at last attacking in strength, putting a stop to the Russians being able to pick them off piecemeal with their constant harrying attacks. Thirty or more T34s raced out of the wood to intercept them and we could see the Soviet tanks in the southwest manoeuvring to join the battle. We were in a unique position to observe the action, on a low hill where we could see for several kilometres north, south and west. The Soviet artillery kept up a ferocious barrage, but so far failed to hit any of our tanks or half-tracks. The T34s joined in, but were equally unsuccessful. Our own tanks scored heavily, decimating the Soviet armour, the STuGIIIs kept up a furious rate of fire and our artillery, concealed in a distant wood, kept up a ferocious rate of counter battery fire that annihilated the Russian guns. For ten minutes the battle raged but it was one sided, we'd caught the Russians unprepared this time and even when their tanks joined in from the southwest there were not enough to turn the tide. A green flare burned brightly in the sky and the Russian survivors turned abruptly and headed east. Behind them they left more than half of their vehicles burned and broken on the battlefield, yet our own losses were light, no more than three tanks and a STuGIII destroyed. My platoon shouted with joy, I almost felt like joining in it was a redoubtable victory. I told the men to get into the Kubi and we drove across the steppe, straight for our own troops. I was counting on the distinctive shape of the Kubelwagen to protect us from itchy trigger fingers.

A Tiger commander, an Obersturmfuhrer, watched warily as we approached, I could see the co-axial machine gun keeping us covered.

"Who are you?"

I explained that we had been caught behind the lines. The presence of an SD Sturmbannfuhrer helped persuade him that we were genuine and I sensed the finger on the trigger of the machine gun relaxing.

"My congratulations on beating the Russians, it was very impressive," I said to him sincerely.

"Thanks, but we'll need to do more than this, they've retaken Kursk."

We were all shocked. Kursk had been bitterly fought over, but our assumption was that it would only be a matter of time before we used it as a springboard for the renewal of the offensive east.

"So what was this lot all about?" I asked him.

"The Soviets had pushed a salient through our lines, they threatened to divide us. Before we can even think about Kursk we needed to re-unite our armies, now that we've beaten them back we can regroup to try and take Kursk again."

So we had to do it all again. I was still new to this, but I knew that my platoon had been involved in the bitter fighting around both Kursk and Kharkov. The bitter disillusionment on their faces was a testament to the failure of our armies to make progress against the Soviet juggernaut. He gave us directions to Deutschland HQ and I thanked him, Voss drove us away in silence. Von Betternich leaned towards me.

"Hubris, Hoffman. Just when you think things are going well, the gods snatch victory away from you."

"I thought it was the Soviets that did that," I snapped back

He smiled. "Yes, of course, you are right."

We drove on in silence. Soon we started to reach the first signs of our division, supplies, ammunition and replacements being rushed backwards and forwards. We stopped next to a Feldgendarmerie post and were given directions. Ten minutes later we drove into the temporary camp of SS Deutschland Regiment, the men scattered to the cookhouse to find food. Von Betternich disappeared into the radio tent, presumably to contact Berlin. Muller appeared, he was in a foul mood.

"Hoffman, where the hell have you been?"

I explained that we were heading for SS Der Fuhrer Regiment when we got caught in the Russian advance.

"That's all very well, but we had our hands full fighting the Russians, as did Der Fuhrer, while you were messing around with that damn SD man. I've a good mind to charge you for dereliction of duty."

"Look, Sir, I don't want this assignment any more than you do. I'd much prefer fighting with the regiment, but the Sturmbannfuhrer insists that this mission is essential for the morale of the whole division. We've lost some good commanders, Sir, including our own CO."

"To partisans, yes, they're always active behind our lines. You know how I feel about this, I'll speak to von Betternich later. Dismissed, Hoffman, get yourself something to eat."

I went to the cookhouse and scrounged up a bowl of stew and some black bread, our division seemed to fight on the same fare every day. Mundt was still there with the platoon.

"What do we do next, Sir," he asked me anxiously. "The men are not happy about this SD business, some of the other units are starting to haze them about it."

I was tired of the whole business too, but I couldn't admit it to an NCO. "Anything you can't handle, Scharfuhrer?"

"Not yet, Sir, but it could get worse. They're asking if our men are here to fight the enemy or to grass them up to the police."

"It's to be expected, I suppose. I think things are coming to a head, the CO is pretty fed up about losing half a platoon to the SD too. Give it a little longer, maybe we'll be able to get out of it."

Mundt nodded, but he was anything but happy.

In the late afternoon, Muller called me to his temporary office, which was a tent fastened to the side of his Horch armoured car. When I went in, von Betternich was already there. It was obvious that they had been arguing. The policeman nodded to me in a friendly way, Muller just glared.

"I want to clear this nonsense up once and for all," he spat out. "This investigation is interfering with the smooth running of this unit, it's got to stop and I want all of my officers available to fight. That includes you, Hoffman."

"Sir!" I acknowledged.

"So Sturmbannfuhrer von Betternich, would you kindly find someone else to assist you and leave my men to carry out their duties, clear?"

"Of course it's clear," the SD man smiled. "But equally, of course, I have my own orders from Berlin."

"Berlin is a long way from here. They have no idea of what kind of a war we are fighting."

"I'll make your feelings known to them, Sturmbannfuhrer," von Betternich smiled gently.

Muller knew he was being played but wasn't sure how far he could go. I pitied him, he was honestly trying to maintain a fighting regiment under difficult conditions. As it happened, an unexpected arrival took the decision of how to cope with the SD out of his hands.

"Achtung!"

There was the sound of vehicle engines and he opened

the tent flap to look out. A convoy of vehicles was coming through the snow, in the lead an armoured half-track flying a general's pennant. A senior officer sat rigidly in the rear looking around at the camp. We all recognised the figure of Obergruppenfuhrer und General der Waffen-SS Paul Hausser, the commander of Second SS Panzer Corps. Muller's face dropped as the vehicles braked to a halt and soldiers jumped out and took up position around the General's car. Then he got out and waited for Muller to approach. He was a tall, immaculate man, wearing a general officer's greatcoat with contrasting lapels. Even in the snow his jackboots gleamed, at his throat was the Knight's Cross he had won during the Barbarossa campaign. Under the command of von Manstein, he was regarded as a superb officer and clever tactician, the right man to turn the campaign on the Eastern Front around. He was well-liked and widely known in Das Reich by the nickname 'Papa'. Muller rushed up to greet him, clicked his heels to attention, right arm straight up in the salute.

"Heil Hitler, Herr Obergruppenfuhrer, this is an honour."

Hausser casually returned the salute. I'm on an inspection of our front line troops, Muller, tell me, how is everything going?"

He took Muller by the arm and led him away in the direction of our vehicle park to look at our half-tracks. All around the camp, men were running to get into their units ready for inspection, pulling on jackboots and helmets and shouldering their weapons. Hausser's entourage followed while he went around and looked at the vehicles, spoke to officers and men and generally made himself known to all of us. As much as anything, it was clearly a morale-boosting mission and it worked.

I was waiting with von Betternich next to Muller's armoured car when the General and Muller came back. They went inside the tent and von Betternich was called in. I heard them talking in quiet voices for a short time, something about Kharkov, then the voices became heated. Finally, Hausser snapped out an order of some sort and they all went quiet again. After a few more minutes, the tent flap opened and Hausser emerged, said a friendly goodbye to the troops and drove off in his half-track. Muller called me into his tent with von Betternich.

"It seems that your platoon is to continue to assist the SD," he said. "I'll leave you to it."

He nodded to von Betternich and gave him a half salute. "Sir." Then he left.

I raised my eyebrows.

"It seems that the Reichsfuhrer has decided to promote me, Hoffman, I am now an Obersturmbannfuhrer."

"Congratulations, Sir."

"Thank you, yes. But I think my promotion is to facilitate this investigation more than for any reason of merit. Now, in the morning we will try again to meet

Standartenfuhrer Werner Stettner, the CO of Der Fuhrer Regiment. Let's hope the Russians do not get in our way this time."

I went to rejoin my platoon, the men had rigged a series of lean-tos, that made our previous accommodation in the church at Korenevo seem positively luxurious. Mundt had made sure that I had a screened off shelter for myself, although I noted with amusement that it was furthest from the campfire that they had built. I decided to try and enjoy some of its warmth before I got some sleep. Merkel poured me a mug of coffee unasked. I was astonished. It tasted like coffee.

"Where the hell did you get this?"

They all looked away and I set my mind to thinking, who would have had access to real coffee on the Eastern Front in the middle of winter? Then it hit me, of course!

"I trust General Hausser can spare this?" I asked them. In the darkness, a soldier said 'General Who?' But I let it go. It was worth it for the coffee.

"What's new, Sir?" Mundt asked. "Can we go back to being full-time soldiers again?"

"I'm afraid not, Sergeant. Not just yet. The Obersturmbannfuhrer wishes to visit Der Fuhrer Regiment in the morning."

They raised their eyebrows when they heard his new rank.

"Maybe this mysterious shooter will put a round

through his brain," someone murmured.

That of course was always a possibility and was in part why we were escorting him. But in that case, it would be proved that one of our own people was doing the killing which meant that the mission really was fully justified. Why the hell couldn't they leave aside their stupid squabbles until the war was over? The Russians wouldn't leave me alone, that was for sure, but at least my own people could. That wasn't too much to ask for, or perhaps it was. I almost wished for von Betternich to meet with an accident, at least a slight wound so that he could be recalled and leave me to continue with my military career. But somehow he seemed to possess a charmed life, a way of deftly avoiding the potholes that life put in his way. Perhaps it was what he had learned as a policeman. Or maybe within the Sicherheitsdienst.

CHAPTER FIVE

"I can give vent to my inmost feelings only in the form of humble thanks to Providence which called upon me and vouchsafed it to me, once an unknown soldier of the Great War, to rise to be the Leader of my people, so dear to me. Providence showed me the way to free our people from the depths of its misery without bloodshed and to lead it upward once again.

Providence granted that I might fulfill my life's task-to raise my German people out of the depths of defeat and to liberate it from the bonds of the most outrageous dictate of all times... I have regarded myself as called upon by Providence to serve my own people alone and to deliver them from their frightful misery."

Adolf Hitler April 1939

I was awoken in the morning with another mug of General Hausser's excellent coffee. I buckled on my kit and rounded up the men ready to accompany von Betternich. Our Kubi was still serviceable, though very battered, and we piled into it ready to leave. The SD officer limped out, I noticed his lapels bore the badges of his new rank. He was reading through a sheaf of reports and barely waved a good morning to me. We drove off, Der Fuhrer was encamped only two kilometres away and we soon arrived in their headquarters, part of an old wayside railway station. A train was stationary in the siding, the engine steaming away in the cold air while soldiers worked to unload supplies of food and ammunition. We were shown into the CO's office, obviously it had been the stationmaster's in happier times. Standartenfuhrer Werner Stettner sat on a peculiar chair in front of the fireplace, a fire was blazing in the hearth and his orderly was throwing extra logs on the blaze. An adjutant was standing nearby, an Obersturmfuhrer, with a sneering expression on his face.

"Gentlemen, do come in," he shouted to us.

Mundt waited outside the door with Merkel and Beidenberg while Voss stayed with the vehicle. Stettner was an interesting sight. A handsome, lean man of about thirty-five, his uniform was battered and well-worn. At his throat, a Knight's Cross hung at a careless angle and he was unshaven. His feet were on a wooden stool warming at the fire, his jackboots on the floor. Next to him was a battle-worn MP38 together with a creased leather belt holding a pistol holster. The picture was clear, probably deliberately, he was a fighting soldier with little time for the formalities.

Von Betternich and I came to attention. "Heil Hitler," we chorused.

Stettner just waved, as if Hitler was of no consequence.

"What can I do for the SD?" His expression was friendly enough, I noted.

My eyes were drawn to his chair, virtually a throne. It had an enclosed base decorated with carvings, the arms and back were also carved. All the woodwork was painted in gilt with rich, red velvet upholstery over the arms and back, though it was very worn and threadbare.

"We are investigating the untimely deaths of several senior officers," von Betternich explained.

"There's a war on, my friend. Doesn't the SD know that?"

"Of course, Sir. May I have permission to look at your unit's movement records, perhaps I could speak with some of your men?"

Abruptly Stettner stood up, his expression was no longer friendly.

"Now listen to me. To the east, we are barely holding, Kursk has already fallen. SS Leibstandarte and some of our Wehrmacht units are defending Kharkov, but reports suggest that the Russians are trying to encircle us and take the city, which could mean the loss of two divisions of troops unless by some miracle they can get out before the Russians complete their manoeuvre. Der Fuhrer has orders to prepare to go to their assistance with other elements of the SS Panzer Corps. Now, you come here and tell me that you want to waste our time by inspecting my records and talking to the men. What would you say if you were me, Obersturmbannfuhrer?"

He'd picked the wrong man to reason with. "I'd obey my orders, Sir," von Betternich said.

Stettner was silent for a moment, and then he nodded. "Very well, but not now, you'll have to wait. You may return after the matter of Kharkov is decided and conduct your investigation then, not before. Clear?"

"Of course," the SD officer said. "Thank you, Sir."

We saluted and walked out of the office, I was astonished that the policeman had given up so easily. I should have known that he knew exactly what I was thinking.

"I got what I came for, Hoffman, don't worry. After they've finished their little squabble over Kharkov we'll be back and do as the CO suggested."

I half smiled at his description of a little squabble, several armoured divisions, perhaps even two Soviet armies as well, manoeuvring to take or defend the city. I didn't however give him the satisfaction of asking exactly what he'd got from this visit, he'd tell me when he wanted to, not before. Merkel was chatting to a Sturmscharführer, they seemed to know each other. We walked back to the Kubi.

"Merkel, you are a friend of that NCO?"

He smiled. "Yes, he helped me out a lot when I was younger. When I joined the Hitler Youth he taught me to shoot."

"Are you any good?"

He smiled. "Artur Vinckmann helped me get my sniper qualification."

"Excellent, that may well come in useful, Merkel."

Von Betternich turned to Mundt, "Did you find out, Scharfuhrer?"

"Yes, Sir. Their Sturmscharführer Artur Vinckmann, as you suggested, Sir."

"Thank you."

He saw my expression. "I merely asked Mundt to find out who is the best shot in the regiment."

"So you think it's Vinckmann?"

He shook his head. "It's too early to draw any conclusions. Don't forget that we're looking into the records after Kharkov is decided, until then we mustn't jump to conclusions. Let's get back to your unit, Hoffman, I need to contact Berlin."

I wondered should I mention that Merkel had known Vinckmann before the war, but I decided to keep quiet. In any case von Betternich probably knew already. I was surprised he'd been put off so easily. Surprised and uneasy, there was something he wasn't telling me. As usual.

We drove back along the icy track. Snow was still falling and the temperature was dropping fast, when we got back to HQ von Betternich commandeered Muller's armoured car and used the long-range radio while Muller stood out in the snow tapping his foot. We waited nearby for our orders. When he climbed out, he was all smiles.

"I am to report to Division, so you and your men will get your wish to go back to being ordinary soldiers, at least for now, Hoffman. General Hausser is sending a car to collect me, the Reichsfuhrer has one of his personal representatives there waiting to discuss my findings."

"Anything more we can do for you, Sir, you've only to let me know," Muller said. I had to hide a smile, he'd done his best to obstruct the SD man ever since he arrived.

"Thank you, Muller. And all of you, thank you for your help, I am sure I'll be seeing you all again once we've decided on our next move."

Divisional HQ was only five kilometres away and ten minutes later a long, black Mercedes limousine drew up and von Betternich got in and drove away. Muller stared after him with relief.

"That's it, Hoffman. You can rejoin your platoon, I'm calling a meeting of all my officers later today, you're aware of the difficulties we're facing around Kharkov?"

"The Russians threatening to encircle, Sir?"

"Exactly. The 1st SS Division Leibstandarte Adolf Hitler is holding the line at Kharkov, but intelligence reports that the Ivans are gathering their forces to attempt a classic encirclement. General Hausser wants his 2nd Division Das Reich to be ready to move against them. Staff meeting is at eleven hundred hours, you'll find out all you need to know then. A good job with the SD man, by the way, you seemed to keep him happy and off of my back."

"Thank you, Sir."

I saluted and left to find my platoon, utterly confused. One moment I was the black sheep of the regiment for escorting the SD officer, now that he had gone I was back in favour. With the departure of von Betternich it was as if a black cloud had been lifted off the regiment. I found the men shivering underneath a canvas shelter and warming their hands on a fire made of wood and old engine oil, it stank terribly. I told the men about the forthcoming operation at Kharkov. There was the usual SS competitiveness.

"So the Leibstandarte need us to bail their arses out, do they?" Beidenberg said with a degree of satisfaction.

"Josef, I think they are facing two Soviet armies, it's hardly surprising that they're having trouble holding the line."

It was obvious from their jeers that they didn't agree with me, but I ignored it and started on an inspection to check our ammunition inventory and equipment. While I was talking, there was the sudden clamour of an armoured half-track clanking into the camp and I looked around to see our Sonderkraftfahrzeug 251 being driven into the camp. Grinning at us from the open cockpit was Stefan Bauer, recovered from his wound. He jumped down and winced as he hit the snowy ground, came up to me and saluted.

"Schutze Stefan Bauer reporting for duty, Sir."

"Are you fully recovered, Stefan?"

"Near enough, Sir, thank you. I am ok to fight, if that's what you mean. I gather we're going to need everyone to deal with this business around Kharkov."

So he already knew, clearly the difficulties of LAH were being discussed all around the Corps.

"Very well, check your weapons and ammunition, we may be in action very soon."

I completed my inspection and had a chance to see the repairs they had done to our vehicle. The mechanics had welded a steel plate over the hole in the bodywork and fitted new wheels and a track. We were fully mobile once more. Almost for the first time since I'd taken over the new platoon I felt confident, the SD were out of my hair and we had a formidable armoured division, Das Reich, that would soon be rolling towards Kharkov to obliterate the Soviet threat to our SS brethren in Leibstandarte. Who knew where we'd go from there, maybe even Moscow, what more could a young officer want? Even the platoon seemed more cheerful and optimistic, no more gloom about thousands of Soviet T34s appearing out of the mist, this time we meant business. The cookhouse even outdid themselves with huge helpings of meat pie and gravy to fill our empty bellies. The meat was a little tough and I recalled seeing a pair of horses being led to an empty building nearby and the sound of two shots. Sometimes it was better to not see or hear certain things. The talk was about what we would be doing after we'd defeated the Russians, Voss was contemplating driving into Moscow in a limousine stolen from one of Stalin's commissars. He was still fantasising about the Russian beauties that he'd get to ride with him in his vehicle when I left them and reported to Muller for the officers' briefing.

There were more than fifty officers present, including two new arrivals, I was pleased to see that I was no longer the most junior officer in the Regiment. Muller outlined the battle plans, which involved a mixed fighting group comprising Der Fuhrer and Langemarck Regiments as well as some of the LAH units to assemble at the town of Merefa, ready to launch the main counterattack that would either destroy or drive the Soviet armies away from Kharkov. Our regiment, Deutschland, was to occupy the flanks and prevent our SS battle group being encircled. Although we faced several Soviet armies, intelligence reported that they were so under strength and ill equipped that they would be no match for a determined attack.

"Is that clear?" Muller asked. There were nods and shouts of assent. "Good. If this goes well, and it had better, we can push on towards Kursk and retake the city. From there, who knows, let's make sure we give the Ivans a bloody nose. Rejoin your men, we're moving off to our assembly points at four o'clock, ready to jump off for the attack at dawn tomorrow."

We hurried back to get started. I outlined the operation to the platoon and they started to load the half-track with supplies and ammunition. At four precisely, we drove away in a cloud of exhaust smoke, at last I was going to war, a proper battle. We drove for two hours and as it was getting dark, the Feldgendarmerie guided us to a temporary camp. A regiment of SS Panzers was already in position with a mix of Tiger tanks and STuGIII assault guns. In the artillery park, rank upon rank of guns was lined up ready to lay down a barrage and we had a dozen vehicle-mounted Nebelwerfers with which to pound the enemy. The Nebelwerfer 41s were fitted to firing frames, grouped together in a bank of six rockets that could hit the enemy at a range of two kilometres. Some said their accuracy was lamentable, others that they had a devastating effect on enemy morale. We also had an anti-tank section with towed twenty-eight millimetre PAK guns that should be able to blunt the effect of the T34s. It was an imposing mix of might and armour and we were only the flank guards, the main battle group would be substantially larger. The following morning we woke up in the dark, a snowstorm was blowing hard.

The camp was alive with the clamour of shouts from NCOs, engines being warmed up and equipment being given final checks. It was still dark, but the real problem was the snow. It literally fell from the sky in thick, rich flakes, visibility was less than fifty metres. Mundt came and told me that the cookhouse was serving breakfast.

"Stew and black bread, Scharfuhrer?"

"How did you guess, Sir?" he answered with a smile. "Snow's going to be a problem."

"More of a problem for the enemy," I replied. "They won't see us coming, we'll roll straight over them."

"Yes, Sir. The armourers have been around in the night fitting new machine guns to the half-tracks, we've got the MG42s now."

"Are they any different to the previous guns?"

"Armourers say they have a much higher rate of fire and they are more reliable, so yes, they'll be an improvement."

"Good. Let's get some breakfast while there's still some left."

I wolfed down the food and went to prepare the platoon, in truth there was nothing much to prepare, the half-track had been warmed up, refuelled and rearmed and was ready to go, the men assembled nearby. Promptly at five o'clock a whistle blew and we climbed aboard, along the line dozens of engines started and we roared off, following the Panzers.

The terrain was crazy, all we could do was follow the vehicle in front who was in turn following the vehicle in front of him. We drove a kilometre and came to a halt, the Russian front lines were immediately ahead. Suddenly our artillery crashed out and began laying a shattering barrage down on the enemy, it went on for an hour. Then the whistles blew again and we started the attack. Ahead of us, I heard the roar as our tanks opened fire, then the flatter sound of the T34s as they replied. How the hell could anyone see to shoot in this, I wondered? Soon we came upon the wreckage of Russian tanks destroyed by our Panzers, then abruptly we were in the middle of the battle. The Soviets had deployed their infantry into anti-tank formations and they were firing at our tanks with their PTRD anti-tank rifles. They may as well have thrown rocks for all the good these feeble weapons achieved. We came upon a huddle of Soviets who had just fired at a Panzer, there was a clang as the projectile bounced off the heavy armour. The Tiger swung its coaxial machine gun around and hosed down the gunners, they were flung to the ground like dust in a storm. The tank charged on without even slowing and we followed it looking for our own targets. We soon found them, a small group of Russians who were desperately trying to deploy a ZiS3 anti-tank artillery piece. I shouted at the driver to turn towards where they were positioned, our half-track swung over and we bore down on the Russian gunners. Bullets hammered all around us, they had a machine gun set up in a defensive position behind a low stone wall. I looked around for support, but we were on our own.

I shouted orders at the men. "Mundt, get on that machine gun, give us covering fire. Voss, drive straight at the anti-tank gun."

Mundt opened up, Merkel had detached the rear-mounted MG42 and brought it to the front of the vehicle, both guns fired incessantly, the loaders continually fitted ammunition belts as the empty ones rolled through the breech. Mundt's gun overheated and he called for a new barrel, we didn't need that in the middle of this fight. The Soviet artillery piece was clearly loaded ready to fire and the gunners were rushing to crank it around to hit our half-track. Then we slewed around, one of our tracks had become detached. We weren't hit, it was probably a faulty pin on the new track they'd fitted, but it stopped us dead. Without thinking, I leapt out of the vehicle and landed heavily in the snow, I scrambled up and ran towards the anti-tank gun, pulling a stick grenade from my webbing and arming it in one fluid motion. The Russian machine gunner saw the danger and swung his gun over. He fired a burst, it went wide and I flung myself to the ground as his second burst ripped over my head, then the grenade exploded. The machine gun stopped firing as the two-man crew was cut to pieces by the flying metal fragments. The anti-tank gun crew looked shocked, one of them was lying on the ground, also hit by my grenade and the others stunned by the force of the explosion. My platoon wasted no time, before I could get up they ran past me and sent burst after burst at the gunners.

"Cease fire, cease fire!" Mundt shouted. "Are you ok, Sir?"

"Yes, thank you, Sergeant. We need to try and get that gun ready to defend ourselves against the T34s, who can fix the half-track?"

"Voss and Beidenberg, Sir, I'll get them straight on it, if it's just a shackle pin we carry spares, we'll soon have it fixed."

We checked over the anti-tank gun, it looked similar to our own. We turned it around and Merkel checked that the breech was already loaded with a shell. The snow was still coming down heavily and there was nothing in sight, none of our armour, no enemy, nothing, we were alone on the steppe.

"What now, Sir, there doesn't seem to be a target?" Mundt asked.

"Destroy the gun and then we'll follow the line of advance, it shouldn't be a problem. Can you double shot the gun and stand back while it fires?"

"Yes, Sir."

They loaded a shell nose into the breech and extended

the lanyard that fired the weapon. I went to check on Voss and Beidenberg, even in the freezing cold they were sweating with the heavy work of lifting the broken track back into place.

"It's almost done, Sir," Voss said. "We slackened off the idling wheel and we've nearly closed the two ends of the track. Another five minutes and we'll be ready to lock up the pin. Say twenty minutes all up."

"Very well, do your best, I don't like hanging around here on our own, we've no idea where Ivan went off to."

"Running like hell from our Panzers, I think, Sir."

"All of them, are you sure about that, Voss?"

"Right, we'll get a shift on."

While we waited, the men rifled through the possessions of the dead Russians. I left them to it, they knew the importance of documents and if they found any food that was edible they were entitled to it. I didn't ask about personal possessions, if they wanted a souvenir Russian pistol or cigarette lighter, I preferred not to ask, there were more important considerations on the battlefront. Like the two surviving crew members of the anti-tank gun being guarded by two of my troopers.

"What do we do about the prisoners?" Merkel asked.

I'd been thinking about that. "We'll search and disarm them, then tie them up and leave them for our support group. If we take their boots it'll stop them from going very far."

I turned around and lifted my MP38, an engine was getting louder as a vehicle approached, but it was the familiar roar and clatter of one of our armoured half-tracks. It stopped next to us and an officer jumped down carrying an MP38 like mine. He was an Obersturmfuhrer from the Der Fuhrer Regiment and I saluted him. He nodded an acknowledgment.

"What's going on here?"

"We're fixing one of our tracks, nearly finished now so we'll be able to follow the Panzers."

He looked at the anti-aircraft gun and the broken machine gun nest.

"Your work?"

I nodded.

"Excellent. The gun is to be destroyed?"

"Double shotted, we'll blow it when we leave."

"Good. What about the prisoners?"

As he was speaking, he walked across to look at the two Russians. One was a private, the other a sergeant from the Thirty Eighth Army of the Voronezh Front, I explained it to the Obersturmfuhrer.

"Have you questioned them?"

"Yes, but they don't know anything worthwhile."

"I see. Well, we can't leave them in our rear and we can't spare any men to guard them, I can deal with this for you."

Before I could protest, he raised his machine pistol,

pulled the trigger and aimed a short burst at the two men. I noticed that he had a gleam in his eyes as he fired, his expression strange and far away, as if he was performing some sort of a private ritual. I realised he was enjoying it.

"Sir, I must protest, they were my prisoners!" I shouted at him.

"They were Russians, man, hardly worth the bullets."

"I believe we have a regiment of Russians within the SS."

He shrugged. "Perhaps these two should have joined it then."

He jumped back up on his half-track. "Good luck, try not to be too late for the party."

As they drove off my men looked at me. It was an unwritten rule in the SS not to shoot prisoners. That kind of behaviour would lead to our own men being shot when they became prisoners of the Russians, even the Fuhrer's order to kill captured Commissars was often quietly ignored. Yet here we had just witnessed what amounted to murder. I cleared my head, it was too late to worry about it now.

"Men, we need to hurry, Voss, how long until you're finished?"

"Two minutes, Sir. We're almost there."

In the event, it took another ten minutes before the job was completed, they started up the engine and we piled into the half-track. Merkel was on the ground and he paid out the string that led to the trigger of the anti-tank gun. We drove fifty metres away, he lay down in a shell hole and pulled the string. The gun fired and instantly blew up in spectacular fashion. Merkel ran up, jumped aboard and we followed the chewed up terrain after our main force. Panzers made a chewed up mess of the snowy ground, which was fortunate, they were not difficult to follow. Voss was driving and he went flat out to catch up. I made sure the men kept a wary eye out on all sides, the threat from both Russian stragglers and partisans was very real. Finally, we came to a halt on top of a long slope that swept away in the distance. The view of the battlefield was incredible. The snowstorm had temporarily stopped and we could see for several kilometres.

The whole of our Panzer Corps was on the attack, charging at the enemy who were firing back from positions at the top of a low rise two kilometres away. The enemy had anti-tank guns deployed and while we watched they found the range of a Tiger tank and destroyed it, but our own gunners were already in action. Our guns fired repeatedly, mobile artillery pieces, STuGIIIs and PAK anti-tank guns kept up a withering rate of fire to add to the onslaught of the Tigers deadly eighty-eight centimetre main guns. I'd seen photos of artillery barrages on the Western Front during the last war, this looked similar, hundreds of guns firing, except that so much of the artillery was mobile. The battle was still very fluid, pockets of T34s and mobile guns stood their ground and took on our armour, others were turning and fleeing. I felt a hand touch my arm.

"Sir, look, the Major."

About half a kilometre from us, I could see a Horch armoured car, the aerial array and unit marking made it obvious that it was Muller's. The vehicle was at a standstill, the reason obvious. One of the wheels had been blown completely off by a hit from a shell, or possibly a land mine. The vehicle was under attack from a trio of the new Soviet armoured cars that I recognised from intelligence briefings as the BA-64, lightly armoured and carrying only a machine gun but they were capable of overcoming the lightly armoured Horch. Normally the Horch would carry a two centimetre cannon, but for vehicles equipped with long range radios, like Muller's, the cannon was removed and all they had to defend themselves with was a single MG34. There were no other units nearby, I didn't have any choice but to go and help him.

"Voss, head for the Sturmbannfuhrer's armoured car. Men, those BA-64s have thin skins, if we can send enough bullets their way we should do some damage. Hopefully enough to drive them off, at least. Use both machine guns and every man that can shoot, do it, plaster those Soviet tin cans. Let's go!"

We hurtled down the slope and closed the gap between us, and the three Russian armoured cars. At first, they didn't see us, until the weight of fire from our MG42s started to hit their armour. Then they turned their attention to us. Streams of machine gun bullets arced towards our half-track, then one of our gunners scored a lucky hit and an armoured car exploded. We were lucky, the car behind it ran straight into the burning wreck and had to waste precious time reversing out of the flames. We concentrated our fire on the third vehicle, seeing it lurch as we managed to hit something vital, possibly the driver or the commander. Then it turned through one hundred and eighty degrees and fled at speed up the slope and away from us. The remaining Russian vehicle disentangled itself and turned to engage but this time he was on his own, and the concentrated fire from us and the stalled Horch turned it into a flaming ruin as their fuel caught fire. One crewman escaped but he was badly on fire, screaming with the agony of the burning fuel that had soaked his uniform. Merkel was on one of the MG42s and he casually sent a short burst that ended the man's suffering. We stopped next to the Horch, Muller climbed out and up onto our half-track, his crew followed him.

"Thanks, Hoffman, I need to catch up with the regiment, they're over to the south of the slope near the bottom of the hill."

"Right away, Sir. Voss, head for the south east, bottom of the hill."

I told him about the broken track that had delayed us but he ignored me. His eyes were bright with the excitement of the battle.

"We're beating them, Hoffman, they're running from us, all the way back to Moscow with any luck. When the Panzers reach their objective they will turn south and we'll have the whole damn lot of them caught in our trap, like dogs. A whole army, maybe two armies! Damn, how stupid they were to let themselves be caught in a trap like that."

I thought about Stalingrad that had recently fallen to just such a trap, but wisely said nothing. It seemed that military stupidity was not unique to any army.

We caught up with our Deutschland regiment and Muller commandeered another Sonderkraftfahrzeug 251 half-track, one equipped with a radio so that he could regain command of his regiment, the luckless crew left to join up with several groups of infantry that were advancing on foot. We followed Muller's vehicle, the T34s and Soviet artillery had disappeared and we had an unobstructed journey through to our objective. We assembled under the cover of a thick wood, the hatch of a Tiger clanged open and General Hausser climbed out. We all leapt to attention and saluted.

"At ease, men. The first part of our operation had gone according to plan. The Soviet Seventh Guards Tank Army currently occupies the ground between us, and Kharkov. If they are not dealt with now the city will be threatened and our troops could even be surrounded. None of us wants another Stalingrad."

There was a grumbling and murmuring amongst the officers. The fate of the prisoners who had surrendered on the banks of the Volga was unknown but one thing was for sure, it would not be a happy one.

"Together with the Leibstandarte and the Wehrmacht 320th Division, we're going to turn the tables on the Soviets and encircle them, if we do our jobs right we can completely wipe out an entire Russian army. The enemy think that they can have things their way since Stalingrad, but there were no SS units involved in that battle, in fact, many of the divisions were not even German. Romanians, Italians, Hungarians and God knows who else, it's no wonder they crumbled. I want to give our Russian friends a real bloody nose, show them that they are dealing with a different class of soldier on this battlefield, so don't let me down. Let's go in and destroy the bastards!"

We all cheered mightily, it was what we wanted to hear, needed to hear. It was quite true, as bad as the fall of Stalingrad had been for German morale, it had been a great morale booster for the Soviets. Since then they seemed to have fought with a new spirit and enthusiasm, we needed to set the record straight and show them how them how the German soldier fought, particularly the SS. As Hausser had said, at Stalingrad they had fought Romanians, Croats, Italians and Hungarians, a real hotchpotch of assorted nationalities. Das Reich and Leibstandarte were purely German SS divisions, a different story entirely. We intended to give them a lesson they would not forget.

Buoyed up by the General's pep talk, we set to preparing our vehicles and weapons, we needed to take on fuel and ammunition, attend to running repairs and finally help ourselves to steaming hot bowls of the inevitable stew from the mobile cookhouse. It was probably the same food as before, but served with a starter of Hausser's morale boosting speech, it tasted like cordon bleu, the black bread was wonderful once you'd scraped the mould off it and even the coffee was hot and cheering. Not in the league of the General's coffee, I thought ruefully, but good enough. We were on the way to Moscow and nothing could stop us now. We settled down to get some sleep, we were due to jump off again at four am and catch the enemy in their beds. I managed to claim a place in the cockpit of the half-track, a prized spot that kept me out of the snow and the bitterly cold wind that swept across the steppes. Three men joined me, the other men rigged a lean-to shelter at the side of the vehicle with a waterproof ground sheet to keep them clear of the snow, but it must have been bitingly cold.

I was already awake when they called stand to, and I only had to rinse my face in a bowl of melted snow that Mundt had left in the vehicle so that it thawed in the morning ready for our ablutions. We rushed to help ourselves to more stew and bread and washed it down with freezing cold water, there hadn't been time to brew coffee, then we were starting engines ready to go. Hausser stood in the turret of his Tiger and looked over his command. He gave an affirmative nod and spoke into his microphone. The driver engaged the gears and got the huge vehicle moving, the rest of the tanks and STuGIIIs followed. Then it was our turn and Voss swung our half-track behind the long column of armour. We were going to relieve Kharkov.

The drive into the city was hell. Soviet snipers had taken up positions in many of the ruins of the suburbs, making the approach a grim business. In the end we dismounted from the half-track, leaving only Voss to drive and Bauer, who I did not feel was fully recovered from his wound, as well as another trooper, Neumann, to man the MG42s. I took four men and walked the south side of the road, Mundt took another four and took the north side, in that fashion we crept carefully from house to house. Whenever a sniper was encountered the machine guns kept them occupied, while we rushed the building and took out the sniper either, with long bursts from our sub-machine guns or hand grenades. At one stage we were attacked by a column of T34s who rushed into the suburbs to try and make a few quick kills. There were perhaps ten or twelve in all and we thought we'd have to make a run for it, but the snowstorm at that time was holding off allowing the Luftwaffe to take off. They were flying over at the time looking for targets and they swooped eagerly on the Soviet armour. The Stukas screamed in for the attack and dropped bomb after bomb. By the time they had finished eight of the tanks were ablaze and the survivors had swung around and were driving at full speed away from the city. We finally met up with units of the Leibstandarte as well as the soldiers of the Wehrmacht 320th Division. They swung into action to help us clear the snipers and by the late afternoon, we entered the centre of the city.

I found our temporary regimental HQ, Muller was barking orders to bring up replacements and reinforcements, more ammunition, fuel and the one hundred and one other things that kept an army in the field. He saw me and nodded.

"Hoffman, any problems?"

"No, Sir, we didn't lose any men, it all went well."

We both looked around as a group of men marched past, Soviet prisoners, dejected, unshaven, but their clothing was of some interest. Warm clothing, unlike ours, the Soviets had clearly been prepared. I suspected that some of their fur boots and hats together with the thick quilted arctic parka coats would 'disappear' en-route to their prison camp.

"Good. We are staying in Kharkov for a few days to conduct mopping up operations and strengthen the city defences, so you can find your platoon somewhere warm to bed down. Watch out for the snipers," he said in dismissal.

Was he being sarcastic, we'd just fought our way

through nests of snipers that had caused a number of casualties, though not to my platoon? No, I decided he just didn't know. For myself I didn't care, but the men had fought well and hard.

"Sir, the men did well, all of them, they cleared out a lot of the snipers when we reached the city and saved our people from taking much heavier casualties."

"Thank you, Untersturmfuhrer, I will thank them when I see them."

It was the best I could do, I found Mundt who had sent two of my troopers to rustle up some food. I heard him shouting at them, "And try and find a pig, the cookhouse is doing potato soup today and I fancy a bit of meat to go with it."

He saw me and winced. "I heard that there are wild pigs running around the city, Sir."

"That's good news, Scharfuhrer," I replied drily. "I imagine there must be thousands of wild pigs running around these Soviet cities."

"Yes, Sir, there must be."

They knew my views on looting. Sometimes, especially in the depths of the Russian winter it was necessary to take food to stay alive. At the other extreme, there was the notorious Dirlewanger Battalion. Doctor Oskar Dirlewanger was an infantry officer during the Great War and won both the Iron Cross 2nd Class and the Iron Cross 1st Class. Subsequently he went back to university and was awarded a PhD in Political Science. While a teacher in 1934 he was convicted of the rape of a thirteen year-old girl, illegal use of a government vehicle and damaging the vehicle whilst under the influence of alcohol. For these crimes he was sentenced to two years imprisonment. Dirlewanger then lost his job, his title of doctor and all military honours. Soon after his release he was arrested again on similar charges. He was sent to the Welzheim concentration camp, which was standard practice for deviant sexual offenders, but was subsequently released and reinstated as a Colonel in the General SS Reserve. This following the personal intervention of his friend Gottlob Berger, the head of the SS-Hauptamt and long-time personal friend of Reichsfuhrer Heinrich Himmler. Dirlewanger later headed the Sturmbrigade Dirlewanger, a penal battalion composed of German criminals. In February 1942, the battalion was reassigned for anti-partisan duties in Belarus. Dirlewanger was known to lead his soldiers into combat personally which was unusual for someone of his rank, he was wounded many times in combat. He was also intensely disliked by many of the SS troopers and officers for the extremes of his behaviour that dishonoured us all. Part of that extreme behaviour was looting, often combined with rape and murder. I was determined to keep a firm rein on my platoon and ensure they didn't even think about going the way of Dirlewanger's men.

By early evening the city had gone quiet and the mobile cookhouse once again served up their potato soup. The men had got a fire going and a pig was roasting on a spit that they'd improvised from the wreckage of a Soviet anti-aircraft mount. I sat around the fire, enjoying the warmth of the blaze, the good food in my belly, the flask of schnapps that was being passed around, thinking how good soldiering could be. For the first time I felt that I belonged in the SS Deutschland Regiment, that I was accepted as a part of it. With men like these, I could go the very length of Soviet Russia and get back in one piece. What a fine profession soldiering was. I bent down to pick up a piece of wood that had fallen from the fire. That was when the bullet cracked out, I dimly remembered hearing it even as everything went black.

CHAPTER SIX

"I am convinced that 1941 will be the crucial year of a great New Order in Europe. The world shall open up for everyone. Privileges for individuals, the tyranny of certain nations and their financial rulers shall fall. And last of all this year will help to provide the foundations of a real understanding among peoples, and with it the certainty of conciliation among nations. Those nations who are still opposed to us will some day recognize the greater enemy within. Then they will join us in a combined front, a front against Jewish exploitation and racial degeneration."

Adolf Hitler January 1941

I heard voices, could see a bright light burning overhead. Surely I wasn't dead, not already. Was this how the afterlife began? But no, my sense of smell was coming to me, I sensed ether, antiseptics, the tang of urine. I had to be in a hospital. The voices got louder.

"I think he's regaining consciousness, Doctor, his eyes are moving."

I struggled to focus and my eyes suddenly revealed the prettiest girl I'd ever seen, a true angel. Perhaps I was in heaven after all. A vision in blue and white, blue dress with white stripes and a white armband adorned with a red cross, white apron, white cap, creamy skin, dark hair and flashing brown eyes, huge, warm liquid eyes that were staring at me gravely.

"How do you feel?"

I had to think about that.

"My head hurts. Where am I?"

"This is the hospital in Kharkov, it has been taken over by the military. Do you know what happened to you?"

I tried to think, I was near the campfire with my platoon, the crack of a bullet.

"I was shot?"

"Yes, you were, Untersturmfuhrer. The bullet came from behind, it lodged inside your skull, you were lucky. The surgeons were able to remove it and nothing vital was damaged. Very lucky."

I tried to move my legs and arms, I didn't feel very lucky. "Did I suffer any other injuries?"

She smiled at me and my world lit up with warm sunshine. "None whatsoever, I think the head wound was enough for now. The doctor is next door, he will be coming back to check on you shortly. Now, I have to attend to my other patients."

"Nurse, would you tell me your name?"

The smile again. "It's Heide, Heide Thalberg. I am a Rotekreuz Helferin, a Red Cross Auxiliary Nurse."

"My name is Jurgen, Jurgen Hoffman."

She smiled yet again. "I know that, Untersturmfuhrer, we have your records."

"Please, call me Jurgen."

She smiled. "Just lie back and relax, the doctor will be here soon."

She turned and walked away. Did she quietly murmur 'Jurgen' or was I imagining it?

I lay there trying to work out what had happened to me, it must have been a Soviet sniper, one that we'd missed. Well, Kharkov was a big city with many tall buildings, we couldn't expect to clear out every single Russian with a rifle. I looked around, I was in a ward with perhaps twenty beds, all full of wounded or sick men. The beds either side of me were both occupied with men who appeared to be wrapped from head to toe in bandages, they were both groaning quietly. Probably tank crew, I reflected. The Panzers carried a heavy load of petrol, when they were hit they often went up like Roman candles. Poor devils. There was a stirring at the door and a harassed medical officer came into the room wearing a Wehrmacht uniform, a captain. He worked his way from bed to bed until finally he came to me.

"How do you feel, Untersturmfuhrer?"

"Just a headache, Sir. When will I be able to rejoin my unit?"

He put a stethoscope against my chest and listened, then moved my head forward and looked at the wound at the back, I saw stars as my head was tilted. He noticed me screwing my face up in pain.

"Hurts a bit does it? Well, that is to be expected. Three days, no less than that. Then you should ok to leave here, but you will need to rest up for another few days before you're fit enough to go back into action."

He made notes on a chart at the foot of my bed and moved on to the next bed. Three days, how could I lie here doing nothing while my platoon was out fighting the enemy? Yet even as I thought about it the door burst open and four of my men came into the ward. I recognised Mundt, Voss, Merkel and Beidenberg. They clustered around my bed.

"How are you feeling, Sir?"

I told them I was ready to come back, it was just the hospital that was keeping me from rejoining them. Mundt looked closely at the back of my head and winced.

"Jesus Christ, they've sure made a mess of you. Lucky it wasn't the front of your head, at least you can grow hair over the wound. You'll still be able to pull the girls, Sir.

Talking of which, we've found a decent bar in the centre of town, just off Red Square."

"I thought Red Square was in Moscow."

"Well, it is, but they've got one here too. The local booze is quite reasonable and the vodka will blow your head off. Not that you need anything else to blow your head off, Sir."

They laughed at his joke and I smiled dutifully.

"Tell me about the platoon, the regiment, what's happening?"

"We're billeted here in Kharkov for the time being, division are fortifying the defences, they're expecting the Russkis to make a counterattack before too long. The half-track is up to scratch, weapons, ammunition and supplies all good. We're short of men still, of course, but so is everyone else, we'll just have to manage."

It was good to hear them and to know that everything in my command was on the top line. They stayed for half an hour, before Nurse Thalberg came to my bedside to throw them out.

"It's ok, we're going. Hey, I wouldn't want to leave here if I had a nurse like you looking after me. What's your name, beautiful?"

She laughed. "Get out before I throw you out, you're disturbing the patients."

"Ok, ok," Mundt agreed. "We'll call in again, Sir. Try not to get in the way of any more Soviet bullets."

"But it wasn't a Soviet bullet, Scharfuhrer. It was one of ours, German."

I knew that voice, surely not, not again. Von Betternich was standing nearby, leaning on his cane.

The men looked at him, but his hard gaze was enough to send them on their way, his companion was no less menacing. Heide took the hint too and went off to attend to her other patients. I felt a pang of disappointment as she left. The SD man was with a stranger, a man dressed in civilian clothes. Black leather coat, trilby hat and he carried a briefcase. I knew that my problems were about to get worse.

"This is my colleague," he introduced the civilian, "Gerd Wiedel."

I nodded at him, "How do you do, you are working with the Obersturmbannfuhrer?"

Von Betternich interrupted him. "Gerd was with me in the Criminal Police before the war, he was my sergeant, and a very effective policeman."

"So you have joined the Sicherheitsdienst?" I asked Wiedel.

"I am with the Gestapo, Untersturmfuhrer. The Reichsfuhrer grows concerned at this criminal behaviour, officers being shot at by our own people. He has insisted that we put a stop to it before it totally undermines the morale of our fighting men on the Eastern Front."

So he was with the Gestapo, as I'd suspected. "It was

a German bullet?"

Von Betternich nodded. "Yes, it was. We have taken charge of the bullet extracted from your head, it appears to be identical to the others that were used to kill those officers. You are lucky to be alive, Hoffman, I gather you leaned down at the critical moment, otherwise it would have hit you in the area of the heart. As it is, it almost killed you."

I recalled the moment of the shooting, when I had leaned down for something, I couldn't remember what it was.

"Why would they target me, I'm the most junior officer in the regiment, almost the whole of the Das Reich Division?"

"Because you were investigating the shootings, Hoffman. Obviously they thought you were getting close to them," Wiedel said.

"That's nonsense, Herr Wiedel."

"Kriminalkommissar Wiedel," he corrected. I knew it was the Gestapo rank equivalent of an SS Obersturmfuhrer.

"It is certainly not nonsense, Hoffman," von Betternich interrupted, "but it is something we can use to our advantage."

"What do you mean, Sir?"

"If they were trying to kill you, they will try again and we'll keep a watch on you, see who makes the attempt."

I had to point out the flaw in his plan. "What if they

manage to kill me before you get to them?"

Von Betternich raised his eyebrows. "But Hoffman, this is wartime. We all have to take our chances, don't we?"

I didn't feel that being shot at by your own people was a reasonable risk to ask a soldier to take, but arguing with the SD and the Gestapo was not likely to change anything.

"What do I do now?"

"First of all you need to recover your strength, my boy, then go about your duties as normal," von Betternich replied cheerfully. "We have some resources in the Deutschland Regiment, they'll keep an eye on things and report back to me if anything looks suspicious."

"Resources, Sir?"

He smiled. "Nothing for you to worry yourself about, Hoffman. You'd be surprised at the number of people that report back to Prinz Albrecht Strasse."

Of course, RSHA Headquarters where both the SD and Gestapo were established. As was Reichsfuhrer Heinrich Himmler.

They left me after another few minutes, promising to return in the next couple of days. Nurse Heide Thalberg returned and bustled around for a few moments, checking my dressing and making sure my bedclothes were tucked in properly. Was it my imagination, or was she deliberately spending a little more time with me than with the others?

"You're doing a marvellous job, Heide. I'm really grateful."

She looked sharply at my use of her first name. Then she nodded. "You're more than welcome, it's no trouble."

I swallowed my nervousness and blurted it straight out. "Could I thank you in a better way, perhaps you'd have dinner with me when I'm discharged?"

She looked at me coolly, of course she would get lots of invitations like that.

"What were you thinking of, an SS field canteen?"

I nearly choked. "No, no, definitely not, there must be a restaurant around..."

Then I saw her smiling, that wonderful smile again. "I see, you were joking. There must be at least one good restaurant around here, I'll find out where it is and book us a table, is that a deal?"

I could see she was considering it. Finally, she said, "I'll think about it. I am very busy at the hospital, we've got casualties coming in all the time. But yes, if I can get away for a couple of hours, I'll probably accept, thank you."

She was going to say yes, I felt on top of the world. As she bent down to re-dress my head wound, I brushed her cheek with my lips and said, "Thank you, Heide. I'm feeling better already."

She coloured red a little, but didn't seem unduly worried, she didn't slap me or call a guard. Excellent, it was worth getting wounded to find a girl like this to take out to dinner. Well, probably, she'd said. I would work with that. Mundt came in the following morning with Merkel, the others were preparing our equipment for the next phase of the operation. But it seemed as if our assault on Kursk may have to be postponed, the Soviets were closing in around Kharkov and before we went back on the attack we had to work to defend what we had already taken. They said there was another matter of a huge shortage of Panzers, they were waiting for hundreds of new Tigers to arrive from Germany. I had another mission for them and I whispered the details when I was sure that Nurse Thalberg wasn't around.

Von Betternich came to see me on the third day, once more with the Gestapo Kriminalkommissar at his side.

"We are making progress, Hoffman, we think that we may have identified at least one of the conspirators."

"Really, who is that?"

Wiedel smiled. "We have arrested Sturmbannfuhrer Muller, under a protective custody order."

I said nothing, it was bad news for Muller. The real power of the Gestapo was called 'Schutzhaft', the power to imprison people without judicial proceedings on the theory of 'protective custody'. This power was based upon the law, which in 1933 suspended the clauses of the Weimar Constitution that until then had guaranteed civil liberties to the German people. We all understood Schutzhaft and did our best to pretend that it didn't exist, or if it did, that it wouldn't affect people like us.

"So who is running the regiment?"

"Ah, that's the clever thing," Wiedel replied. "I applied for, and was granted, dispensation for Muller to continue as acting CO for the time being. They've lost one CO, it would not be good for morale to lose another so quickly."

"It simply means," von Betternich continued, "that Muller's freedom of action is somewhat constrained. If he's innocent, it will of course be proved in the course of my investigation."

I ignored that, we both knew that Schutzhaft was the mark of guilt for any German citizen who fell foul of it. Muller's career was in ruins and his future freedom in considerable doubt.

"As a matter of fact, he's coming in to see you later, Hoffman."

How on earth did they know that, I wondered? But then again, what didn't they know? Except for the identity of the shooter, of course."

"Be careful what you say to him," Wiedel said, "he is under suspicion and he may lead us to the other guilty party, or parties."

"He may be innocent, Sir," I replied.

He smiled coldly. "Naturally, Hoffman, there is always that possibility. In the meantime, do not give him the impression that it was anything other than a Russian sniper that hit you, is that clear?"

"Yes, Sir."

"Excellent. We will see you when you report back for

duty tomorrow."

That was news to me, I had hoped it would be tomorrow, but obviously the SD and Gestapo were privy to more exact information than mere mortals. The two men left and I spent the morning longing to see the beautiful apparition of Nurse Thalberg appear beside my bed, but it seemed that she was off duty. Her replacement was a burly woman from Bavaria with all the personality of a suet pudding, but rather less beauty than the popular German recipe. She nearly ripped my head off looking at my wound and applying a clean dressing, bellowing at me to make sure that I had regular bowel movements so that the whole of Kharkov could hear. In the afternoon, Muller came to see me. He was a wreck, a shocking sight, his strength and optimism, the burning drive and ambition that had pushed the Deutschland Regiment into the recent counterattack was completely absent. Instead he was faltering and unsure of himself.

"Hoffman, it's good to see you're looking better."

"Yes, Sir, thank you for coming to see me. How are things at the regiment?"

"We're gearing up to repel a Soviet counterattack on Kharkov, no doubt you've heard?"

"Yes, Sir, I have."

"Have you also heard about my problems?"

"Problems? No, Sir," I lied.

"I'm under a Gestapo protective custody order. Still in

command of Deutschland Regiment, but for some reason the fucking Gestapo have got their claws into me. What happened to you, was it the same sniper, one of ours?"

"I don't think so, Sir, there were Soviet snipers in the city. It was just a case of me being in the wrong place at the wrong time. Not one of our people."

"Good, that's good."

We chatted for five minutes or so about aimless things to do with the regiment, then he abruptly left. One thing I knew for sure, Muller was nothing to do with the shooter. It was absurd and made no sense to even accuse him. At the end of the afternoon Heide Thalberg came back on duty. I had found out her shift hours from a medical clerk and knew her dinner break was at ten o'clock that evening. At nine o'clock I slipped out of bed, washed, shaved, and put on my best field grey uniform that Mundt had brought in for me. Then I went back to the ward and got into my bed, pulling the covers over to hide my clothes. Just before ten, Heide walked through the ward checking on the patients and came to my bed.

"How are you, Untersturmfuhrer?"

"I am well, thank you, Heide. Are you going for something to eat?"

"Yes," she said, surprised, "why do you ask?"

I swept the covers aside and got out of bed, resplendent in full uniform and gleaming jackboots. Her eyes goggled.

"Because I'm taking you to dinner, Fraulein."

She was laughing now. "But they won't let you into the staff canteen."

"Which is why I have a table booked at a local restaurant."

I had mounted a devastating surprise attack and she had no choice but to capitulate. She tried the usual female excuses, 'I've nothing to wear' and so on, but I brushed them aside, and following Mundt's detailed directions led her to the restaurant. As it was run by a Ukrainian who hated the Russians, the Scharfuhrer assured us we were unlikely to be poisoned. When we went into the building, our table was ready for us with candles lit and a bottle of champagne waiting in an ice bucket. Her eyes were shining. "Jurgen, this is wonderful, how did you manage it?"

I had to admit to her that I'd got my sergeant to fix it up, but she was still impressed. Most of the tables were full with SS officers, some of them with female companions. Not all of them looked totally respectable. I hoped she wouldn't notice, but it was a forlorn hope, she knew instantly.

"I hope they don't think that I'm one of those women, those, harlots," she said.

"Of course not, especially in your nurse's uniform. Besides, some of these women are undoubtedly with our army, clerks, nurses like yourself, some SS Helferin."

She calmed down. "Very well, then. I am impressed, the officers here all look like important people."

I smiled. "Probably not, don't let the uniforms fool you, they're probably clerks mostly, quartermasters and administrators. Most of the fighting soldiers will be with their units."

I noticed a chubby Hauptsturmfuhrer at a nearby table look at me sharply, but my head covered in a huge bandage, and my nurse companion, made it clear that I was a fighting soldier. His immaculate uniform made it eloquently clear that he was not.

We ordered the food, a Ukrainian veal speciality rather like our Wiener Schnitzel.

"Heide, tell me about yourself, I'm fascinated."

"You mean what's a nice girl like me doing in a place like this?" she smiled.

"Something like that, but how did you get here, were you always a nurse?"

"Not at all. I'm not really a nurse, just an auxiliary helper. No, I was at university, training to be a teacher but I thought that our fighting men needed me more, so here I am."

"What is your home town?"

"I was born in Dusseldorf, but eight years ago we were forced to move to Bremen."

"Really, why were you forced to move, that sounds very dramatic?"

She looked cautiously around the restaurant. "My father is a communist, he was getting a lot of trouble from the locals."

I thought about the Nazis' persecution of the communists. Along with the Jews, they regarded them as their mortal enemies.

"It must have been difficult, the state gives communists a hard time."

"Yes, it was hard, he was beaten up, thrown in the cells a couple of times. Finally he was threatened with a Schutzhaft, you know what that is?"

"Yes, I've heard of them."

"Well, we moved on to Bremen and he found work there in a shipyard. Of course, he'd left the communist party by then, or at least it had been made illegal and so we were able to live our lives as ordinary citizens."

"It must have been bad for you."

"Not really, we coped, somehow. It wasn't as bad as the disgusting treatment given out to the Jews. That was really terrible."

Her voice had risen slightly, it was obviously something on which she had passionate views.

"Heide, please don't think me rude, but this restaurant is reserved for SS officers and high ranking Nazi party members. It would be as well to not discuss certain subjects."

She looked around angrily, some diners glanced at her with puzzled expressions. She opened her mouth to make a sharp retort, then relaxed and smiled that wonderful smile. "You're right, it's the wrong place and the wrong time."

The food arrived just in time, a wonderful meal rich with local spices and flavours. Afterwards we had apple pie with cream, real cream, and coffee, real coffee too. I ordered a brandy and cigar to finish, but she declined both. "I don't smoke and I'm going back on duty, Jurgen, so I can't drink."

Afterwards I took her back to the hospital and she allowed me to give her a long, passionate kiss of farewell. Then it was back to business.

"You get those clothes off and back into bed, Untersturmfuhrer, or I'll call the ward sister."

"Jawohl, Fraulein Helferin. Sofort!"

I folded my uniform neatly, put my nightshirt back on and got into bed. I lay there for a long time, enjoying the glow of recalling the evening with her, hoping that she would come into the ward before I dropped off to sleep, but she'd been assigned elsewhere and I was out of luck. Nurse Suet Pudding came in and chided me for not being asleep, how could I ever recover if I didn't get my sleep and so on? The following morning there was still no sign of Heide. The doctor called round and said I could be discharged once my dressing was removed. Two hours later I reported back to SS Deutschland Regiment. Muller had just called an officers' briefing and I went straight into the room of the old school that he was using as a headquarters.

"The Soviets are trying to retake Kharkov," he announced without any introduction. "Our job, gentlemen, is to stop them!"

He unrolled a large chart of the area and we immediately saw the problem. The eastern, northern and southern edges of the Kharkov district were surrounded by arrows, that indicated the Soviet line of advance.

"I want our regiment deployed before first light tomorrow, that's when we expect the first of the new Soviet attacks. If they get through, it means that any hope we have of retaking Kursk is going to be pushed back a long time."

He went on giving orders and directions, our unit was pulling out at two am. I left the briefing and went to check on my platoon. The moment they saw me, my men let out a ragged cheer and I had to endure several minutes of their obscene jokes about my dinner with Heide. Then I called for quiet.

"Listen, you've heard about tomorrow morning?"

"We have, Untersturmfuhrer, the unit is all ready to go. The half-track is fuelled up, ammunition and supplies all set," Mundt said.

"Thank you, Scharfuhrer. I'm going back to the hospital. I want to see Heide before we go."

"Is that wise, Sir? I mean, just hours before we kick off the offensive, the Feldgendarmerie would have a field day if they caught you."

I touched my bandaged head. "I'm wounded, I need to get the dressing changed before we pull out."

He nodded. "That should do it."

I set off immediately, this time I was prepared for battle, wearing my steel helmet and carrying my MP38 machine pistol, the Walther PPK in its holster, a pair of grenades in my webbing. There were snipers still operating in the city and as the Soviets drew nearer, they would become bolder. When I reached the hospital, the desk clerk told me that Heide was on duty on the ward. I marched through the door and saw her at the other end of the long room, talking to another nurse. They looked at me in alarm. Then she recognised me.

"Jurgen, what are you doing here, you look as if you are off to fight a war?"

"I'm afraid we are. The regiment has been called out to fight, the Russians are trying to break through."

"Are they near?"

"Smiyev."

She started, it was a suburb only a few kilometres away. The other nurse was listening avidly, I asked her to give us a few minutes and she moved away.

"Do you think they will reach here?"

"No, we'll stop them, but..."

"They could break through then?"

"Look, I just don't know. Heide, be careful, I have to

see you again."

"I'd like that. I'll be fine, it's not as if I'm on the front line. You be careful."

"Don't worry, they're fighting the SS now."

She indicated the long rows of beds. "Almost all of these patients are Waffen-SS, Jurgen."

"I'll be careful."

She bent forward and kissed me, then we were holding each other tightly, I winced as she pulled against the strap of my helmet, causing it to press on the wound. She noticed instantly.

"Let me dress that for you before you go, I can give you some spare dressings too."

I sat and enjoyed her fussing with my head wound. Afterwards she gave me a bag of spare dressings and told me not to wear the helmet for as long as possible as it would aggravate the wound and prevent it healing. If she'd asked me to go into battle naked I think I would have. We held each other and kissed long and hard, then the other nurse said that she needed her and I had to leave.

I was sad walking back to my unit, I had no idea when I would ever see her again, if ever. The Feldgendarmerie did stop me, a private soldier checked my papers and called for his officer. The man stepped out of the building that they were using as an office and came up to me with a sneering look.

"And where do you think you're going,

Untersturmfuhrer?"

"To rejoin my unit."

"Really, and you have a pass to leave them and come into the city?"

"I was injured, Sir. I needed to go to the hospital to get my wound dressed."

I still had my helmet off, the bandage on my head was already damp, I knew the wound would be leaking again."

"That's no excuse, you need a pass."

"To get injured, you mean?"

His look darkened. No one made jokes at the expense of the Feldgendarmerie.

"Anyone without a pass can be arrested and shot without trial, you know that?"

I was about to reply when another man came out of the office, a civilian in a black leather trench coat and trilby hat. Kriminalkommissar Wiedel.

"Let him go."

"But, but Sir..."

"Now!"

"Yes, Sir. Untersturmfuhrer, you may go."

I nodded at Wiedel and walked on. I wasn't too sure that having a Gestapo officer as my guardian angel was a good idea. It wasn't as if the Feldgendarmerie were going to shoot a line officer returning to the fight. After all, my wound, and the fact that I was walking from the hospital back to the regiment proved my story. Finally, I got back to my platoon and slept for a couple of hours on an old straw filled mattress that Mundt had found for me. In the early hours after midnight, we prepared to pull out and go into battle against the Slavic hordes that Stalin had once more sent to attack us. The camp was alive with exhaust smoke as engines rumbled into life, soldiers beating their arms against their bodies to try to get warm in the chill of the snowy night. The loud roar of the Panzers, even more deafening, as they started to move and their tracks clanked on the hard ground. Then it was our turn, Voss put the half-track into gear and fell in behind another vehicle. I felt the excitement of being a part of the mighty machine of the Waffen-SS, off to do battle against the Soviets. We were heading for Smiyev.

We reached the front and were directed to laager in prepared positions. They looked like remnants from the last time this ground had been fought over, only weeks before. The Tigers and STuGIIIs deployed in a line facing the expected path the enemy would take when they came towards us. All around my half-track were light armoured cars, motor cycle combinations of the Langemarck Regiment and rows of artillery lined up ready for the coming action. We waited. Our task was to remain in defence and be prepared to go at once should the Panzers see an opening to move forward, in which case we would follow behind them to mop up the enemy infantry. On paper it seemed so simple, in practice I wasn't so sure, the

Soviets always seemed to have so many men and so much equipment. Before dawn, Muller came amongst us to wish us well and check that we were prepared. The prospect of action had heightened his mood and he had some of his old fire back. Then he went back to his command half-track and we waited. Snow fell, enough to obscure our view of the Russian positions but not enough to hide them completely. Then our artillery opened up to soften the enemy, every time a shell exploded in their lines it kicked up showers of snow mixed with the more normal detritus of explosions, earth, stones, men and equipment. The artillery pounded on, then the Russian artillery started and shells started falling around us. The barrages continued for over an hour until the Russians decided it was enough. In the distance, we saw movement, almost as if the ground was moving. But it wasn't the ground, it was thousands of men, tens of thousands, moving forward in a mass attack more reminiscent of the 1914 war.

The Panzers fired first, round after round of high explosives that ripped huge gaps in the Russian lines. The artillery changed their aim and joined in the carnage, but there were so many of them, life was cheap to these Russian generals. No matter how many men fell more rushed forward to fill the gaps. Then they were within machine gun range.

"Open fire," officers shouted frantically, but they could have saved their breath. Even as they spoke, our MG42s and MG34s were sending their rain of horror and death towards the enemy. A few of our men started to fire with their machine pistols but I told my men to wait, the enemy were still outside of effective range and ammunition wasn't inexhaustible. It seemed incredible that anyone could survive that cauldron of hot steel that smashed through their ranks, but they kept coming, there were hundreds of them in the leading ranks and thousands more still behind them. They got to within three hundred metres and I gave the order.

"Fire!"

Our two MG42s had already been firing in short, consistent bursts to stop the barrels from overheating. Now the men joined in with their machine pistols. Merkel had a Kar 98 that he was using to snipe at individual targets, the rest of us just hosed down the enemy ranks as fast as possible, emptying clip after clip at the Russians. Our artillery and Panzers had to stop firing, the enemy had now closed to with a hundred metres of our positions and they would have endangered us with shrapnel from their shells. It was up to us and we poured on the fire, the machine guns grew dangerously hot as belt after belt of ammunition sped through them. No time now for short bursts, it was all or nothing, survival or die. As the Russians got even nearer I saw the front rank fall as thousands of machine gun bullets raked over them and they fell in neat, wide lines. Their comrades stepped over the bodies and kept running, I could see the Soviet battle police, commissars and NKVD men behind them, urging them on, threatening to shoot them if they faltered. But there was only so much flesh and blood could withstand. They were almost within fifty metres of us when they faltered, they had run into a wall of lead that was simply too much to pass. They turned and ran, still pursued by our gunners. The artillery and Panzers opened fire again to finish off the survivors and soon the battle was over. For now.

"Did we take any casualties?" I called out to the men.

They looked around them, but we were all here, no one was injured. Firing from the shelter of the half-track we had been protected from the worst of the Soviet small arms fire. Several of our vehicles were wrecked, two were on fire, victims of the Soviet shell fire. Many of our men were dead and wounded, not all of the platoons had been so lucky. I thought then of Heide, she would be busy attending to the fresh influx of casualties. Soldiers were running around with boxes of ammunition to replenish our supplies, the danger of a second attack was very real. Then there was the sound of aircraft engines, we looked up, ready to take cover but they were our own, Stukas, soon they peeled off one by one and descended on the enemy positions, aiming to take out their armour and artillery. The Stukas punished them for fifteen minutes in endless bombing attacks followed by strafing passes, then they left. During the lull in the battle, I ordered Mundt to stand the men down to eat. We sat around drinking water, someone had stowed a bag of loaves of bread in the half-track, they handed them around and we ate breakfast.

"Do you think they'll come back again?" Merkel asked me nervously.

I looked at Mundt, he was the experienced veteran.

"They usually do, Dieter, but look on the good side. The ones we killed won't be coming back, so the more they attack us, the less they're able to attack us next time. The second wave will be nothing, they'll be the newcomers, inexperienced. We'll slaughter them, easily."

I thought about the counter argument, the Soviets were known to use their green troops to soften up the enemy for the veterans that would come and finish us off. Their lack of concern for casualties was staggering. But perhaps this time it would be different. A flight of aircraft flew overhead and we anxiously looked up at the sky.

"Stukas?" someone asked.

"No," Mundt said, "Sturmoviks."

But they weren't aiming at us, for some reason. Their target was the city itself, perhaps our command and control centres, possibly our supply dumps. Whatever they were aiming at it was the civilians' turn to suffer, as the Russian ground attack planes bombed and strafed the centre of the city. At least they were leaving us alone, but then I thought of Heide. The hospital, oh God, no, surely they wouldn't attack it? I made a vow to make sure she was safe as soon as we got back from this mission. Muller came around to check on us.

"Any problems, Hoffman?"

"No, we're good, thank you, Sir, no casualties and no damage."

"How about ammunition?"

"They brought around some belts for the MG42s, but not enough if the Soviets attack in similar strength, we could do with more."

"You'll have to manage, I've issued everything we've got and I've sent a message to Division requesting more supplies. I'm sure they'll get replacements to us very soon, in the meantime, well, do your best. Good luck."

He went on to the next platoon. The men looked at me, horror struck.

"Sir, we can't hold them with what we've got," Mundt said. "We've only got half of what we used to fight off the first attack."

He'd already forgotten his reassuring words about killing off the worst of the enemy in the first wave.

"I'm afraid we'll just have to manage, Scharfuhrer."

"With what?"

"We'll have to make the ammunition count. We'll wait until they're closer before we open fire with the MG42s, the same for the machine pistols. Merkel, use your Kar 98 as soon as they get in range, that was fine shooting last time, the same for anyone else that can shoot straight and has a Kar 98. When they get in range, we'll hit them with grenades. Who can throw the furthest?"

Merkel put up his hand. "That would be me too, Sir, I always threw almost twice the distance of anyone else on the ranges."

"Good, make sure you have plenty of grenades, take some from the other men if you haven't got enough. We will manage, don't worry! Don't forget, it's only until the supplies come up from Division."

Then someone shouted. "They're coming!"

CHAPTER SEVEN

'The war against Russia will be such that it cannot be conducted in a knightly fashion. This struggle is one of ideologies and racial differences and will have to be conducted with unprecedented, unmerciful and unrelenting harshness.'

Adolf Hitler March 1941

Fortunately for us Mundt's analysis was proved correct. The suicidal enthusiasm of the first assault troops was nowhere in evidence, the second wave was of a very inferior calibre. They came forward piecemeal, small groups leaping from shell hole to shell hole, hiding from our fire, only going forward when urged on at gunpoint. When they did get near they were cut down by short, accurate bursts from our MG42s.

"Hitler's Saws, they call them, the Russkis," Mundt said.

"They are noisy bastards too, I guess, just like a sawmill."

"As long as they give us the bullets to use them," Voss said sourly.

He was correct the new machine guns were devastating as long as they had the belts of ammunition to keep them firing. A small group of Russians, more determined than their comrades, did get quite close to our half-track and Merkel got the chance to demonstrate his skills with grenades. His throws were incredible, he drew his arm back, looked carefully at the target and then launched. The soldiers must have been fifty metres away, a group of Russians sheltering in a nearby shell hole that we couldn't dislodge. The stick grenade flew unerringly into the middle of them and exploded, their screams echoed towards us. They carried on screaming for a long time, but they were no longer shooting at us. The attack quickly petered out, the last of the Russians retreated to their positions and the battlefield was empty, except for the corpses that were strewn across the snow, smears of red blood and dismembered body parts giving it the appearance of some kind of surreal camouflage. A runner came around with a message from Muller, we were pulling out to re-arm, a regiment of the LAH would take our places in the line.

Shortly afterwards we heard the noise of engines as the half-tracks, armoured cars and Panzers of our relief began to arrive. We started up and Voss drove us back to our assembly point. Muller was already on the ground surrounded by a group of officers, I dismounted and went to join them.

"The pressure on Kharkov is off for now, Division report that the Soviets are pulling back after the bloody nose we gave them. It looks like we've got a clear front open for us, we're going forward again."

We all cheered, at last, it was what we were here for, seeking and destroying the enemy, not waiting for them to come and attack us.

"HQ want us to get in position to counterattack Kursk, it's time we drove the Soviets out of that city. Our immediate objective is Korenevo, we aim to retake the ground we lost recently. If all goes well, we'll set up our HQ back in the monastery where we were before. We'll take today to re-arm and re-equip, some of our half-tracks need repairs and I'm waiting for new barrels for some of the MG42s. Attend to your men and I'll try and get the cookhouse to rustle up some food. We leave at two am tomorrow. That's all."

I went back to my platoon and passed on the news. There was more than a little grumbling.

"We're going backwards and forwards like a fucking see-saw," Beidenberg said. "You'd think they'd give us the tools to finish the job, a few more Panzers and some air support from the Luftwaffe and we could run these Soviets the length of Russia."

There were murmurs of agreement. I didn't say

anything, our commanders weren't fools. If they had the equipment and troops they would have sent them forward, but I suspected the cupboard was bare. We'd heard of heavy Luftwaffe losses over the past few days, apparently the Russians had new types of aircraft in increasing numbers over the front, our flyers were stretched to breaking point trying to contain them.

We spent rest of the day replenishing our stocks of fuel and ammunition. In the afternoon a Kubelwagen drew up next to us. I tried to ignore it.

"Untersturmfuhrer, a word if you please."

It was Kriminalkommissar Wiedel of the Gestapo.

"Yes, Sir, of course."

We moved off out of earshot of the men.

"Have you seen Obersturmbannfuhrer von Betternich?"

"No, Sir, not today."

"We were observing the battle when he went to check on something that worried him, he saw movement in a nearby building but he never came back. I went to search for him but he has disappeared, the building is empty."

I assumed he meant that observing the battle meant watching to see who would snipe at me.

"Perhaps he was wounded, Sir?"

"The building was subsequently hit by a Russian shell, but there is no sign of him inside. I want you and your platoon to make a search of the rear area and see if you can find him."

"We're departing for Korenevo in the early morning, Sir."

"I know that," he snapped, "so you had better hurry. I'll be with Sturmbannfuhrer Muller, report to me what you find."

The men grumbled about having to be roused to go on a wild goose chase, 'just to look after an SD man', especially when the rest of the regiment was getting some rest, but I pushed them into action. I left two of my private soldiers to guard the half-track, the rest of us went over to the ruined building to start the search.

We scoured the rubble but found no sign of him. Then Merkel shouted, he'd found some traces of fresh blood. We spread out to search a wider area, there were more traces of blood some thirty metres away. We followed the direction of the red trail and found more blood. There was a collapsed wall and as we approached calling out for von Betternich, we suddenly heard a groan. There was a pile of masonry, that looked as if it had been a grain store or something similar, another groan came from inside. We started to move the rubble aside, pulling off bricks and rocks to reach the trapped man, finally we made a hole through to a hollow in the middle of the stones, a hollow big enough for a man. Von Betternich's face peered out, white with dust. We ripped away at the bricks and made a hole large enough to pull him free. By a miracle, he was unhurt.

"I took shelter in here from the bullets, Hoffman, but the building was hit by a Soviet shell and collapsed around me."

"The Soviets were certainly chucking everything at us, Sir, you're very lucky."

"Perhaps, but it was not Soviet bullets that I was sheltering from. Someone else shot at me while the battle was on. Have you seen Kriminalkommissar Wiedel?"

I told him he was at regimental HQ with Muller.

"In that case you can escort me there now, Hoffman. Thank you for rescuing me."

He was quite able to walk and we made our way to where Muller was talking to his officers. Wiedel was nearby using the HQ radio, he saw von Betternich and signed off, then came to greet him.

"It's good to see you, Sir," Wiedel said.

"Yes. Listen, Wiedel, they tried to kill me, did you know that?"

"No, Sir, I didn't. Who tried to kill you?"

"I don't know who it was, but I would recognise him if I saw him again, he came quite close to me. What is happening here?"

"We're pushing forward again, the LAH have taken over our positions around Kharkov, we are heading back to Korenevo prior to jumping off for Kursk. Departure is set for the early hours of tomorrow morning."

He looked around it was growing very dark.

"Very well, I'll do the rounds of every man in the regiment when we stop at Korenevo and see if I can find the swine that shot at me."

"Assuming it was one of our SS Deutschland soldiers, Sir."

He looked at me thoughtfully. "Yes, that's right, assuming that it was. We will see in daylight when we arrive at Korenevo. Bastards, they tried to kill me!"

I got back to the platoon and settled in for a short night. We bivouacked next to the half-track, again my position as officer in command gave me a privileged place in the cockpit, so I was out of the snow. The men passed around another bottle of schnapps, they seemed to have an inexhaustible supply, I didn't complain. My thoughts were elsewhere and I was happy to drown my sorrows.

"The men won't be sorry to get back to Korenevo, Sir, that church was a lot warmer than out in the open."

"That's true. Has anyone heard any news of Kharkov, the Russian bombing? Did they hit the hospital?"

"You're worried about the nurse, Sir?"

I admitted that I was.

"I heard from someone that they hit several buildings but not the hospital," Voss said. "I'm sure she'll be safe."

My hopes lifted, but when I'd be able to get back to Kharkov and check for myself I couldn't be sure. This battle seemed to be endless, it had started before I arrived for my new posting and there was no sign of it ending. First we took ground, the Soviets counterattacked and retook it, then we took it again, when would there be a real conclusion? I thought about what the men had said, that the Russians had seemingly endless supplies of men and equipment. Our own supplies were becoming more and more intermittent, it was a sobering thought that the 6th Army had perished in the snows of Stalingrad almost entirely through lack of food and ammunition. We all remembered the radio broadcasts, Reichsminister Goering promising to resupply by air, Reichsminister Goebbels constantly assuring us that the city was in our hands, even the Fuhrer claimed that the 6th Army would prevail right up until the end. They had all been wrong. It struck me like a body blow that if the assertions of the men were true, then the Russians would always have the advantage in men and materiel. In that case, the end would surely be pre-ordained, we couldn't beat them. We had just won a good victory, beating back the fresh Russian offensive at Kharkov. I recalled that they'd sent wave after wave of troops against us as if they did indeed have thousands, possibly millions more to take their places when they fell. Was the war in Russia then doomed? I tried to put that thought out of my mind, as it was unthinkable. Yet at the current rate of attrition, we could win battle after battle and still lose the war, eventually we would just run out of troops, of tanks, of fuel and ammunition.

I helped myself to more schnapps. Mundt raised his eyebrows, but said nothing. I realised how much I depended on the tough, reliable sergeant, he always seemed to be there, always did the right thing. When I drifted off to sleep, I thought again of Heide. It seemed that almost as soon as I'd shut my eyes I was being shaken awake. It was Beidenberg, "Sir, we're getting ready to move out, we've made a pot of coffee. Merkel managed to get some loaves of bread from the cookhouse, so you'll want some breakfast before we leave."

I groaned, my limbs were stiff with cold and the cramped position I'd slept in.

"What time is it, Beidenberg?"

"One thirty, Sir."

We had half an hour before we left. I quickly strapped on my webbing, checked my MP38 and went towards the smell of hot coffee. As usual, it was foul, but at least it was hot and soaked into the bread in my stomach.

"Are we anticipating much resistance, Sir?" Merkel asked.

I smiled, he was obviously keen to follow up on his grenade throwing exploits.

"I suggest you keep a supply of grenades handy, Merkel, you never know."

"Yes, Sir."

"And keep that rifle handy too, we could find having our own sniper might useful."

He nodded and smiled.

When I climbed into the half-track I discovered that Merkel already had a fresh wooden box of grenades by his feet, the lid off and ready to use. That suited me, if we ran into Soviet resistance a well-thrown grenade could well tip the balance in our favour. Then there were shouts for us to start up, there was a massive roar of engines, smoke swirled over the vehicles, even the light of the campfires disappeared into the dark cloud as the leading vehicles pulled away. We were advancing again, yet I felt little optimism, I was being carried further away from Heide. Even after knowing her for such a short time, she was uppermost in my thoughts. Whatever it took I would get back to see her, whatever.

We were well on the way when I heard the sound of a shell being fired up ahead, one of ours. Two more shells were fired, then there was the chatter of machine gun fire, after that everything went silent, obviously a Soviet outpost that had been taken by surprise. We accelerated and after another kilometre more firing broke out, this time shells and bullets whistled overhead, it seemed that we were engaging the enemy. A flare lit up the sky and I saw the amazing sight of an entire Soviet army encamped on the steppe immediately in front of us. How on earth they'd failed to realise we were heading towards them I couldn't imagine, except that they may have mistaken our tanks for their own. But it was a golden opportunity, by the light of the flare I could see the tankers jumping into their vehicles, clouds of exhaust smoke as they started the engines, men running out of tents, pulling on boots and grabbing equipment. Some of the men were already firing back at us, camp sentries, anti-aircraft guns probably, but it was all too little too late. We smashed through the Twenty Fourth Army, part of the Voronezh Front, as if it was made of paper. The Panzers and STuGIIIs were firing constantly and the Soviet tanks were exploding one by one, as our shells hit the easy stationary targets. The machine gunners of our tanks and half-tracks poured belt after belt of ammunition at the hapless Russians, some tried to regroup to shoot back but there was a desperate panic in the camp, that blocked men's minds and stopped them thinking sanely. Then we were in amongst them.

Merkel lobbed his grenades in quick succession. A small group of soldiers were crouched behind a pile of rubble, popping out to take quick shots at our troops. Two stick grenades sailed over their heads to land, one behind them, one in their middle and they exploded in a shattering mixture of smoke, brick dust and body parts. Mundt was firing the forward MG42 and Beidenberg the rear, they swept the ground of live soldiers, leaving only corpse strewn devastation in their wake. Voss was driving, several times he swerved to run down a group of fleeing Russians, Beidenberg finished off any survivors as we rushed past. Several tanks had started their engines and were fleeing the battle but our Panzers and STuGIIIs pursued them and finished them off. An armoured car, a command car probably with its large aerial array, was totally destroyed, almost certainly incinerating its occupants including the commander of this outfit, possibly a Soviet general. Our half-tracks were braking to a halt, soldiers jumping out and going around on foot to finish off the survivors. Our job now was to protect the Panzers from infantry attack from the rear, the Russians had a nasty habit of popping up behind our Panzers and hitting them in their vulnerable, thinly armoured rear. We went from cover to cover, shell hole to shell hole, rooting out Soviet resistance and taking prisoner any that surrendered. Not all were quick enough, some soldiers were too slow to throw down their guns and put up their hands and our men mowed them down in droves. I shouted at my men to be careful and spare those soldiers that surrendered, but their blood was up, they were both terrified and exhilarated in the fierce heat of battle and they were hard to rein in. Finally we had cleared the area of the enemy, the prisoners were being herded back to begin their captivity and we pressed on non-stop to Korenevo. The track was clear of any enemy and we were able to drive straight to the monastery and make camp just as if we had never left.

I was surprised to see the monks still in their camp. When we checked out the church and monastery it was obvious that the Soviet army we had just decimated had used them as a headquarters, there were signs everywhere that they had made a hurried departure. We simply moved our possessions back in and took over as before.

"Weird, those monks camped out over there still," Mundt said to me. "They must be dedicated."

Merkel was watching them too, an uneasy expression on his face, no doubt he had been religious once. Perhaps he still was.

"It's almost as if they're waiting for something," he said. "They give me the creeps."

I laughed at his nervousness. "Merkel, they are waiting for something, they're waiting for the soldiers of both sides to go home and leave them alone. They suffered under the communists, Stalin had tens of thousands of their priests shot. Now we've arrived and they've got freedom of religion but they are stuck in the middle of a war zone with soldiers occupying their church."

"That's right, Merkel, they just want us all to bugger off and leave them alone," Mundt added.

"Well, they still make me uneasy, seeing them waiting there, silently. I'm going to go over and see what they want."

Some impulse made me get up and shoulder my MP38. "I think I'll come with you, Merkel, you've aroused my curiosity."

The platoon looked astonished. "Are you religious then, Sir?" Voss asked.

"No, I'm not, I'm just curious, as I said. After all, they're our neighbours, I want to see what they're like."

"Make sure they don't convert you," Mundt shouted after us.

Merkel half turned and flipped a rude sign back at him.

We walked over to the camp, there were six tents, some large, some small. The monks, twelve of them, were sitting on cut logs they had dragged around a campfire to use as stools. They eyed us warily as we approached, I remembered that we were still armed to the teeth, I had two unused stick grenades clipped to my webbing, my Walther in the holster and the MP38 on its strap around my chest. With the steel helmet on my head, it was hardly an encouraging sight. An older man looked up at me, then got warily to his feet.

"I am Bishop Demchak, how may I help you?"

I tried to give him a reassuring smile. "Jurgen Hoffman, Bishop. Don't worry, I want nothing from you, nothing at all. I just came visit your camp and to ask why you are still here."

The older man hesitated for a moment. "And where would we go, Untersturmfuhrer?"

"You know of our SS ranks?"

"I make it my business to know who is occupying our church."

"I'm sorry, it must be difficult for you."

He shrugged. "It has been so for a long time, the

communists have not made our life easy. But to answer your question as to why we are still here, we must guard what is ours."

"The church and the buildings, you mean?"

"Our order of monks has many riches, Untersturmfuhrer, not all are visible to men. But yes, the buildings are of course important to us."

"And the other riches, the ones not visible to men?"

He looked alarmed for a moment, then relaxed. I guess he remembered that we weren't a communist raiding party.

"God has many mysteries, my son. We preserve what we can."

I was growing tired of his cryptic way of speaking, I felt as if he was in some way trying to dazzle me with the benefits of redemption.

"Come on, Merkel, let's get back to the others and see if they've managed to find any food."

"Yes, Sir."

"Herr Hoffman," the Bishop called after me. "If you are in need of spiritual guidance, do come and see me again, I will be pleased to assist you."

I waved my hand in acknowledgement as we walked away. Then a thought struck me, how did he know my name was Hoffman? I looked around but he had gone, probably disappeared into one of the tents.

The cookhouse had prepared their inevitable stew and brewed more foul coffee. I took a steaming bowl of potato soup mixed with some indeterminate meat, a hunk of coarse bread and a mug of coffee and sat with the men. My head had started to ache again badly after the excitement of the early morning engagement and I was glad of a rest and hot food.

"So what's the next move, Sir," Voss asked me. "Is this the beginning of the attack on Kursk?"

"Why Kursk, why are you so keen on Kursk?" I asked him.

"I had a woman there, bloody beautiful, can't wait to get back to her. We were in love, you know, she was the nicest girl I'd ever met, said she'd come back to Germany with me after the war, unless of course I settled here on one of these farms."

"You do that and the bloody partisans will cut your balls off, you know," Mundt said. "They don't take kindly to our settlers."

"But Oberschutze, she could be dead by now, you should prepare yourself for the worst," I said to him.

"Oh, I have, Sir. She had a couple of sisters so at least one of them is bound to have survived."

I heard the men laughing, I tried but couldn't hide my astonishment at human nature. "I hope it turns out well for you, Voss."

"Yes. What about your girl, Sir?" Voss asked me. "You know, the pretty nurse at the hospital, do you reckon she's ok?"

"Fraulein Thalberg is in perfect health, I'm happy to say," a voice said from the other side of the half-track. Von Betternich, as always standing in the shadows where you least expected him. But this time he was welcome.

"Sir, it's good to see you. So you have news of Heide?"

"Yes, the hospital was untouched by the bombing and shelling, she is fit and well and going about her duties even as we speak. A word with you, Untersturmfuhrer."

I moved away from the men and we found a quiet spot.

"I found the man I was looking for."

"One of our men, from the Deutschland Regiment?"

"As it turned out, yes, he was."

"Was, Sir?"

"Was. He had been shot, not a rifle bullet this time, as far as we can tell. A shot to the side of the head, doubtful he even saw it coming. When the surgeon has time I will get him to extract the bullet, but I have little doubt it will prove to be one of ours."

"So you think the sniper is one of our own people?"

"Certainly a German, yes, but not necessarily from this regiment. No, he could be from another regiment, Der Fuhrer, perhaps, we have unfinished business there, if you remember. We are due to go back and visit them, I will naturally want you to accompany me."

"Sir, I thought I was finished with all of that business?"

"I need you, Hoffman, to watch my back. It seems you need me too, to watch your back," he looked significantly at my head wound, covered by the bandaging.

"I'm sure I can take care of myself, Sir."

He smiled. "You don't want the men thinking you're being watched over by a policeman, eh? But what about Fraulein Thalberg?"

"What about her?"

"You have been helping us, naturally we are concerned for your welfare and that of your friends. You are aware that the Kriminalkommissar has made it his business to keep an eye out for Fraulein Thalberg's well-being. War can be a very dangerous business, you know."

So that was the quid pro quo, but it was a price well worth paying. And he knew that I would pay it, gladly and in full.

"I appreciate that, Sir."

"Good. Der Fuhrer have set up their HQ outside the city of Kharkov, Hoffman. We'll be going there in the morning, perhaps there will be time for a visit to the hospital if you wish. You could take the opportunity to get your dressing changed and attend to other more personal business. Now, I have some matters to attend to with Sturmbannfuhrer Muller, I will see if he has a Kubelwagen that we can borrow. Half-tracks are so uncomfortable, aren't they? And entirely too warlike, quite the wrong impression for a policeman."

He nodded and walked off, leaving me once more wrapped up in the dark tentacles of the SD. And now, of course, the Gestapo. But tomorrow, I may see Heide, I could deal with the SD and the Gestapo if meant spending some time with her, even a few precious minutes.

An hour later, a runner came to find me.

"Sir, you are to report to Sturmbannfuhrer Muller, at once!"

"Very well."

I heard the men muttering about their platoon commander being in the shit again, it was entirely possible too, I wondered what I was being accused of this time. I went into Muller's outer office in the monastery, the orderly sent me straight in and I saluted. Kriminalkommissar Wiedel was with the CO, whose face was red with anger. The Gestapo man was as calm as ever.

Muller spoke first. "Hoffman, I've had my attention drawn to some of your reports of the actions you've been involved in since you've been here. I've checked the reports from other officers and talked to the men. Do you have anything to add to what you have already said?"

I thought hard, what the hell could I have said that would have given the wrong impression?

"No, sir."

"I see. Well, I am pleased to inform you that I have decided to promote you to Obersturmfuhrer, effective immediately."

"What, er, I see. Thank you, Sir, thank you very much."

If I had made a list of the one hundred things least

likely to happen to me, promotion would be at the very top.

"Congratulations, Hoffman. It is unusually early to promote an officer this quickly, but your actions have been a credit to the regiment and to the SS. See the quartermaster and he will issue you with new rank badges. That's all, dismissed."

I saluted. "Heil Hitler." He returned the salute and I left the office. How things could change, one minute I was on Muller's shit list, the next he promoted me to Obersturmfuhrer. I was walking away, feeling slightly dizzy when Muller's office door opened and Wiedel came out.

"Congratulations, Hoffman."

"Thank you, Sir. Was it von Betternich who pushed the Major?"

He smiled thinly. "He may have mentioned something, but believe me, the merit of your actions spoke for itself. As a matter of interest, I wanted to speak to you about your young nurse, Fraulein Thalberg."

My pleasure at the promotion turned to an icy feeling in my stomach.

"She is well? Has something happened to her?"

"Do not concern yourself, she is in perfect health. At least, as far as the Russian efforts are concerned. You know of her politics?"

"She told me her father was a communist, yes."

"Quite so. However, she is on a watch list that I brought

with me from Berlin. She has certain unwise political views herself, did you know that?"

I was about to say I didn't when I thought to that time in the restaurant, she'd mentioned something about the treatment of the Jews.

"I suspect she may be a little outspoken, that is all, no more than that."

"People have been shot for being a little outspoken, Hoffman."

I reeled. "Is she in any danger?"

"No, not at the moment. But listen to me, the Reich has stern policies in place in certain areas."

"You mean the Jews?"

"Yes, that is one such area. It is not advisable to question the State in these matters. Or even the wishes of the Fuhrer."

"What is happening with the Jews, Sir? It's not the first time that I've heard someone mention this."

"They are being resettled, Hoffman."

"So why is that a problem?"

Wiedel was silent for a few moments.

"Take my advice, Obersturmbannfuhrer, forget the Jews and do not make any enquiries. It would be sensible to pass that message on to Fraulein Thalberg. People meddling in State affairs risk everything, do you understand? Everything! Good day to you, Hoffman."

He walked away, leaving me more puzzled than ever. I

rejoined my men and we spent the rest of the day making repairs to our equipment, the re-arming and refuelling that were part of the routine after any action. After the evening meal we had time to ourselves, the men had a camp fire blazing outside the church and coffee brewing in a battered kettle. I joined them and nursed a mug of coffee, feeling more confused than ever. The business with the Gestapo and the SD was obviously more ominous than I had realised, of course they had their teeth into Heide, I knew that now. I wished they'd all go away and leave me to fight a simple, straightforward war.

"Mundt, what have you heard about the Jews?" I asked my sergeant abruptly.

He looked up and by the light of the fire I saw his eyes narrow.

"Nothing, Sir."

"Nothing? How is it that none of us knows anything? Where have they gone?"

Mundt shrugged. "No idea."

"For Christ's sake, man, they can't have disappeared into thin air. How many are there in the Reich, a million, two million. Where are they?"

"Begging your pardon, Sir, but I prefer not to talk about the Jews."

I was wasting my time, I knew that. But something was odd, they'd been bullied and beaten, their property confiscated in many cases. They'd been thrown out of their jobs and evicted from their homes. The same had happened to the communists and anyone else the Fuhrer blamed for the problems of Germany under the Weimar republic. It was cruel, sure, but the politicians said it was necessary. But what had happened to these people, especially the Jews, where had they gone? I recalled when I was very young seeing communists and Nazi stormtroopers brawling in the streets, but Jews never, they seemed like well-behaved model citizens. I decided to speak to Heide, she obviously knew something. Despite what Wiedel had said, I wanted to know what was happening in my own country, I had a right to know, didn't I? But I thought of the dark, mysterious power of the Gestapo and the SD. Perhaps I didn't have that right, I remembered instinctively asking Heide to keep quiet in public about the Jews. My heart told me I wanted to know, my head told me that some knowledge could be very dangerous. At least war was simple, kill the enemy before he killed you.

In the morning we had an early start, von Betternich and Wiedel climbed into the back of the Kubelwagen with me. We left the camp just after dawn, Voss drove with Mundt and Merkel crammed into the front with him. We drove for an hour to the city of Kharkov, just outside the city we bumped into the camp of SS Der Fuhrer Panzer Grenadier Regiment. It was a farm, it must have been prosperous before the war, the farmhouse looked to be in good repair and quite large. The sentry stopped us at the gate to the farmyard but Wiedel showed him his Gestapo identification disc and the man waved us through. The ground was littered with half-tracks and equipment, men working on the vehicles, a few standing in line at the cookhouse for breakfast, just like our own HQ at Korenevo. A soldier stood guard at the door of the farmhouse, his MP38 at the ready. Once more, Wiedel showed his Gestapo disc and we were waved through. An orderly knocked on the door of the CO's office, the two security men and I were shown in. Mundt and the others stayed outside.

"Good morning, Sturmbannfuhrer," Stettner said coldly, nodding at Wiedel and me.

"Obersturmbannfuhrer, Sir, I was promoted."

"I see. Congratulations," he said sarcastically, "what can I do for you?"

He wasn't on his own in the office, the Sturmscharfuhrer sat on a chair by the blazing log fire, a rifle on his knees, a Kar 98 with a telescopic sight. He took his time but finally got to his feet, a Sturmscharfuhrer was the highest rank of NCO in the SS, he wasn't about to let any officer forget his status.

"This is Sturmscharfuhrer Artur Winckmann, he keeps things in order for me around here. Now, tell me what you want, we are very busy!"

The two security men were on thin ice. Stettner was senior to both of them and he was a line officer in the middle of a major military action. Strangely, I noticed that he was still sitting on the ornate, gilt throne, it was obviously a treasured possession of his. But a little over-ostentatious, I thought, for an SS officer, more suited to a nobleman. Was that what he thought he was?

"Sir, you said you would have your regimental journals and movement records ready for us to inspect, we were interrupted by the Russian attack. We've come to look at those documents now."

"Then I am afraid you have wasted you time. They were lost during the Russian counterattack."

There was silence in the office. We all knew what should happen next, a formal enquiry, officers and men questioned, a search mounted for the missing documents, equally we all knew that it would not happen. The CO was blatantly hostile to von Betternich and Wiedel and we all knew that in this place he could please himself. Perhaps he really did think of himself as a nobleman after all.

The SD man and the Gestapo officer exchanged glances, and then nodded formally at Stettner.

"In that case, we need not waste any more of your time," von Betternich said. "Thank you, Sir. Heil Hitler."

We all three saluted and left the office, I could swear that Winckmann was grinning from where he stood near the fire. Outside, we got into the Kubi and Voss drove away and into the centre of the city.

"We have some administrative matters to attend to,

Hoffman, we'll drop you outside the hospital and collect you in two hours, your men will be perfectly safe with us," von Betternich said.

"Yes, thank you, Sir"

I rushed through the doors and asked the clerk on the desk about Heide.

"She is on the ward, Herr Obersturmbannfuhrer."

I went through the double swing doors, the familiar smell of ether, urine and unwashed bodies hit me full in the face but she was there, she looked up, saw me and came towards me, then stopped a metre away.

"Jurgen."

"Heide."

Then she was in my arms and we ignored the cheers, jeers and catcalls from the patients in their beds.

"I thought you might have been killed," she said.

"No, it'll take more than a bunch of half-arsed Russians to kill me, Heide."

But she saw through the bravado and didn't smile. "I'll see the sister and get someone to cover for me, how long have you got?"

"Two hours."

"Then we must make full use of the time we have. One moment."

She came back after three minutes with another nurse who gave me a cryptic smile and walked on into the ward to take care of the men.

"Come with me, there is somewhere quiet we can talk," she said.

We went up two flights of stairs and she opened the door into a tiny room with just a chair and a bed.

"This is the on-call doctors' restroom, it is where they sleep when they may be needed at short notice."

We looked at one other for all of five seconds, then we were in each other's arms, kissing, caressing and tearing the other's clothes off until we were both naked. We fell on the bed and her hands were all over me, our mouths clamped together, I pulled my mouth away and bent to kiss her beautiful, firm breasts, the nipples were hard and erect. Then I put my hand down and felt between her legs, she was already wet with arousal, her own hand was on my penis, softly stroking me.

"Fuck me, Jurgen, now, my darling."

I entered her and we held each other tightly as I moved my hips gently backwards and forwards, she held me, almost as if I might want to leave. I showered her with kisses and she reciprocated, we worshipped each other's body, revelling in the sheer beauty and innocence of this most basic yet magnificent fulfilment of our needs, a tiny temporary oasis away from the filth, terror and horror of the war. Our bodies clamped together even more tightly as we made love for what seemed like an eternity, then all too soon it was over as we both surged to a climax. Afterwards we lay together, touching and holding in wonder at the newness of the love we had found.

"You know I shall never let you go after this, don't you, Jurgen?"

"That suits me, my darling. I'll be happy to stay with you forever."

But we both knew that our forever was an illusion. We constantly had to check our watches, I only had a half hour left. We slowly got dressed.

"This damn war, will it never end?" she said to me. "I hate this place, the dirt and squalor of Russia, the snow and the cold, the dark, I want you to take me away somewhere it is always warm."

"I would if I could, you know that, Heide?"

"Yes, I do," she gave out a huge sigh. "These fucking Nazis! You're not a Nazi, are you Jurgen?"

I was able to reply honestly to that one. "No, I am not and never have been."

"Yet you joined the SS?"

"Of course, I was in the Hitler Youth, it was an honour to join such an elite regiment as SS Deutschland."

"But some of your people are so brutal, Jurgen."

"Which people?"

She hesitated for a moment, but then she went on. "I was stationed first at a hospital in Poland, there was an SS unit there, they were called an Einsatzgruppe."

"Yes, one of our Task Forces, probably on anti-partisan duties."

"They boasted that they were rounding up Jews, not partisans, Jurgen. Rounding them up and shooting them, murdering them."

"Perhaps they were partisans."

"They were women and children, children as young as two and three, together with their mothers. I saw the bodies. And then there were the camps."

"Camps?"

"Yes, concentration camps."

"I see, they're used to intern political prisoners, that's all."

"No, there are dozens of trains travelling east every day, packed with Jews, they take them to the camps and then they disappear. Jurgen, they're murdering them!"

"That's ridiculous, why would they do that, they're German citizens?"

But even as I was denying it, I sensed the truth of what she'd said. I had known Jews in my childhood who had long disappeared. The Reich propaganda maintained that they were parasites that should be cleansed from the earth. Until now, I'd assumed it was just words, that they were being sent to territories somewhere far from the Reich. Then I remembered Wiedel.

"They're watching you, you know. The Gestapo."

"I don't care, I'm going to write to the Fuhrer, he has to be told of this."

I was horrified. "The Fuhrer, are you totally mad?"

"What do you mean?"

"Nothing happens in the Reich without the Fuhrer's consent. You would just be advertising your opposition to the government, to the Fuhrer himself."

"So what can I do?"

"Please do nothing for now, my darling. When the war is over we will make our voices heard together."

"You mean when the war is won?" she said anxiously.

I didn't reply.

"Is it that bad?" she asked.

I think for the first time since I'd joined the SS I faced reality. The enormity of our government murdering our own citizens, Jews and communists, the overwhelming odds we faced on the Eastern Front, and they seemed to be getting worse. I hadn't been here long, but I had seen and heard enough to know the way things were going.

"We haven't lost yet," I tried to reassure her. "Just be prepared for any eventuality."

She gave me a pale smile, the message was obvious, look out for yourself. We both had to get back to our duties. We kissed long and hard, and made promises to each other, then I said goodbye to her at the hospital entrance. The half-track was waiting outside.

"You look thoughtful, young man," von Betternich said, "is anything wrong?"

"No, I'm fine," I said, trying to appear relaxed, but I got the impression that there was little about me he didn't understand. I shivered, hoping that his and Wiedel's protection of Heide would continue for now. If it didn't, I worried for her future. And I realised that I loved her, it was not just the aftermath of wonderful sex, I loved everything about her, the way she looked, the way she talked, the way she smelt, the way she styled her hair, the way she walked. I knew that I would lay down my life for her. I felt that it might just come to that too, with all of the complications that surrounded our relationship.

CHAPTER EIGHT

"Man has discovered in nature the wonderful notion of that all-mighty being whose law he worships. Fundamentally in everyone here is the feeling for this all-mighty, which we call God (that is to say, the dominion of natural laws throughout the whole universe). The priests, who have always succeeded in exploiting this feeling, threaten punishments for the man who refuses to accept the creed they impose.

When one provokes in a child a fear of the dark, one awakens in him a feeling of atavistic dread. Thus this child will be ruled all his life by this dread, whereas another child, who has been intelligently brought up, will be free of it. It's said that every man needs a refuge where he can find consolation and help in unhappiness. I don't believe it! If humanity follows that path, it's solely a matter of tradition and habit. That's a lesson, by the way, that can be drawn from the Bolshevik front. The Russians have no God, and that doesn't prevent them from being able to face death. We don't want to educate anyone in atheism."

Adolf Hitler July 1941

We drove through along the snow-covered tracks back to Korenevo. I felt as if this dismal, dreary place had become the epicentre of my world. If the Soviets wanted it, they were welcome to it as far I was concerned. The men must have known that Heide and I had made love, I knew that people have something about them when they have just been to bed with someone they are passionate about, a faraway look, maybe even the smell of their body, the sweat of a man mixed with that of a woman. They just knew, but tactfully they kept their silence. When we got back to the regiment, von Betternich and Wiedel asked me to follow them to their office. They had taken the same office as before, the Soviets had even left the furniture as it was. Their orderly had got a fire going in the grate and it wasn't totally freezing in the office, though not as warm as Stettner's luxurious quarters. Von Betternich limped in and sat behind the desk, Wiedel stood in front of the fire warming his hands and I was left standing rigidly in front of the desk, once more the naughty schoolboy about to be told off by the headmaster.

"It seems we have much to discuss, Hoffman."

"Yes, Sir." About Heide? Surely not!

"We are nearing some conclusions about this shooting business, give me your impressions."

I was astonished, I thought they were stalled, hadn't any idea as to who may have done it or why.

"I don't have any, Sir."

"Really? Young man in love, eh? How was the delightful Fraulein Thalberg today?"

"She was well, thank you."

He looked at me with a smile on his face. "That much is obvious, Hoffman. You did not discuss politics with her, then?"

I hesitated only for a moment. "Not really, Sir, no."

"No? You are very wise. Well, perhaps we will come to that later. After the war, perhaps?"

I made no reply.

"Well, back to the shooting of our officers. An open and shut case, yes?"

"Sir, how can it be open and shut, it seems to be a major conspiracy, the Soviets could well be behind it."

I must have betrayed my naivety, they both looked at each other in amazement.

"Conspiracy," Wiedel said in a surprised voice, "what conspiracy?"

"The conspiracy to shoot our senior officers, Sir."

They both smiled. "My dear Hoffman, I have been a policeman for many years. With a very few exceptions, murder is either a crime of passion or an act of criminal gain. This was clearly for gain."

Wiedel nodded. "You'd better explain it to him before he starts a major panic."

Von Betternich nodded. "It is quite simple, my friend. We know that certain high-ranking officers have taken it upon themselves to relieve the population in occupied territories of valuable artworks, paintings, sculptures and other artefacts. Russian icons, in particular, are well regarded, as are paintings by Renaissance masters, Van Gogh, Titian, Rubens and so on. I believe I mentioned that Reichsmarschall Goering has a large collection at his estate, Karinhall, generously held in trust for the German people."

He lips twitched in a small smile as he said that and even Wiedel grinned. He went on.

"Reichsfuhrer Himmler has established a special unit to search out these confiscated artworks and make sure that they are sent to the Reich through official channels, to stop individuals pilfering these historical treasures. The unit reported that many pieces of art were going missing before they reached them and the indications were that these thefts occurred in areas fought over by the SS Das Reich Division. We have been investigating the various regiments within the Division to find out who is responsible. We thought we were getting near to the culprits when the shootings started, someone seemed to want to prevent us from talking to certain officers. Our current investigation centres on locating a stolen crucifix, solid gold and encrusted with precious stones and worth millions of marks. It was stolen from the church here at Korenevo. This crucifix is regarded by the Orthodox Church as one of their most precious possessions and dates back to the second century, it was made by a Greek craftsman and taken to Russia when Christianity was first brought to this country. It is a priority to both the church and the Fuhrer that this artefact is recovered."

"Senior SS officers stealing valuable artworks, looting churches, committing murder, are you serious?"

"It's not unique, Obersturmfuhrer," Wiedel said. "The Gestapo has many similar investigations in progress. But now, of course, it has taken a more sinister turn, the killings are interfering with our ability to prosecute the war."

"Do you know who is responsible for these thefts and murders?"

"Standartenfuhrer Stettner of Der Fuhrer Regiment is the person who is at the centre of it, yes."

Stettner? It did make a mad kind of sense, his obvious preoccupation with artworks, I recalled the gilt antique throne he used to sit on in his office.

"Surely you need to locate the crucifix before you can arrest him?"

They exchanged glances. "It is not quite that simple, Hoffman," von Betternich replied, "we know where the crucifix is, certainly, but arresting him is fraught with danger."

"You know where it is? Then why not just go and get it to prove his guilt? Where does he keep it?"

"In the base of that antique throne he uses."

"Really? How do you know that?"

"Because it is the one possession that he has with him at all times and carries everywhere, guarded and protected. Where else would he put a solid gold artefact worth millions of marks?"

"But why were the other officers killed?"

Von Betternich smiled broadly. "A simple falling out amongst thieves, my friend. I sometimes tire of hoping that criminals will one day come up with a more interesting motive, but that's what it usually comes down to. Simple greed, and when the thieves fall out, it is by no means unusual for them to start killing each other. They were all in it, all of the officers who were killed, even Brandt, your own CO, I'm afraid."

I was staggered by the terrible implication that our own commanders couldn't even be trusted.

"So you know who the culprit is and where the crucifix is yet you can't arrest him, I don't understand."

"He is surrounded by several hundred heavily armed troopers who are fiercely loyal to him and we're in the middle of one of the bloodiest wars that has ever been fought. If we went in to make the arrest, he would probably order his men to shoot us and blame the partisans."

I recalled Stettner's Sturmscharfuhrer with his telescopic rifle. "So his sergeant is the sniper?"

"Yes, probably, we checked the marksmanship of every man within Das Reich who could shoot that well, Vinckmann is one of the best they have, if not the best. There is Merkel, of course, from your own platoon. But Vinckmann looks most likely, he just missed the 1936 Olympic Games rifle shooting competition due to illness and he is Stettner's right hand man. Yes, almost certainly, it's him."

"So what will you do next?"

I had a vision of hundreds of Gestapo and SD personnel arriving in lorries to hold back Stettner's regiment while they went in and made the arrest, but it was ludicrous. Back in Germany it would be easy, we had rules and laws people generally obeyed. With us here in the wild snowy Russian wastes, there was little or no rule of law, and very little order. The commander of a Waffen SS Regiment possessed huge power in a region where our own legions had stormed in declaring that 'might is right.'

"We will go back to Der Fuhrer tomorrow and speak to Stettner. With any luck, we will gain an opening and be able to make the arrest. If, for example, we can reveal the location of the stolen artwork, that may persuade his men to let us arrest him, and Vinckmann too if he is the sniper."

"Couldn't you just have him recalled to Berlin, then question him there?"

Wiedel smiled. "We are not amateurs, Hoffman. Do you honestly think he would arrive carrying the crucifix in his suitcase? We would have no evidence and besides, the man is a war hero, Iron Cross First Class and The Knight's Cross with Oak Leaves. He is distantly related to Reichsleiter Bormann, the Fuhrer's secretary and has connections with several high-ranking members of the Nazi party. Without evidence, he could well turn the tables and have us arrested on some trumped up charge. No, we need to tackle him again, but carefully and cautiously, to see if we can literally catch him red handed. We will require you and three members of your platoon to accompany us again tomorrow. We will revisit Stettner and try to get him to incriminate himself, perhaps he will even give himself up, although I'm afraid that is very unlikely. We will leave at eight am, we won't have the opportunity to go sightseeing in Kharkov this time, I'm afraid."

"No, Sir," I saluted and left. As I walked away, I could only reflect how politics could be both the making and the ruination of any man. As, of course, could war.

I walked back to my platoon, noting with approval that Mundt had made sure that everyone was working on repairs and restocking the ammunition. They already had a fire going and I sat around it going over the unending paperwork that is part of an SS officer's lot. Mundt brought me a hot mug of coffee.

"Are we all finished now with the police stuff, Sir?"

"I'm afraid not, Mundt. I want you and two other men, we're going back to Der Fuhrer in the morning, they have more questions for the CO, I believe."

"Any chance of some time off in Kharkov?" he asked. "Maybe a few hours?"

"None at all, I'm afraid. They've said it will be a quick visit."

He grunted and was about to say something more when someone started shouting, "Alarm!"

We ran for cover, the nearest for us was the stone structure of the church. I looked up and saw a Sturmovik swooping down on us. Too late our anti-aircraft battery opened fire but the Russian was gone before he could find its range, the bomb dropped straight down and exploded on the perimeter of our camp, destroying a water tanker and killing several men who were clustered around it. It was firing its machine guns and cannons in long, raking bursts as it pulled out of its dive, flew over the camp and soared away. The second aircraft followed, another Sturmovik, firing continuously as he dived down on us, released his bomb and roared away, pursued by anti-aircraft fire. The bullets and cannon fire stitched a line across the camp, killing several unfortunate soldiers who were in its way, but the bomb failed to explode. We waited in the shelter of the church, but there were no more aircraft. The bomb bounced up in the air a couple of times, finally came back down to earth and rolled across to lie next to a half-track that was in process of being repaired, the engine had been pulled out and was hanging on chains from the framework of a portable crane positioned above it. Two mechanics for some reason had sheltered inside the fragile thin armoured body of the vehicle. They looked over the side at the bomb lying next to them, their expressions as frozen as the ground we were camped on.

The whole camp stopped, where normally people would carry on almost as if nothing had happened after a raid, except to repair the damage and carry away the dead and wounded. Now it was like a frozen tableau. Then one of the mechanics gingerly jumped down from the half-track and looked closely at the bomb. We heard him calling for tools from the vehicle and his companions handed them down to him. In front of the eyes of the whole camp, he calmly unscrewed the housing that held the fuse in place and gently removed it. He looked at it for a moment and then tossed it to one side.

"It's ok, the fuse is defective, it's rusted solid, couldn't go off if you hit it with a hammer. Look."

He picked up a hammer.

"Rottenfuhrer, no!" a voice roared across the camp.

It was Muller, who no doubt admired the man's bravery as much as the rest of us but had no wish to see any further demonstration of it. The man put down the hammer and we all relaxed.

"I think another mug of coffee would go down well, Scharfuhrer." I needed something to calm my nerves, it had been nail biting to watch that mechanic disarm the bomb.

"I'll see to it now, Sir."

I sat down to get on with my paperwork. Merkel was staring at something on the perimeter of the camp and I noticed it was the monks, huddled in their own shabby camp, hunched around a tiny fire. Did Christianity keep them warm, I wondered. Their ripped and ragged habits seemed to offer little protection from the biting cold, although they did wear fur boots on their feet rather than the more traditional sandals. Merkel was looking at them with a glance that seemed like hate, he'd behaved very strangely when we went over to see them. Perhaps he was a true atheist, a Christian hater. I'd better keep an eye on him, the last thing I needed was for one of my men to start giving the monks a hard time. After all, we were supposed to be more civilised than the previous rulers of this place, the Soviets.

We spent the rest of the day watching the sky for a return of the fighter-bombers and going about the daily business of a fighting regiment. Muller ordered the anti-aircraft defences doubled and called Division for some additional artillery. They must have taken his request seriously for within two hours a vehicle mounted 20mm

Flakvierling 38 anti-aircraft gun rolled into camp. Until now our anti-aircraft defences had consisted of two sets of twin MG34s mounted on a frame arrangement, the gunner sat behind an emplacement of sandbags and endeavoured to target enemy aircraft, it was an unenviable task. Mostly they missed completely, frequently low flying raiders strafing the camp targeted these gunners and they had a high mortality rate. The Flakvierling 38 was a different matter, mounted on a half-track chassis the gunner sat behind an armour-plated screen. Additionally, the guns themselves were 20mm cannons, four of them putting up a fearsome rate of fire. If nothing else, the men all visibly relaxed when the new gun was installed in position. There were no more raids that day and we were able to work on getting the regiment ready for the next day's operations without interruption. The following morning I got Mundt, Bauer and Beidenberg to ready the borrowed Kubelwagen. I had intended taking Merkel but Bauer took his place, apparently Merkel was suffering from stomach pains and had gone to report to the medical officer. We collected von Betternich and Wiedel, crammed into the vehicle we made our way towards Kharkov and Der Fuhrer's HQ.

We never made it. Halfway there Mundt had to grip the wheel as we hit a series of rough bumps in the track. We thought they were corpses, frozen in the snow but it was a trap, logs placed to slow us down for an ambush.

Three shots rang out in quick succession and smashed the windscreen of the vehicle, two of them whistled past my head, between Wiedel and me. The third hit von Betternich in the upper arm. Mundt was desperately trying to steer the Kubi, he regained control and swerved off the track and drove into the trees, out of direct line of sight of the sniper. We jumped out with our MP38s and looked for the position of the sniper. Wiedel was pulling off von Betternich's tunic to dress his wound, thankfully it didn't look too serious. I shouted orders to my men.

"Mundt, take Bauer and start working your way around to the left, I'll go with Beidenberg to the right! We need to flush out this Russian bastard before we can get out of here. Are you able to use your pistol, Sir?" I said to Wiedel. "There may be more partisans hiding in the woods, so be ready just in case."

He nodded, "I'll be ready, don't worry about us, Hoffman, just get the bastard!"

This was what I had been trained for, dealing with enemy riflemen. I directed the men to follow a series of shallow ditches, to keep us out of the shooter's sights. The Russians had made much of their snipers at Stalingrad, even distributing leaflets shouting about the skills of Vasily Zaitsev, who they said was their best man and the best sniper in all Europe. It all sounded like bullshit to me, but still like the other soldiers on the Russian Front, we all hoped never to meet with this Zaitsev or any of his companions.

Mundt and Bauer were making quick dashes from cover to cover, twice shots rang out and bullets clipped the bark from trees next to where they were sheltering. I rushed forward with Beidenberg, we had almost reached the next tree when a shot clanged on my helmet, wrenching my head back and leaving my ears ringing, but at least I was alive. Beidenberg sent a burst from his MP38 in the direction of the sniper to keep his head down and we dashed forward again, I could see Mundt and Bauer fifty metres way doing the same. But the sniper had picked his lair well, he was in a clump of trees another fifty metres ahead, surrounded by clear ground, we would be totally exposed rushing across the open space. There was nothing else but to rush it. I gave Josef my MP38.

"Can you fire both of these at once, empty the magazines at the sniper and I'll run at him?"

"Sir, that's crazy, he'll get you for sure."

"Just keep his head down, Josef, I'll have to run a little faster than usual, that's all."

He looked at me as if I was truly mad. Perhaps I was, but no way was that Russian bastard going to shoot up my platoon without me doing my damndest to finish him. I pulled out my Walther PPK checking the clip. It was full. I cocked the weapon and took off the safety.

"Now, Josef!"

He opened fire with both machine pistols, putting a

barrage of 9mm bullets towards the enemy. Mundt and Bauer caught on immediately and laid down a storm of fire, I ran. The clump of trees was fifty metres away, forty, thirty, I dodged to the left as a bullet cracked past where I had just been running. Beidenberg had reloaded, another hail of bullets lashed out from his position towards the sniper. Mundt and Bauer were still firing bursts from their own machine pistols. Then I threw myself down behind a tree as another bullet cracked out overhead, once again I'd missed death by a split second, but I was behind cover.

For some long minutes, there was silence then I started to crawl forward, moving from tree to tree. There was no more shooting. I crawled forward again then I heard a rustling, someone moving through the trees, moving away from me. I didn't want him to get away so I jumped up and ran, but he cut the main track where there were thousands of boot and vehicle marks where an army had passed backwards and forwards. I'd lost him, I couldn't see which way he'd gone so I retraced my steps. Mundt, Bauer and Beidenberg were coming up, I gave them the bad news.

"Beidenberg, go and guard the officers, we'll try and find the sniper's stand, perhaps we'll find out more about him."

We spread out and walked through the clump of trees where the shots had come from. There was a shout from Beidenberg and we went across to where he was gesticulating. He was standing beneath a huge, old tree.

Low branches had enabled the shooter to climb into it from where he could cover anyone coming along the track. I saw something on the ground and bent down to retrieve a cartridge case, ejected from the breech when he'd fired. I put it in my pocket and started to search for more. I found another four, while I was bending down searching the ground von Betternich and Wiedel came up with Beidenberg.

"Show me," Wiedel said, holding out his hand for the brass cartridge cases.

I put the ones I was holding in his hand and he looked at them then passed them to von Betternich. "7.92mm. Almost certainly a Kar 98, a German rifle."

"Often used by partisans," I said.

He smiled. "Sometimes, but used all of the time by our own men. Let's go and ask Stettner what he knows about this little episode, ambush, I imagine would be the best way to describe it."

We were only three kilometres from Der Fuhrer's camp, when we rounded a bend and literally ran into a band of partisans who were hacking a hole in the frozen ground, almost certainly to lay mines. There were eight of them, they were wrapped in thick furs and were so noisily hacking at the ground with pick axes that they hadn't heard us until the last moment. Mundt didn't hesitate, he accelerated the Kubi and charged straight at them. They scattered, one of them picked up a weapon, a rifle, but we stood up with our MP38s and fired burst after burst. After the debacle with the sniper, we were determined not to let these Russians get away. Three of them were bowled over by our hail of bullets, the other five managed to reach the shelter of the trees, one to the left, four to the right of the track.

"We'll watch the man on his own, Hoffman, you take the others," von Betternich ordered. He was still in pain but the wound was in his left arm. With his right hand, he fumbled his pistol out of the holster, a beautiful Luger Parabellum. Wiedel reached under his coat and took out a PPK like my own. Then they started after the Russian at a surprisingly fast pace.

"Spread out," I said to the men. I didn't want to bunch together and get caught in a fusillade of rifle fire. I'd only noticed the Russians with one rifle, I hadn't seen any automatic weapons, but who knew what they were armed with? We moved rapidly through the trees, ahead of us we could hear them crashing through the foliage. Then the noise stopped. We slowed down and went cautiously ahead, it sounded as if they were waiting in ambush for us. We got within ten metres of where I estimated they had stopped. Then a Russian stepped out, holding a prisoner in front of him, an SS officer, barely recognisable, ragged and filthy.

"That's far enough, Fascist," the Russian shouted, speaking good but accented German. If any of you come another step nearer your comrade will get a bullet in his head."

He held a pistol, probably a Tokarev, pushed into the side of the officer's head.

"You will go back to the track and we will leave. If you try to attack us, your man dies," he continued.

I saw Mundt slide to the ground and crawl away to the right. Good, he was an experienced fighter, if anyone could surprise these partisans, it would be him. I called out to the Russian to gain time.

"If we leave, will you release that officer to us?"

The man laughed. "No, that is out of the question. He is a prisoner of the Russian People."

"What would it take to persuade you to let him go?"

"Are you mad, does your own army give up their prisoners? Besides, if we release him you'll start shooting at us."

So why would that worry him, I wondered? Partisans were notoriously brutal fighters, often known for fighting to the last man to rid their land of the German invaders, surely they would do their best to kill us all, there were several of them. Then it struck me, they were almost unarmed apart from the single rifle. The Russians used penal units extensively in many battles. Although our own army used them too, Soviet penal units were much harsher, considered to be certain suicides. They were often brought forward and issued weapons moments before they were ordered to attack, then their machine-pistol armed NKVD guard companies would herd them into the teeth of German fire. Sometimes they even had to attack without any weapons at all. Frequently they were forced to march through minefields, their bodies marking the cleared passage for the Red Army to pass through. In many Soviet attacks entire penal battalions were completely wiped out. The partisans had a similarly ruthless attitude to prisoners, especially those regarded as politically unreliable. It seemed likely that most of these partisans were prisoners, coerced into digging holes to plant mines. It made our task much easier. I wondered about von Betternich and Wiedel, were they pursuing a partisan or a prisoner? Well, they were trained to deal with it, they would have to cope.

"I can't leave here without that officer," I shouted back. "Either you leave him with us or we will be forced to attack."

"Then he will die!" the man shouted back. "Get out of here, SS men. I will count to ten, if you have not started to leave your man dies."

He started counting, "One, two, three..."

I saw movement in the trees five metres to the right of where the Russian stood with his prisoner.

"four, five, six..."

I could see Mundt clearly now, he was standing behind a tree only three metres from the Russian.

"seven, eight, nine…"

A short burst from Mundt's MP38 ripped across the short gap between him and the Russian. The man was thrown to the ground, leaving his prisoner still standing, thank God he hadn't been hit. Then Mundt was beside the prisoner, his machine pistol covering someone else behind the trees that I couldn't see. I went forward cautiously with Beidenberg and Bauer, we stepped behind the trees and saw the other four partisans standing with their hands held high. They were unarmed.

"Cover them," I ordered the two men. Then I went to check out the prisoner. He was a Hauptsturmfuhrer, his cuff title showed him to be Das Reich Division, like us, but he was from Der Fuhrer Regiment, one of Stettner's officers. Two shots rang out from across the track where the two security men were hunting the single partisan, they sounded like pistol shots.

"Scharfuhrer, would you go and check on von Betternich and Wiedel, make sure they're not in any trouble."

Mundt nodded and went at a fast pace towards the location of the two security men.

I attended to the SS officer, his hands still tied with thin rope and I got out my knife and cut him loose. He rubbed his hands together to get the circulation moving.

"I'm Max Mosel, Hauptsturmfuhrer, my thanks to you, Obersturmfuhrer. That bastard was aiming to kill me."

Before I could reply, Mundt returned with the two officers.

"They were already on their way back, they dealt with that Russian," he said.

I nodded. "Was he a partisan or a penal unit prisoner?"

Wiedel shrugged. "He was Russian."

I introduced the released prisoner to them. "We can crowd him into the Kubi, we were going to his regiment anyway."

"What about the others?" Mundt asked.

Beidenberg and Bauer were covering the four men with their machine pistols. I asked Mosel which of them was penal unit and who was a partisan. He pointed to one Russian, a man slightly less ragged than his companions with a thick, bushy black beard.

"Him, he's the only partisan, apart from the man you shot."

"Does he speak German?"

"No, only the one you killed."

"Perhaps we'd better try and question him," von Betternich said.

I was surprised. "But he doesn't speak German, Sir."

He was still clutching his Luger. "That's not a problem, Hoffman, I have something that speaks a universal language."

"Sir, you can't shoot an unarmed man, a prisoner."

He looked at me with a cold gaze. "Yet the Fuhrer

has decreed exactly that, Hoffman, where combatants in civilian clothes are captured. Would you argue with the Fuhrer, your Supreme Commander?"

I felt sick. "No, Sir."

"Good, Wiedel, let's see if this man can come up with any words of German."

They took him a few metres away, I heard their raised voices trying to bully him into speaking German, but his replies were all in Russian, his voice terrified, clearly he had no idea what they were talking about. Then a pistol shot rang out and we heard something heavy hit the ground. They came back.

"All done," Wiedel said cheerfully. "What will you do about the others?"

"They're penal unit, Sir, I'm going to let them go, they've got more to fear from their own people than they have from us."

"I'm not happy about that, Hoffman."

"Damnit, Sir, we're talking about men who were prisoners already, they were unarmed and they weren't fighting us. Chances are that they'll do some damage to the Russians, God knows they hate them enough."

"That is true," Mosel added. "They are all Ukrainians, they do hate the communists."

Wiedel considered. "Very well, let them go. You'd better be right, Hoffman."

One of them understood a little German, I told him to

go. They all looked grateful, but wary. They backed away from us, when they were ten paces away they suddenly turned and fled. Poor devils, they suffered Stalin's Red Hordes devastating their homeland, now they had us to contend with.

"We'd better press on to Der Fuhrer and finish our business, otherwise we'll be pushed to get back to Korenevo before nightfall," I said to them.

"What was your business with my regiment?" Mosel asked.

None of us answered and von Betternich and Wiedel studiously ignored him. I shrugged, as if to say 'I've no idea'.

"I see," Mosel said heavily, looking at Wiedel's leather coat and trilby hat, the uniform of the Gestapo.

We walked back in silence and piled into the Kubi, it was too small for all of us but we crammed ourselves in and Mundt drove away.

The two security men were busy talking to each other when Mosel turned to me and spoke quietly.

"Was it the thefts?"

There was an abrupt silence. Wiedel overheard him and fixed him with a hard glare.

"Which thefts are you referring to?"

"Just before I was captured, someone was talking about the Gestapo investigating the theft of artworks, I assumed that it was something similar."

Von Betternich and Wiedel exchanged glances. "We were looking into the unexplained deaths of some senior officers, Mosel. But do tell us about the thefts."

Mosel went bright red, he realised he'd opened his mouth prematurely. He didn't reply.

"Mundt, stop this vehicle," Wiedel shouted. "Turn around and take us to Division, perhaps we can show the Hauptsturmfuhrer how the Gestapo interrogates its prisoners."

Mundt pulled in to the side of the track, Mosel's face paled. "No, there's no need for that. Look, we all knew that some senior officers were stealing artworks and selling them on. I thought all of the regiments were doing it."

"How do they dispose of these artworks?"

"There's a quartermaster from Division, when they go to collect supplies they hand them over to him in exchange for cash and he ships them back to Germany."

"So which of the Der Fuhrer officers are involved?"

"I can't, he'll kill me."

"Would you prefer me to get it out of you in a Gestapo cellar, Hauptsturmfuhrer?"

He was silent for a few moments. "No. It was the CO."

Von Betternich and Wiedel got out of the Kubi and walked a few metres away to talk quietly between themselves. Then they ordered Mosel to join them and I heard them arguing, voices raised in anger, Mosel started shouting, both fear and anger in his voice. They came back to the Kubi.

"Change of plan, Hoffman. The Kriminalkommissar has put Hauptsturmfuhrer Mosel into protective custody. We are going back to the Deutschland HQ at Korenevo, we have much more to discuss with this officer."

I saw Mosel's face go several shades whiter. The dreaded 'Schutzhaft' meant that he was now in the clutches of the Gestapo. It seemed to be a card, that Wiedel played often, but I could see the logic of returning to Korenevo. If we pushed on to Der Fuhrer with Mosel, the presence of the Gestapo and SD would tip them off that von Betternich and Wiedel had made a deal with the officer. Instead, the Schutzhaft would be like a collar around Mosel's neck, no matter what he did it would stay in place until Wiedel decided to remove it. In the meantime he now belonged to them, body and soul. Wiedel explained that they were going to get someone else to return Mosel to Der Fuhrer and keep his testimony secret. It had been a stroke of luck for them when we came across the Der Fuhrer officer with the partisans and a witness literally dropped into their laps. We got back to the monastery and they whisked Mosel away to their office. Wiedel curtly dismissed me, and the men, to go back to our duties until they needed us again. Mundt drove over to the vehicle park and left the Kubi with the Scharfuhrer in charge, then we walked back to our quarters in the church.

I'd already sworn them to secrecy about the

investigation, on pain of being placed under arrest by the Gestapo. They resented it until I told them that I was under the same threat.

"It's not as if we'd shout our mouths off if we were told to keep quiet," Mundt grumbled.

"I'm sorry, Willy, but it's out of my hands. You could talk to them about it if you wished."

"Very funny, Sir."

At least he understood that we were held on the same leash.

"So what next, are we still in the service of the SD and Gestapo?" he asked me.

"We are to remain ready to escort them whenever they wish."

"It's crazy, why don't they get a squad of Gestapo here instead?"

"To take on an SS regiment, Scharfuhrer?"

His jaw dropped. "Is it that serious? A whole regiment?"

"No, not the whole regiment, but it involves certain senior officers who could persuade their men to deal harshly with anyone that tries to arrest them. This is not Berlin, my friend. This is the Russian Front. Rather like the Old West in the American cowboy films."

We reached the church, the men still had a merry fire going outside. Merkel was putting some extra logs on it, we came up behind him."

"Merkel, how are you feeling now?" I called in a

friendly greeting.

He abruptly dropped the logs he had been carrying and whirled around. "Obersturmfuhrer, I didn't expect you back yet."

His face was pale. "Well, here we are," I replied wearily, "you still don't look very well, what did the medical officer say?"

"I didn't see him, Sir, but I'm sure it's nothing, it'll be gone after a good night's sleep."

That was strange, I thought he'd been ill, but it was his business. "Fair enough, would you try and rustle us up some coffee."

He went away and I spoke to Mundt. "I saw Merkel looking at the monks with a strange expression on his face, Scharfuhrer. I've got a feeling it may be some religious thing, perhaps he's troubled by us occupying church property or it could even be the opposite, maybe he hates them, I'm concerned about him."

Mundt looked dubious. "He's never said anything to me, if he is a bible-basher, or even bible hater, he's certainly kept it quiet."

"Perhaps I'm wrong."

I looked across at the monks in their ragged camp. They were holding some kind of an outdoor service, one had a censer, an ornate metal container on the end of chains that contained burning incense. He was swinging it from side to side, the smoke from burning incense swirled out of it. I couldn't hear him from this distance but he appeared to be reciting some kind of ritual.

"They're probably praying for us to go away," Mundt said.

"True. They'll get their wish before long, I would think, we'll be on our way soon."

"Will we be heading east or west, Sir?"

I knew what he meant, but it was a dangerous question with SD and Gestapo in the camp.

"Why don't you go and ask Wiedel?" I replied lightly.

Mundt laughed. "He'd tell me we were going north."

"And von Betternich that we were going south?"

"You've got it, Sir."

"Mundt, I'm sure that the Russians are at the limit of their capabilities, they're exhausted and I doubt they have many resources left to hit us with."

As the last word came out of my mouth, the air-raid siren started to wail and our new four-barrelled Flak gun started turning to seek out a target. Both of our twin MG42s were alerted and swinging around to engage the enemy aircraft. The first one swooped down on us, mentally I ran through my aircraft identification lessons at training school, it was a Lavochkin LaGG-3, a Soviet fighter equipped with both machine guns and cannons, I seemed to recall they also carried rockets for ground attack. Streaks of fire leapt out from under the wings, that at least cleared up any doubt about rockets. As soon as they were released the pilot started strafing us with machine gun and cannon fire. He came so low that I could make out his face through the glass of the cockpit, then he zoomed back up into the sky as the second aircraft came in to attack. Mundt and I had jumped behind a solid pile of broken masonry near the church. He looked at me.

"What were you were saying about the limit of their capabilities, Sir?"

I realised that I had in fact spoken far too soon. They were obviously a long way from being out of ammunition and resources.

CHAPTER NINE

"Stalin is one of the most extraordinary figures in world history. He began as a small clerk, and he has never stopped being a clerk. Stalin owes nothing to rhetoric. He governs from his office, thanks to a bureaucracy that obeys his every nod and gesture. It's striking that Russian propaganda, in the criticisms it makes of us, always holds itself within certain limits.

Stalin, that cunning Caucasian, is apparently quite ready to abandon European Russia, if he thinks that a failure to solve her problems would cause him to lose everything. Let nobody think Stalin might reconquer Europe from the Urals! It is as if I were installed in Slovakia, and could set out from there to reconquer the Reich. This is the catastrophe that will cause the loss of the Soviet Empire."

Adolf Hitler July 1941

The second salvo of rockets roared out from their wing pods and hammered into our vehicle park, the machine gun and cannon fire chattered again. It didn't hit near where we were sheltering. I looked up and saw to my horror that there were at least another ten aircraft in the sky, some already diving down on us, the others circling, awaiting their turn to begin their attack run.

Unlike the Sturmovik the LaGG-3 was a single seater. The aircraft carried two heavy calibre 12.7 mm Berezin machine guns, a single 20 mm ShVAK cannon and six rockets. It was a lot of firepower, especially when attacking ground forces.

The third and fourth aircraft came in and unleashed their cargo of devastation onto the camp, then the four-barrelled Flak cannon hit the fifth one. The shells ripped through the cockpit and shredded the pilot, the massive firepower seemed almost to stop the aircraft dead in the air, then it exploded, showering the camp with broken and burning pieces of aluminium and rubber, as well as bloody flesh and bone. The other aircraft were undeterred, they roared in one after the other, turning our camp into a scrapyard filled with broken metal and bloody human tissue. The Flak gun managed to down another aircraft, it went away burning furiously, too low for the pilot to parachute out. It had barely disappeared from view before a huge explosion and sheet of fire shot up into the sky, marking its final resting place. Finally we got up to survey the damage, we had been hurt badly.

Immediately in front of me our half-track had been struck with machine gun bullets, the bodywork had several new holes in it. Fortunately none of the Soviet rounds appeared to have damaged anything vital, at least, not vital to the vehicle. Two of my men had been sheltering underneath it, Bosch and Kramer, they were both beyond help, their bodies riddled with Soviet heavy calibre bullets. I looked around the camp and could see that we had taken extensive damage. Everywhere men were helping to get their wounded comrades to the medical aid station, a large tent with a red cross that was miraculously undamaged. Some of our half-tracks were clearly wrecked, as were a number of other vehicles and motorcycles, two Kubelwagens were burning fiercely and piles of stores were ruined, blown to pieces and flames leaping out of them. Our ready use drums of petrol had been untouched, but even as I was looking at them flames licked around their base, probably one of them had been leaking and a spark had ignited it. As I watched, the flames rocketed up and around the drums and within seconds they exploded in a shower of burning petroleum. The cookhouse tent was only twenty metres away, some of the burning debris descended on the canvas and men ran to put out the flames before everything was destroyed. I could have made it over there to help them, but they had enough men to deal with it. The attack weighed heavier on me than I could have believed possible, one moment we were a proud, fighting regiment, now we were a smouldering heap of scrap. Muller started around the camp to inspect the damage.

"Any casualties, Hoffman?"

I told him about my two men.

"That's about it, Sir, most of our equipment is undamaged. What about the rest of the regiment?"

He looked grave. "It's not good, we were already understrength and waiting for new equipment to arrive. We are down to less than two hundred men, even with so few we have barely enough transport. Fuel is critical, but Division is bringing more up," he laughed bitterly. "With any luck we can put a company into the field to fight the next Russian attack, that's about it."

"When do you think that will happen?"

"It could be as soon as tomorrow morning, who knows?"

I thought I'd heard wrong. "Tomorrow morning, but that's impossible!"

He smiled. "Sadly, the Russians are unlikely to see it your way, Hoffman. The pattern of Soviet attacks is consistent. The Soviets use their aircraft differently to the way we use ours, particularly the dive-bombers. Theirs are more of a preliminary softening up process, probably as much psychological as much as anything, they're damned good chess players, after all. First the ground attack fighters, then the artillery barrage, after that they send in the infantry and the tanks, often the infantry in front."

"To clear the minefields?"

He nodded. "Exactly, they send over the penal units first, then their weaker divisions and finally the T34s with the Guards tank rider regiments."

"So what do we do, Sir?"

"I'm waiting for replacements and fresh troops to come up with new vehicles and more fuel. We need anti-aircraft guns, of course, that Flak gun really paid off, but four of them could have prevented the worst of the Soviet attack. Ideally, we would move out so that the Soviets waste their shells on an empty area, but we are part of a defensive strategy, we're the neck of the Panzer Corps salient. If we leave here, the Soviets could come through and cut off an entire division, so here we stay until we are ordered to move. Cheer up, Hoffman, there's going to be some hard fighting but we'll beat them in the end, even if we only have one or two platoons left when we get to Moscow. We'll beat the bastards, Hoffman, we'll beat them."

I only wished that he sounded more convincing.

I returned to my platoon and set them to repairing the damage to the half-track. There were no spare mechanics, they were all overburdened after the raid and we needed to have a working vehicle. Fortunately, there was no serious damage and with a few patches and repairs to some of the wiring, the half-track was ready to go into action by the evening. The church had not been hit during the raid but I didn't expect that to last, we ran the half-track into a nearby gully that would hopefully shelter it from the worst of the artillery shells, it would shelter us as well. Three other platoon commanders noticed what we were doing and followed suit, we moved our blankets and bedding next to the half-track and rigged a temporary shelter to keep out the worst of the weather. We stocked our makeshift shelter with as much ammunition, water and supplies as we could find and settled for the night, there were perhaps fifty of us crowded into the makeshift trench. We had fifteen half-tracks left and a variety of other equipment, including two Kubelwagens and the mobile anti-aircraft four-barrelled gun. We were well equipped with MG42 machine guns and stick grenades, we also had two anti-tank guns that were towed behind the half-tracks. That was almost our entire compliment, Muller was right, we would be hard pressed to field much more than a company. If the Russians shelled us badly in the morning and then followed up with massed infantry attacks backed by tanks, we may not be in a position to hold them off at all. I wondered where our Panzers were, they were the key to the forthcoming battle. With a couple of regiments of tanks, we could hold off a Soviet army, maybe two Soviet armies. Where were the Panzers? And just as importantly, where were the Luftwaffe? That last raid shouldn't have happened, our own aircraft should have been in the air to prevent it. Didn't they have enough aircraft, enough fuel and pilots to operate on the Eastern Front, surely they did? Or could what the men were suggesting be true, that the overwhelming Soviet advantage in men and munitions was swallowing us up like a giant shark? But no, that was not possible, we had the toughest, the most feared armies in all Europe, the best aircraft and guns, the best armour. And we had our soldiers, of course, we prided ourselves that we were better trained, tougher, more dedicated and more professional that any other soldier on the battlefield. I resolved to discuss these issues more with the men, they should know that we were a part of the most feared army on earth and we were going all the way to Moscow. Weren't we?

I slept badly that night, constantly waking to expect to hear the sound of the Russian guns. At four am the camp started to wake, I stood up to see that everyone was dispersed under cover, finding niches and holes in the ground like us. Just as dawn was breaking we heard the drone of aircraft engines, a large number of them, it grew to a roar but it was coming from the west. It meant they were ours, soon the distinctive shapes of Luftwaffe Heinkel He 111 came into view, dozens of them, there must have been almost fifty aircraft. I knew that our Heinkels could carry two thousand kilos of bombs, they would do enormous damage to the enemy. They droned past us, when they were about eight kilometres away I saw the bombs falling from their bomb bays and explosions that sent smoke and flames soaring into the sky. There was no doubt they were hitting the Russian artillery hard, I think we all prayed that their aim would be accurate and there would be no Russian guns left to shoot at us. Then the Soviet fighters arrived, swarming out of the sky to take on the bombers, but our fighters were ready. The Russian fighters were more LaGG-3s, I could see them distinctly through my binoculars. There were fifteen of them, a deadly threat to the Heinkels. On their first pass two Heinkels started to billow smoke, one exploded, the other turned west for home. Our fighters swooped, eight Focke-Wulf 190s, they tore through the Russian LaGG-3 s and their cannon destroyed four of the enemy on the first pass. The Russians broke off the attack to defend themselves and a dogfight developed, allowing the Heinkels to release the remainder of their bombs.

The sky was a kaleidoscope of noise, smoke, movement and colour, the fighters ranging wider and fighter, battling each other in whirling circles as each manoeuvred for the advantage. The Heinkels were still not entirely unopposed, Russian Flak hurtled up towards them from the artillery positions beneath them, streams of tracer from lighter weapons and puffs of smoke exploding amongst the bombers from their heavier anti-aircraft artillery. Another of our Heinkels was hit and literally exploded in mid-air but the rest had finished their bombing runs and turned for home and out of the range of the Flak. The Focke-

Wulfs had lost two of their number but the Russians were reduced to only six fighters, the others had fallen to the superior performance of our 190s. Two more LaGG-3s were downed before the Focke-Wulfs broke off the fight and turned east to escort the bombers home, the Russians circled for a few minutes and then tore off to the east, apparently they'd had enough.

"Quite a spectacle, Hoffman."

I turned quickly, it was Muller, making another round of the camp.

"Yes, it was, Sir. We gave the Reds a good hammering."

"We did indeed. You've found a good position here, is everything buttoned down?"

"Yes, we're ready, Sir."

"Good. I'm expecting the Russian barrage to start soon, they'll quite likely follow it up with another counterattack, so be ready to move. We may yet have to pull back again."

I was appalled. "But we were told to hold here, Sir. Can't we fight them off, they must have taken a pounding from the bombing raid?"

"We'll do our best, of course. You're right, it is vital that we hold as long as possible to stop the Leibstandarte in the salient being cut off."

"Can't the Leibstandarte pull back to straighten our line?"

"The Fuhrer says no, Hoffman. They have been ordered to hold, Das Reich is to defend the salient for as long as possible. In fact, the Fuhrer has ordered our Division to hold to the last man, but General Hausser had made it clear that he will not see his troops slaughtered for nothing. We will just have to hope for the best."

He looked across at the monks' camp. "Don't they realise the artillery will be shelling this place before long?"

They were sitting around a campfire, talking, possibly praying.

"Probably not, Sir."

"Very well, go and get them under cover, Hoffman, I don't want the poor sods to be killed."

"Yes, Sir."

I walked over to the camp. The older priest in charge, Bishop Demchak, stood up to greet me.

"Bishop, are you aware that we are awaiting a Russian artillery barrage, it's due to start at any minute?"

He looked calm. "I was not aware of it, but thank you for warning us."

"You will need to take cover, Sir. All of your people, it'll be bad, anyone not under cover is likely to be slaughtered."

"We have no cover, Obersturmfuhrer, so we shall have to take our chances. But I thank you again for the warning."

I thought about our makeshift shelter, three platoons crammed into the gully with the half-tracks. But it was all we had, it would have to do."

"Bring your people, we have a place that will shield you

from the worst of the barrage."

He smiled. "I think we would prefer to stay here than join with your soldiers."

I felt irritated, his calm patience, his unflappable manner in the face of the metal storm of death we expected the Red Army to throw at us. But I had my orders, 'get them under cover' Muller had said.

I unslung my MP38, pointed it at them and shouted. "Now listen, there's a Russian barrage expected at any minute, I've been ordered to get you under cover so you will come with me. Now! If you do not get under cover I'll shoot you myself!"

The monks all looked at the Bishop, who shrugged. "Very well, we will accompany you."

He nodded at them, they got to their feet, and I led them over to our gully. Before we reached it, the sound of gunfire sounded from the east, the barrage had started. Within seconds, the first of the shells landed in the camp, a pressure wave hammered at us as I pushed the last of the monks down into the shallow defile. More guns joined in and the whole camp was swept by explosions and hot steel, that shredded everything in its path.

As the last of them got under cover, Merkel saw them and flinched, surprised that they'd joined us, I assumed, although his look was one of guilt. He tried to push past the Bishop and move to another part of the gully.

"Merkel, what's the problem? Stay where you are,

there's no need to move."

"I don't like bloody monks, that's the problem."

I was amazed, I'd seen him staring at the monks' camp before and assumed it was because of his religious affiliation. Obviously, I'd been wrong, mistaking his hatred for genuine concern.

"My son, we don't mean you any harm," the Bishop said.

Merkel brushed him off. "Just leave me alone, stay away from me."

He scuttled off to find somewhere else in the gully to shelter, but as he left I caught sight of his face, mixed with the rage there was something else, it definitely looked like guilt. Demchak saw it too. In the town where I was brought up there was once a scandal involving a priest, not a monk, who had been accused of buggering one of the boys that attended catechism classes. The priest was quietly transferred to another parish, we never knew for sure how genuine the allegations were, everyone denied it and it was only the boy who insisted that it had happened. He never went to church afterwards and I once saw him catch sight of a priest, that was the look he had on his face, a combination of hate and guilt.

"I'm sorry your man is so unhappy with us being here," Demchak said.

I nodded. "Maybe it's something in his past, something that causes him to dislike men of the cloth."

"Yes, I'm sure it is. It is the past that shapes our future actions, does it not? For good or for bad."

I waited for him to explain what he meant, but he had already turned away. So I had a Bishop prone to vague philosophical statements and a Schutze who seemed to hate everything religious, to cope with. Apart from the Soviet bombardment, of course.

The barrage lasted for an hour, both the church and the monastery were hit, though neither were completely destroyed. The monks' camp, the few tattered tents totally swept away by the heavy explosions from dozens of shells, I felt better at getting them down into cover. Several shells struck near us and fragments of metal spun all around, though most over our heads. A few of the men in the gully were hit but they suffered only minor wounds. Not all of the camp was so lucky, our remaining stores of fuel went up in a spectacular explosion, as did one of our anti-tank guns and three of our half-tracks. When the guns stopped, we stepped out to survey the damage. We had lost about thirty men killed and wounded, but we were still a fighting unit. Muller was out in the open with his radioman, calling for new supplies of fuel, vehicles, anti-tank guns and men. His voice shouting and snarling at Division rang around the camp, he was clearly having a hard time getting what he needed.

I heard the first rumble of tanks in the distance but it was our own armour, a unit of our Sturmgeschutz assault guns, the reliable STuGIIIs advancing to take on the expected T34s. Behind them, came a regiment of our SS Panzers, Tiger tanks, the formidable armour that could slice through the T34s. More tanks and mobile assault guns arrived and took up position, then they halted. I began to understand, we were setting an ambush. When the Soviets swept in here expecting to find a decimated Panzer Grenadier Regiment, they would run straight into our armour. Everyone was heartened by the huge show of force. We backed our vehicles out of the gully and began to prepare for the coming action. Muller came around again to check on his troops.

"Impressive, eh, Hoffman? None of us had any idea what they were planning, trust General Hausser to have something up his sleeve. Did you take any casualties?"

I explained that we only had minor casualties, then asked him what we all wanted to know. Exactly how much of our formidable Das Reich Division was coming?

"All of it. Der Fuhrer Regiment is deploying about two kilometres away and our Artillery Regiment has dug in ready to fight off the expected Soviet attack. All three of our Panzer Abteilungen have come forward, it's the biggest show of force on a narrow front since we reached the outskirts of Moscow."

"Why now, Sir, what's the strategic thinking?"

"Kursk, Hoffman. That city is the key to our forward campaign on the Eastern Front, but in order to take Kursk we have to secure Kharkov, it's the hub of a vital road and rail network. As you know, it has been a yo-yo battle so far. The Fuhrer knows how critical the two cities are to support the renewal of our campaign, as does Stalin and his Generals of course. The next few weeks will be critical."

"So the Russians are being lured into a trap?"

"That's our sincere hope, Hoffman. General Hausser has prepared this plan carefully, the Fuhrer is unhappy about his frequent retreats from positions he'd ordered to hold. However, conserving his men and equipment has enabled him to harbour his resources and keep his Panzer Corp intact. This is his big plan to regain the initiative."

Muller went away to speak to the next platoon and I gave the men the news.

"So you see, this is the big one. We have not been abandoned and the Russians have not got the advantage in men and materiel, we're going to hammer them."

Mundt got one of his unending bottles of schnapps out of his pack. "I'll drink to that, Sir."

"Just a small one, Mundt, we're expecting the Russians at any moment."

We had a quick drink to celebrate the new beginning on the Eastern Front. He barely had time to put the bottle away, before a battery of guns opened fire. They were tank guns. Shells landed around our position, Russian shells, they were here.

Our Panzers roared into action, Tigers and STuGIIIs, soon the new day was a chaos of smoke and flame, the roar of engines and the constant gunfire and shells exploding.

"Deutschland, let's move!" Muller shouted across the camp.

Voss started up the half-track and we moved out to follow the Panzers. We drove onto the flat steppe outside Korenevo where our forces had surprised the Russian advance, our Panzers had tangled with T34s and vehicles manoeuvred for advantage as shell after shell flew across the battlefield. Russian tank riders were jumping off their vehicles and setting up positions in shell holes, quickly bringing their anti-tank rockets into play. As we watched, a rocket hit the armoured side of a nearby Tiger tank and bounced off the heavy armour, but a hit on the thinner rear plate or on the more lightly armoured assault guns could be devastating.

"Voss, over there, head for that position," I shouted, "eleven o'clock, about sixty metres ahead!"

"Got it," he shouted back, wrenching over the wheel and heading for the Russians in a breakneck charge.

Mundt was manning the frontal MG42 and he emptied a belt at the Russians to keep their heads down. They ignored the machine gun bullets that buzzed all around them and started to deploy their own light machine gun, a Degtyarev DP with its round pancake magazine. Several rounds buzzed overhead before Mundt corrected his aim and fired off a hail of bullets that knocked out the gunner and wrecked the gun. Two heads popped up and started shooting at us, one had a PPSh sub machine gun, the other a Mosin-Nagant rifle, but the weight of machine gun fire was too much for them, the PPSh gunner was flung back when several rounds took him in the chest, the rifleman ducked back down. Then we were adjacent to the shell hole, we simply leaned over and poured fire down from our MP38s until the Russians were all dead.

All around the battlefield our half-tracks were doing the same deadly task, protecting the attack from enemy infantry. We moved on to the next enemy position and proceeded to deal with it in the same way, it was brutally effective. Within a few minutes, hundreds of the enemy were dead or wounded, burnt out tanks and broken Russian artillery pieces littered the battlefield. Then the Russians hit back with the Katyushas. One moment the distant slope was empty of Soviet armour and then it was lined with thirty or more cumbersome looking lorries, each carrying the framework that supported the Katyusha rockets. When they opened fire it was devastating, the eerie 'whoosh' as they fired and hurtled over the battlefield, trailing smoke from their exhausts, then the explosion as they hit.

"Should we take cover, Sir?" Mundt asked.

I considered it for a second, then I saw the CO's half-track rushing towards the far slope, accompanied by three other half-tracks.

"No, head for the Katyushas, we'll see if we can't knock some of them out. Voss, move it!"

He drove like a demon across the battlefield. Several times we passed pockets of Russians shooting at us, we fired again and again, both machine guns flat out to cause the maximum amount of death and destruction.

"Merkel, the grenades, give them a present or two as we go by."

"Yes, Sir," he grinned. He seemed to have recovered from that bad moment with the Bishop, I felt sorry for him if as I thought, a priest or a monk had abused him as a boy.

His aim was devastating, we passed the first shell hole, the machine guns hammering at the defenders and Merkel simply leaned out and lobbed two stick grenades into their position. A few metres further on we heard the explosions behind us as another Russian irritant was removed from the battle. We had a bad moment when a small group of Russians launched an anti-tank rocket directly at us, we held our breath as it struck the rear bodywork of our half-track, then it went straight through the other side before impacting itself into the ground and exploding. It was a good omen, we were untouchable, we were the lords of the battle, the Soviets couldn't even touch us. We caught up with Muller and the other half-tracks, two more joined us in our mad dash. He smiled across as he saw us. Then he bent down to use the radio fitted inside his vehicle. We were about two hundred metres away, the Katyushas had little hope of hitting us, several Russians had begun to shoot with rifles and sub-machine guns but the lorries were manoeuvring to turn around and flee. They had left it too late, within seconds we were among them. They had miscalculated badly, half of them were trying to flee, the other half trying to defend their position, they were in total chaos. We tore through them, machine gunning them and lobbing grenades amongst the soldiers and the vehicles. Several of them got away, driving crazily for the safety of a wood in the distance, but two STuGIIIs had come up to join our action and they fired shell after shell at the retreating Russians. I estimated that we had knocked out more than twenty of their Katyusha launchers, a considerable result. Then the tide of battle ebbed and the firing stopped, apart from the odd single shot.

We spent some time on the battlefield, mopping up Soviet pockets of resistance and repositioning our defences against a possible Soviet counterattack, but we had scored a major victory, they were unlikely to be back. Muller called us in for a briefing.

"I've heard good news over the radio, Der Fuhrer has wiped out two divisions of Soviet infantry and armour, virtually an entire army. We've done it, men, this is a major setback for the Soviets, they'll think again before they launch any more attacks! Well done, all of you. We are moving to the outskirts of Kharkov, we'll return to Korenevo first to collect the remainder of our people and supplies and then pull out. Next stop Kursk and then Moscow!"

We all cheered, at last, through all the snow, the wet, the cold and the misery, all of the setbacks the regiment had suffered, we were back in the game. We drove back to Korenevo in triumph, I was convinced that nothing bad could happen now, but as I had learned, hubris is not a good thing. Laughing at the gods carries a strong risk that they'll have the last laugh on you. So it proved. I was checking the inventory of our stores and equipment to make sure that nothing got left when we moved into Kharkov when I heard a voice from behind me.

"An excellent result, Hoffman."

Von Betternich.

"What can I do for you, Sir?"

"I need an escort to take Wiedel and me back to speak to Standartenfuhrer Stettner."

"Sir, Der Fuhrer is in the middle of a fight against the Russians."

He smiled. "I have it on good authority that they won their action, like your own regiment. It seems that the Soviets have been driven away from the main areas of Kharkov, Der Fuhrer is even now being directed to set up their new position on the south western side of the city."

"We're redeploying too, moving to our new camp."

"Of course you are, Hoffman. Fortunately our destinations are similar, Wiedel and I will accompany you, we just want you to detour to Der Fuhrer's new camp on the way."

"We're taking the half-track, Sir, it's not very comfortable." I was doing my best to dissuade him, our camp was in chaos as everyone prepared to move, it would be no less chaotic when we arrived at our new position, Der Fuhrer would be no different.

"In that case the Kriminalkommissar and I are in for a bumpy ride. Shall we say one hour? That should give you time to refuel and re-arm, perhaps get something to eat as well. I understand the cookhouse has a good stew on offer today. The meat is even edible. Don't worry about Muller, I'll speak to him now."

He limped away smiling and left me cursing.

An hour and a half later we were bumping along the trail towards Kharkov.

"Is this business likely to take long?" I asked von Betternich.

"Why, are you in a hurry, Hoffman?"

"Only to get everything settled into our new quarters, Sir, otherwise no, of course not."

"I am pleased for you. Your pretty nurse is likely to be at Der Fuhrer Headquarters tending to the wounded."

"What? You mean Heide Thalberg, what the hell is she doing there?"

"Der Fuhrer took heavy casualties during the battle. The hospital was overrun, literally no more space to attend to the wounded and so they sent out some nurses and a doctor to help on site, so to speak. They've set up a triage centre and an emergency operating theatre too, your friend is assisting."

I could hardly believe it. Yesterday I'd wondered if I would ever see her again, if I'd be killed or wounded in battle, if she would fall victim to an air raid. Now I was heading straight towards her, where she would be working. We arrived at their new camp, they had obviously suffered very badly, there were only six half-tracks that I could see in working condition, three more were being frantically repaired by the mechanics. The Headquarters building looked like an old barn, Stettner had set up his office inside and the wounded were being attended to in a huge white tent with a red cross on it. The duty officer told Von Betternich and Wiedel they would have to wait an hour to see Stettner as he was busy. They just smiled and nodded, and said they'd wait, it was no problem. Von Betternich suggested I find Heide, but to be back within the hour in case they needed me.

I walked across the camp through rows of terrible devastation. Almost everything had been damaged during the fight, broken vehicles towed back to await repair, men lying in disconsolate positions on the ground in the snow. Even the unwounded seemed tired and demoralised beyond hope. Outside the Red Cross tent the wounded were a piteous sight, there must have been nearly a hundred men lying on the ground, just left in the snow. I went inside and walked straight into Heide. Her eyes were like saucers, as if I'd just landed from an alien planet.

"Jurgen! What are you doing here?"

I took her in my arms and held her to me, then I bent down and kissed her, ignoring the stares of the men around me. Amidst the death, the stink and the destruction it was like meeting a vision from a beautiful dream. I explained that I had been detailed to escort the SD and Gestapo. Her nose wrinkled in disgust.

"It's a pity, I wish you didn't have to help those people. But enough of that, tell me how you are, did your regiment suffer badly?"

"Nothing like this lot, no. We're not too bad, just a few casualties."

"Until the next time."

"Heide, you shouldn't worry, I told you I'd be ok."

"Don't be crazy, of course I'll worry, you can't stop an artillery shell or a bomb with words, can you? None of us will be safe until this stupid war is over. Look at these poor devils here!"

She forced me to look around. There were men with no arms, men with no legs, men blinded, men screaming in agony. It was sickening.

"I have to get back," she said, "they need me urgently,

there are so many of them."

"Look, Heide, my regiment is camped nearby, I'll try and get over to see you again tomorrow."

"We could be back in Kharkov General Hospital by tomorrow."

"In that case I'll come and find you there. You can't keep me away, you know."

She smiled, but it was a tired, wan smile. "I shan't complain, then, Jurgen. Come back safe to me."

We exchanged kisses and she hurried away to deal with the wounded. I went back to the half-track to check on the men. Normally there would be plenty of banter between them and troopers from the other regiment, but not this time. I thought about Muller's optimism. If many more of our troops were hit this hard, we would never even get to Kursk, let alone Moscow.

Von Betternich and Wiedel were standing nearby, drinking mugs of coffee that one of my men had found for them. As usual, they were relaxed and calm.

"How was your young lady, Hoffman?"

I told them she was fine.

"Good. We have a unique opportunity here, Der Fuhrer has taken a battering. It could be a good time to deal with Standartenfuhrer Stettner."

"Very well, Sir, what do you want me to do?"

"Make sure that all your troopers are armed and prepared to move. I want the half-track kept manned and ready to leave at a moment's notice, then you can accompany us, bring one of your men, Scharfuhrer Mundt would be a good choice, I think. I suggest you leave Oberschutze Voss in command."

"Right, Sir."

"And make sure that you and Mundt have your machine pistols with you."

"Yes, Sir."

An orderly came out of the barn and told us that Stettner was ready to see us. We walked into the wooden building and into a separate room, it was like a storeroom that had been hastily set up for the CO to use. It was freezing cold there was no heater. I was amused to see Stettner still sat on the gilt throne. Like before, Sturmscharfuhrer Vinckmann was with him. In the corner, the Kar 98 rifle with the telescopic sight I'd seen before was leaning against a chair.

"What can I do for you gentlemen that cannot wait?" Stettner asked.

"It is quite simple," von Betternich replied. "I have come here to recover a stolen artefact, a gold cross, a solid gold crucifix inlaid with precious stones."

Stettner stared at him, his gaze as cold as his office. Vinckmann shifted uncomfortably.

"Why would I have such a thing?" Stettner asked.

"Intelligence suggests that you do, Standartenfuhrer. Will you please hand it over to us?"

"Damn you, von Betternich, you and your Gestapo

friend! I haven't got your cross and you can get out of my headquarters before I call my men to put you in chains for your damned impudence. I could have you shot!"

Wiedel had moved next to Vinckmann. He pulled out his Walther and put it against the Sturmscharfuhrer's body. "Vinckmann, would you prefer to cooperate with the Gestapo or would you prefer to risk being sent back to Berlin in chains for execution like your commanding officer?"

"But, I don't know anything..."

"Shut up, Vinckmann!" Stettner snapped. He jumped up and made a grab for his machine pistol but Mundt and I were ready.

"Stop, Sir," I said to him. "Leave the gun, I'll have to shoot you if you reach for it."

"You'll never get away with this," he snarled. "If I give the order my men will be all over you, you'll never get out of here alive."

"We'll see about that," von Betternich said in a menacing tone. "Scharfuhrer Mundt, break open the base of that throne, let's see what 'King' Stettner has been sitting on."

"Don't you dare touch that throne," he shouted, "I'll have you shot if you go near it!"

Mundt looked at me and I nodded. "Do it!"

He smashed the butt of his machine pistol against the base of the throne several times before it splintered and a hole opened in the side. He gave it several more blows with the MP38 until the hole was wide enough to see inside. He put his hand in and withdrew it clutching the most beautiful object I'd ever seen, a richly jewelled crucifix, the metalwork had a dull yellow sheen, the sheen of solid gold. Vinckmann's face fell, we all noticed. He obviously didn't know.

"Standartenfuhrer Stettner," von Betternich said solemnly, "I arrest you on the charge of looting state property and murder. You will be returned to Berlin for trial. It may be that the SS want to try your case as a military matter but it is unlikely, I think the Gestapo will arrange everything. Do you wish to make a statement?"

"Fuck off, Gestapo man," Stettner hissed, "you won't get ten paces from here before my men shoot you like rabbits!"

"Put the handcuffs on him, Wiedel."

The Gestapo man stepped forward and put the manacles on Stettner's wrists.

CHAPTER TEN

"The heaviest blow that ever struck humanity was the coming of Christianity. Bolshevism is Christianty's illegitimate child. Both are inventions of the Jew. The deliberate lie in the matter of religion was introduced into the world by Christianity. Bolshevism practices a lie of the same nature, when it claims to bring liberty to men, whereas in reality it seeks only to enslave them. In the ancient world the relations between men and gods were founded on instinctive respect. It was a world enlightened by the idea of tolerance.

Christianity was the first creed in the world to exterminate its adversaries in the name of love. Its key note is intolerance. Without Christianity, we should not have had Islam. The Roman Empire, under Germanic influence would have developed in the direction of world domination and humanity would not have extinguished fifteen centuries of civilization at a single stroke. Let it not be said that Christianity brought man the life of the soul, for that was in the natural order of things."

Adolf Hitler July 1941

"Well, that all went well, didn't it?" von Betternich smiled.

"Did it, Sir?"

"Of course. Now, before we go any further, Sturmscharfuhrer Vinckmann, tell us what you know of this business?"

"Nothing, Sir, absolutely nothing! Good God, I wouldn't do anything like that, it's sacrilege to steal from a church."

He crossed himself, the look of horror on his face was evidence enough, clearly he'd not known of his CO's theft. And worse, the murders.

"You are a sniper, Vinckmann. There have been some murders committed by a skilled marksman, what do you know about it?"

"I'm a sniper, that's true, it's how I got my promotion to Sturmscharfuhrer. But murder? No, Sir."

"I thought not," von Betternich said, "but in that case, I wonder who did do it?" he said it almost with the fake puzzlement way of a stage conjurer about to pull the rabbit from the hat. In the background, Stettner laughed, a grating, sneering laugh.

"You should have got your act together before you got here, you clumsy oafs. Now you know that Vinckmann is not the sniper, how do you know that the real one is not outside waiting for you to leave the barn?"

"Thank you for your warning, we will be sure to take precautions," von Betternich said, still infuriatingly calm.

"How will we find the sniper?" I asked him. "He's right, the man could be waiting outside for us."

"I'm sure he is outside, when he does makes himself known to us we will arrest him."

"Unless he shoots us first," I muttered.

"Quite so," the SD man replied. "Would you ask your Scharfuhrer to arrange for the half-track to be brought near to the door of the barn and we can take this gentleman into custody."

"Don't be stupid, von Betternich, you'll never get away with it," Stettner hissed.

The SD man ignored him and Mundt went out to arrange for the half-track. At least I'd feel better having my platoon around me in the armoured vehicle. Wiedel spoke sternly to Vinckmann, he told the terrified NCO to use what influence he had with the men to help get us out of here. In return, he would escape being charged with the thefts and murders. His guilt or innocence was of no consequence, all that was required was his frightened cooperation. It was a masterly way to handle everything,

I thought, the two security men coming here for Stettner and using his sergeant-major against him when the regiment was at its lowest ebb after a devastating battle. But the question of the real sniper still worried me. If it wasn't Vinckmann, who the hell was it, and was he waiting outside for us? Mundt came back into the office.

"The half-track is outside now, Sir."

"Thank you, Mundt."

"Scharfuhrer," von Betternich said to him, "would you ask Schutze Merkel to come in here to assist us?"

"Merkel?" Mundt looked puzzled. "You want Merkel in here?"

"Yes, if you would."

I had been looking at Stettner, when the name of Merkel had been mentioned he'd gone pale. Then it clicked, of course. When our CO, Standartenfuhrer Brandt had been killed by a sniper, Der Fuhrer hadn't been anywhere near him. The best marksman by far in our regiment was probably Merkel. I remembered the easy way he'd handled the rifle, his skill with grenades. But why?"

"I can see the puzzlement on your face, Hoffman. But it is really quite simple, once you've eliminated Vinckmann as the most likely suspect. In fact, I did eliminate him as a probable suspect some time ago. He wasn't anywhere near when your Standartenfuhrer was killed. So I checked out the background of every trained sniper attached to the Division. We were naturally interested in Merkel because of his skill as a marksman and of course the fact that he had the opportunity. He and Stettner are from the same town, which was an interesting coincidence. Apparently Merkel came across Stettner when he was a member of the Hitler Youth and Stettner was in charge of weapons training for that splendid organisation. When he found out that Merkel his protégé, had been abused by a local priest he was so enraged that he took up the case personally, and demanded that the priest be prosecuted. I believe he wanted to shoot him at one time. The church moved him out of the area and covered up the case, but from then on Merkel hated everything religious and was prepared to do anything for the man who had championed his cause, anything at all, including murder."

So it was Merkel, a member of my platoon. I thought of the victorious moment only hours earlier we looked to be on victorious path to Moscow. Now I knew that one of my men was a thief and a murderer. Mundt came rushing back into the office, his face grave.

"When I told Merkel you wanted him he grabbed his weapons and ran for it, I'm sorry, he was too quick for me to stop him. Was it something important?"

I explained quickly why we wanted him.

"Do you want me to go after him, Sir? I can get the platoon to mount a search, perhaps Der Fuhrer would assist." He saw our faces, the prisoner Standartenfuhrer Stettner sat at his desk enjoying our discomfort. "No, perhaps not. What do we do?"

"Tell Voss to stay with the half-track and get one of the men in here to guard the prisoner. We'll go out with the rest of the platoon and look for him."

"Right, Sir."

"Vinckmann, stand outside the door and don't let anyone in here for any reason. Remember, man, your life depends on it!"

He nodded.

"We'll locate him," I said to von Betternich.

He smiled thinly. "I hope so, good luck, Hoffman."

We walked out to the half-track and I asked Mundt which way Merkel had gone.

"I last saw him running over there, towards the Red Cross tent, Sir."

Heide! Damn, if he put a finger on her I'd rip his guts out and hang him with them.

"Right, bring the men and let's go and find him. No shooting, remember, there are wounded men and nurses in there."

We rushed across the camp. Several Der Fuhrer troopers looked at us with curiosity but no animosity, their faces bore the deep, etched scars of defeat on them. Even though they had technically won the battle, they had lost more than half the regiment in doing it. A pyrrhic victory indeed.

I told the men to wait outside the huge tent and I

unslung my MP38 and walked in. There were lines of groaning men, nurses and medical orderlies struggling to ease the worst of their pain, a doctor moved up and down the lines rapping out orders to the nurses. A clerk was stationed just inside the tent flap with a portable field desk piled with stacks of papers.

"I'm looking for one of my men, Schutze Merkel."

"Merkel? Was he the one carrying the rifle?"

I nodded. "That's him."

"He came in here and said that Obersturmfuhrer Hoffman needed to speak urgently with Nurse Heide Thalberg."

"Where are they now, quick, man?"

"I've no idea, Sir. They left a few minutes ago, went out of the tent and turned to the left, I believe. Towards the vehicle park."

I rushed out. "They're heading for the vehicle park, let's go!"

"They?" Mundt asked.

"He's got Heide, Nurse Thalberg, probably he wanted her as a hostage once he realised the game was up. I expect he's going to try to steal a vehicle, we need to stop him!"

We reached the compound, a Scharfuhrer was inside the guard tent talking to one of his men. He came outside when I shouted.

"Did a trooper come through here a few minutes ago with a Red Cross nurse?"

"Why, yes, he did, Sir, said he needed to borrow a Kubi to go out and attend to one of our officers, seriously wounded on the battlefield he said."

"Come on, let's go," I shouted at them. If the man had stopped to think for a moment, he'd have realised that they'd send a field ambulance, not a Kubelwagen to attend to a seriously wounded soldier. But he'd just come out of a hard fought battle and wasn't thinking straight, none of this regiment were. We ran into the vehicle park just as a Kubelwagen shot out from between a wrecked half-track and an armoured car. Merkel was driving, his face wild but determined, Heide was sat next to him, cowed by the pistol that Merkel had in his hand. He lifted it as he saw us and fired two shots but both went wild. One of the men raised his machine pistol and was about to fire when I stopped him.

"He's got the nurse with him, man, don't shoot unless you're certain of your target!"

"Sorry, Sir."

"Back to the half-track, we need to get after them."

We dashed back to our vehicle, climbed aboard and I shouted at Voss to follow the Kubi. We roared out through the camp gate, the sentries only looked at us briefly as we swept past, still too numbed to care after suffering so many losses.

"Voss, give it everything you've got, the trail forks about a kilometre up ahead, I don't want to lose them."

He floored the pedal and we roared along the trail, Voss took the bends at high speed but the caterpillar tracks kept the 251 stable. Too stable, we were a slow, top-heavy lightly armoured half-track, Merkel was in a Kubelwagen, though by no means a racing car it was lighter and faster than us. Except that he only had a two-wheel drive. Merkel turned his head to look at us, then left the main track to drive into the woods, obviously hoping to lose us in the trees. We bumped and pitched after him, but he was still drawing ahead. The wood opened out into a clearing almost half a kilometre wide, he was nearly the other side and about to drive into the next patch of dense woodland when he hit a snowdrift, his wheels sank in deep and we heard him gunning the engine and slipping the clutch, trying to free the Kubi. He looked around again and saw us drawing nearer and nearer, realised that he wasn't going to make it and dragged Heide out of the vehicle and started running across the snow and into the woods. We could see him clutching the sniper rifle as he ran. We were gaining on him fast but then he made the shelter of the woods and disappeared. Thirty seconds later we reached the spot where he'd gone into the trees and we stopped.

"Everyone fan out, we'll have to sweep through on foot to find them, watch for that rifle, he's a marksman, remember."

I took the lead in the middle of our line, there were thirteen of us, six on either side with me in the middle. I shivered slightly, it was an unlucky number, but I dismissed the thought, there was only one person who was going to suffer bad luck today, and that was Merkel. I turned to Mundt who was the next man to my right.

"Watch out for Heide, remind the others not to shoot if there is any risk to her."

He nodded and passed it on to the next man. I told the man to my left who passed it on. We trudged through the wood, moving from tree to tree, trying to make best use of the cover. At every step I cringed, waiting for the crack of a rifle shot, for the moment when a bullet hit me. Would it all end here, killed by a German bullet from a German gun fired by a German soldier? What a useless waste, after all my plans for a glorious military career, killed by a criminal in a cold Ukrainian wood. I cursed the policemen for getting me into this, then there was a vicious 'crack' and I felt a tug on the sleeve of my tunic as a bullet snapped past, ripping the cloth and grazing my skin.

"Down!" I shouted to the men, but they didn't need my warning, they'd gone to ground instantly, crouched in the snow behind the nearest trees. Mundt crawled over to me, keeping behind cover. "I could crawl around to the flank and try and take him that way?" he suggested.

"That's our normal tactic, Scharfuhrer, he'll be waiting for it. We need to try and get nearer to him and see if he makes a mistake. Let's go forward some more, tell the men to keep low."

He grinned. "No need for that, none of them are looking to get shot, especially by a shit like Merkel."

We crawled forward to the next line of trees. I peered around the trunk and a bullet lashed into the bark of the tree, I snatched my head back. We were close, very close. I looked around for Mundt, he was only two metres away, hiding behind the next tree.

"I'm going to try and negotiate with him to distract him, try and flank him, if you get a clear shot, you know what to do."

He nodded. "I'll do it, but are you sure you know what you're doing?"

"Not really, but I've got to do something, the only way we can get at him is to distract him."

"Rather you than me, Sir. Good luck."

It wasn't the most encouraging remark I'd heard that day, but I had to do something. I shouted out to Merkel.

"We need to talk, Dieter, how can we resolve this? If you give up the girl we'll let you get away."

The reply came back immediately. "You must be joking, Hoffman. As soon as I let the girl go, you'll rush me and shoot me."

"Let me come forward and we'll talk about it, Merkel. I'll be unarmed."

There was a silence for a few moments. Then he shouted back, "Ok, come forward, slowly. If I see a gun in your hand I shoot the girl!"

I put down my MP38 in the snow, took out my Walther, and tucked it into the rear of the waistband of my trousers. My combat knife went into my boot, I needed some kind of an edge with which to deal with him.

"I'm coming out now, Merkel, no tricks, I'll show you my hands."

I walked out into the open, my heart thumping, and walked towards him. I advanced twenty metres and then saw him ahead of me, kneeling down in the gap between two trees whose lower branches formed a V shape, in which he had rested his rifle. It was a perfect sniper stand, offering both concealment and a support for accurate shooting. I couldn't see Heide.

"Where's the nurse, Merkel, has she been hurt?"

"Worried about your girlfriend, Hoffman? She's fine, she's lying on the ground by here. I've got my pistol handy, if your men try to rush me she gets it, understand?"

"Yes. Now how can we settle this, Merkel? You want to get away. We want the nurse. If you wish I'll give you the half-track, you'll have no trouble getting through the forest in that."

I waited for half a minute while he considered my offer. Finally, he agreed.

"Pull all of your men back to the vehicle, no tricks. All of you lay down your weapons and stand with your hands up. I'll come to you and take the half-track and leave the girl."

"Agreed, we'll do as you say. Don't do anything stupid, we can all get out of this alive."

He didn't answer and I called out for the men to return to the vehicle. We didn't hide behind cover, we just walked back in the open to show that we would keep our side of the bargain.

"Men, put your weapons on the ground where Merkel can see them and we'll stand to one side with our hands up, I don't want anyone doing anything stupid."

They looked uneasily at one another but finally put their machine pistols in the snow. Then we all raised our hands. Merkel stepped out from behind a tree, pushing Heide in front of him, a pistol pushed into her back. He looked around suspiciously.

"How much fuel is in the half-track?"

"I believe it's about half full."

He sneered. "Excellent, thank you, Obersturmfuhrer. He looked at the platoon. His expression was crazy, his eyes wide and staring, he uniform was even more dishevelled than usual, he'd crumbled in minutes from being one of my troopers to a crazed felon.

"I've got no quarrel with you men, so I'm going to leave you alone. But you, Hoffman, you had to stick your nose into our business, didn't you? It was only those fuckers from the church, after all. They're a bunch of perverts, you know that?"

I nodded tiredly. "Yes, some of them are, I know that.

But not all. Let the girl go, Merkel."

He ignored me. "It was worth taking their stupid treasures to get back at them, you know. They abuse little boys but when it comes to losing their precious toys, they get upset. They deserved to lose them, you know, deserved all of it!"

His voice had risen to a shout, spittle was coming out of his mouth.

"You don't know what they did to me, do you?"

"Yes, I do know, and it was terrible. But those senior officers you killed didn't deserve to die because of it."

"Didn't they?" he laughed hysterically. "You don't know anything, anything at all. They were all in on it, you didn't know that, did you? Even Brandt, our own commanding officer, he was part of the robberies."

"Brandt, so why did you kill him?"

"It was because of Stettner, he killed one of the monks when we stole that crucifix, Brandt called him a murderer and said he was going to report him. He contacted the other officers involved to get their support, he wanted to make a deal with the SD to hand over Stettner in return for immunity from prosecution. They'd all agreed, the only way was to silence them."

I was astonished that the conspiracy went so high. I'd joined the SS on a wave of enthusiasm, believing the newsreels and the glossy recruiting banners. They had given the impression that we would be the elite, a new breed of chivalrous warriors, tough fighters but honest and loyal, and the senior officers were regarded as shining examples for the men to follow. SS officers were famous for leading their men into battle from the front, they were known for their courage and sacrifice. All that lay in ruins, now they would be known for being little more than thieves, looters and murderers. It seemed that the only difference between the SS and other branches of the military was that when they went crooked, they did it in a more brutal fashion. To kill their own officers during such a desperate campaign was unthinkable, despicable, leaving men leaderless and confused at a time when they were desperately needed to fight the seemingly limitless Soviet hordes. Merkel was speaking again.

"I'll take that half-track now, Hoffman. Tell your men to move to one side."

I ordered them to move back. He grinned and pushed Heide to the ground where she lay sprawled in the snow. "Now, Hoffman, I'll be leaving you. Just one thing before I go, I'm going to give you what's coming to you."

So that was it. I should have realised.

"What's that, Merkel?"

"A bullet, Herr Obersturmfuhrer. It's what you deserve for wrecking everything. Kneel down in the snow."

"No. If you're going to kill me, you can do it standing up and look me in the eyes."

He leered at me. "Brave to the end, eh? Fair enough,"

he stepped forward.

"This is what happens to officers who stick their noses into other people's business," he said to the platoon. Then he looked puzzled. "Where's Mundt?"

"I'm here, Merkel."

He whirled around and Mundt stepped out from behind the tree with his machine pistol raised. He pulled the trigger and emptied the clip into Merkel who dropped his pistol as he was flung to lie in the snow, now streaked with the bright red blood that flowed from his broken body. Heide got to her feet and ran to me and I held her in my arms.

"Is it over, Jurgen?"

"Not quite, I'm afraid, we need to get back to Der Fuhrer's HQ. I suspect that von Betternich and Wiedel may need us."

We climbed into the half-track and Voss drove rapidly back to the camp. We left Merkel's body at the side of the wood, nobody wanting to be soiled by touching the corpse of one who had murdered his own comrades. Heide sat next to me on the front seat.

"Are you expecting trouble at the camp?"

I nodded. "There could be trouble, yes, it depends how the men take the arrest of their CO."

"So what do you think will happen when you try to take him away?"

"Either we'll leave with him or without him," I said

airily. But it was nonsense, of course. If his men freed Stettner from arrest, he would not want us to leave the camp just to call up a squad of troops, possibly one of the Einsatzgruppen that fought the partisans, to storm in with the Gestapo and SD to re- arrest him. I was troubled about Heide's safety, but I had few options. Leaving her out on the Russian steppe with a couple of men to guard her was not a good plan. When we drove back into the camp, my worst fears were realised, a crowd of soldiers was gathered around the barn, Wiedel was talking to them from the open doorway, Vinckmann was next to him.

Voss pulled up the half-track behind them and we listened to Wiedel while I tried to decide on the best course of action. First things first.

"Heide, climb down from the vehicle and go back over to the medical tent, no one will notice you and you'll be safe there."

She shook her head. "No, I'm staying here with you."

"Heide, there could be some shooting!"

"In that case you'll need me more than ever, won't you?"

The typical female logic, they always seemed to get the last word.

"Men, stay here and cover us, Mundt, I want you to come with me. Voss, you're in command. For God's sake look after Heide!"

"I will, Sir."

We climbed down from the half-track and I pushed my way to the door of the barn with Mundt. There were no officers present, only troopers and NCOs, Wiedel nodded to me. Vinckmann looked very nervous and was sweating, even in the bitter arctic temperatures. I stared at the Der Fuhrer soldiers, "All right you men, what's going on here?"

A burly looking Scharfuhrer spoke arrogantly to me. "It's damn all to do with you, Obersturmfuhrer, they're trying to take our CO away and they're not getting away with it."

"So you want to be an accessory to murder, do you?"

He shifted nervously. "There's no proof that the CO had anything to do with any murder, this is a war zone, we're trying to kill Russians, not our own people."

I explained what had happened, that Merkel had confirmed all of it, but of course, Merkel was dead, his bloody body lying back along the track. Vinckmann shouted at them and told them to stand down but they ignored him.

Wiedel stepped half out of the door, he had his Walther in his hand, his face was furious.

"I'm telling you men to get back, how dare you interfere, this is a Gestapo matter. I could have you all arrested as accessories, now get back. We are taking Stettner away for trial and that's final!"

"No way," the NCO shouted, "get them, men!"

They surged forward, there must have been forty

of them, far too many for us to deal with. Behind me I heard the loud 'click' of weapons being cocked, then a single shot rang out, I whirled around expecting to see more Der Fuhrer troopers threatening us with guns, but it was Hauptsturmfuhrer Max Mosel clutching a smoking Walther PPK pistol, he was at the head of a platoon of men, all armed with MP38s.

"What the hell's going on here?" he asked.

"It's this Gestapo shit and his friends, they're trying to take the CO," the NCO replied angrily.

"Scharfuhrer, get back to your duties!" Mosel shouted angrily. "Standartenfuhrer Stettner has got a serious case to answer, are you men really trying to defend a murderer?"

The NCO looked aghast. "You mean he might have done it?"

"I certainly do, I have seen the evidence and he looks guilty as hell to me. Do you want to let someone who shoots his own men in the back go free?"

They looked around at each other, there was a loud murmuring and shuffling of feet but the fire had gone out of them, Mosel's passionate argument had won the day. The Gestapo had probably leaned on him, of course, but in this case it was justified, the arrogant bastard knew about the thefts and was as guilty as hell. The troopers drifted away with sheepish looks on their faces. Wiedel went back inside the barn, soon the door opened wide and they led Stettner out, still manacled. He was red faced with anger, shouting at his men, his voice hoarse.

"You men, they're trying to arrest me, your Commanding Officer, I need your help. Stop them!"

When they turned away and ignored him it was a joy to see the bewildered expression on his face. We led him across to the half-track. I helped Heide down from the vehicle before he got in.

"Sir, I'll escort Nurse Thalberg back to the medical tent, I'll be five minutes."

"No more than that, Hoffman," von Betternich replied.

I walked her across the camp. "What happens next, Jurgen?"

"Oh, we'll take him back to Division, I imagine that he'll be sent to Berlin for trial as it's such a complicated affair."

"I meant between us?"

"Us?" Her question left me totally confused.

"Well, I intend to get away as often as I can and come and visit. Will you be based permanently at Kharkov Hospital?"

"Yes I will, at least for now. If the war changes things I could be moved elsewhere, who knows?"

"I think this front may be static for some time, the Russians have taken a hammering and they're in no position to mount any major offensives. Division needs to bring up spare vehicles and ammunition, as well as more men to cover the losses."

"Won't the Russians be doing exactly the same thing?"

I thought about that. "Yes, probably they will."

"So it looks as if you will have to do it all again."

"I'm sure we'll beat the Russians, it's just a matter of time."

She was thoughtful. "Jurgen, lots of people at the hospital say that we can't win this war, that no matter how many Russians we kill, no matter how many tanks we destroy, they'll just keep bringing up more and more until we're smashed into the ground."

I didn't know how to answer her, I tried to think of something clever to say, something that would defeat that argument, but I couldn't.

After a few moments, she said, "So it could be true, we could lose this war?"

"Schh, don't say that, my darling, it's not the done thing to sound defeatist."

"Well perhaps if they are true we should say these things so that we can leave this miserable country."

"Heide, I have to go, I'll be back in a few days and I'll look you up in the hospital."

I kissed her passionately and we hugged each other. Then I broke away and went back to the half-track. The men carefully avoided my eyes, but they must have seen our embrace. Von Betternich was not so tactful.

"Very touching, Hoffman, and such a pretty young woman, a credit to the Reich."

"Thank you, Sir."

I noticed that he was holding the gold crucifix. Would that find its way to some high-ranking Nazi, to be held in trust for the German people, I wondered.

Voss started the engine and we drove away. Stettner sat in the back glowering all the way to Division, where we handed him over to the SD unit that based there. The two security men disappeared for half an hour to speak with General Hausser, afterwards they came back with us to our HQ to collect their things. When we arrived, Muller came straight out to greet us.

"Gentlemen, how did it all go?"

"Very satisfactory, thank you," von Betternich said. "You heard about Merkel? No? Well, he was involved in the conspiracy, he won't be returning to your unit, he was killed during the operation to arrest Stettner. They were in it together, they knew each other in Germany."

"So it's all over?"

"Yes, it is, Sturmbannfuhrer, all the loose ends are tied up."

"And what about my Schutzhaft?"

"Rescinded, of course," Wiedel said. "No need for any of that, you are free and clear."

"Thank goodness," Muller said.

"Just a little tip, Muller, General Hausser may well be paying you a visit sometime soon."

"Hausser? My God, I'll need to make sure everything

is in order."

He bustled off to start shouting orders to his clerk to make sure his paperwork was up to date. Von Betternich held out his hand. "Thank you for your invaluable help, Hoffman."

"You're welcome, Sir."

"We're always looking for good young officers for the SD, you could make yourself a valuable career with us."

It was a tempting offer. I had no wish to be a policeman, but I thought about what it could mean to Heide. I would have much more freedom to see her and with her rather radical political views, could protect her from the worst of the damage she caused herself. But would she want that? No, of course not, it was an organisation that people like her would fear and detest.

The RSHA was the organisation that administered both the SD and the Gestapo, when Reinhardt Heydrich combined the police units they had various sections, including Amt IV, the Gestapo under Heinrich Muller. Walter Schellenberg became Chief of Amt VI, the Sicherheitsdienst-Ausland. Ernst Kaltenbrunner was named Chief of the RSHA by Reichsfuhrer Himmler after terrorists assassinated Heydrich. Their functions would include the investigation and imprisonment of anyone expressing views that were in any way critical of the Nazi Party, which would include defeatist talk about the war.

I had little doubt that if I joined the SD she would

tell me to go to hell. Besides, I wasn't cut out to be a policeman, I was a fighting soldier, an officer in the elite of Europe's armies, perhaps the world's. Except that I had serious misgivings about the war I had been sent to fight. I had no way of knowing the truth, back home in the Reich it had all seemed so clear. I served in the Hitler Youth rising to the rank of Oberscharfuhrer, I also did duty as a Flakhelfer, manning an 88mm Flak gun to defend our cities from the British and American gunners. Because of my early military experience, I'd been able to enter the SS as a junior officer and the day that we marched past Reichsfuhrer Himmler on our passing our parade, when I'd been awarded my SS commission was the happiest day of my life. I was a soldier, a warrior, about to be sent to defend the Fatherland from its many enemies.

After only a short time, I already had strong doubts. When I had been defending the Reich it seemed so simple, they were bombing our towns and civilians, and we did our best to stop them. But now I was on foreign soil, fighting against an enemy that seemed unstoppable and after all, they were only defending their soil against us, a foreign invader. Even discounting the morals of our invasion of the Soviet Union, and there were surely many good arguments, we had clearly been misled. Just before leaving Germany, we'd heard so much about the heroic Sixth Army that was sweeping all before it at Stalingrad. Now it seemed that a quarter of a million of our soldiers were either dead, wounded or captives of the Russians, after all of the promises we'd heard, some from the Fuhrer himself, that Stalingrad had been captured. Then there were the stories of the sub-human Russians, cowardly soldiers who would run at the first sight of the German Army and SS. Yet I had seen them advancing in heroic human wave attacks, attacks doomed to fail with fearful casualties and still they came on. In short, I had been lied to. I felt like a mercenary, perhaps like one of the Hessians, German soldiers who'd sold their services to the highest bidder to fight in foreign wars, strangely many for the British. Was that my lot, to roam foreign battlefields bringing death and mayhem?

"Hoffman, one moment, would you accompany me to the monks' camp?"

He was still holding the crucifix, I could hardly believe my eyes when he gave it to Bishop Demchak.

"For you, Bishop. With the apologies of the Fuhrer that it was stolen from you. Our Leader understands it is important to you and your church, we will do our best to protect it in future from looting by our soldiers."

The Bishop looked totally stunned, too astonished to speak. The look on the faces of the monks was amazing, as if Christ had just descended to earth. Von Betternich just nodded and smiled and we walked away.

"What the hell was that all about, Sir?"

"Politics, my young friend. The Fuhrer has had protests

from the Russian Orthodox Church about the theft of that cross, it means a lot to them. The SS is in the process of building an army of Russians who can be loyal to the Reich, the issue of the cross was threatening everything, Reichsfuhrer Himmler was very angry about the whole business. It was vital that we returned it and punished those responsible."

He explained further. "Look, Hoffman, our General Staff persuaded a certain Russian General, Andrey Vlasov, to become involved in aiding the German advance against the rule of Stalin and Bolshevism. Vlasov agreed , he even wrote a memo to our military leaders suggesting cooperation between anti-Stalinist Russians and the German Army. He was taken to Berlin under the protection of our propaganda department. Together with other captured Soviet officers, he has been drafting plans for the creation of a Russian provisional government and the recruitment of a Russian army of liberation under Russian command. He has even begun the foundation of the Russian Liberation Army. Together with some other captured Soviet generals, officers and soldiers, this army's goal will be to overthrow the Soviet state. A lot of our Russian prisoners, as well as soldiers who received Vlasov's propaganda leaflets, are interested in becoming a part of his new army. It was all threatened by the theft of that damned crucifix. Bloody fools, all of them, but you see how important it was to get it back and stop all of this nonsense."

"Perhaps you should have told me, Sir, it would have made things easier to understand."

"You were told everything you needed to know to do the job required of you, Hoffman."

"And if the Reichsfuhrer hadn't needed those Russians to join the SS?"

He shrugged. "Priorities, Hoffman, that's what war is all about."

"What about those officers who were murdered?"

He spread his hands. "But they were criminals, my friend, just a band of thieves, hardly a task for the SD to concern itself with. I am sure the Gestapo would have dealt with them in due course."

I thought of all of the deaths, murders and misery that had occurred so that these people could play their games, games of politics and deception. A Russian army fighting for us, it sounded like a fairy tale. It all seemed such a waste, especially for me when all I wanted to do was to fight.

"Hoffman, are you certain you won't consider joining the SD? You really should consider it. You could make a fine career for yourself and of course, protect your friends. The SD always looks after its own."

"No, thank you, Sir."

"Very well," he smiled, "just remember that I did make the offer, Hoffman."

What the hell did he mean by that, why wouldn't this man just come right out and say what he meant? I felt confused about everything, who was my friend and who was my enemy? Did the SD and the Gestapo have that effect on everyone they associated with?

My misery didn't last long, I looked around the camp and saw my platoon grouped around our half-track. Damnit, I was an SS officer so whoever came up against us was going to have a fight on their hands. I was a member of the finest fighting elite in the world. If that wasn't enough I had a girl who was one of the prettiest girls for five hundred kilometres, or maybe a thousand.

"Right, men, what's the deal with the half-track, are we fuelled up and ready to go for the next action?"

"We're attending to it now, Sir," Mundt said.

"Thank you, Scharfuhrer. And Willy, thank you for taking out Merkel, you saved my life."

"No problem, Sir, the little shit deserved to die."

"That he did, Scharfuhrer."

There was a sudden flurry at the entrance to the camp and a black limousine roared in, followed by a Horch armoured car. My God, I'd forgotten, General, or rather Obergruppenfuhrer und General der Waffen-SS Hausser, commander of the SS Panzer Corps.

"Men, get your kit, look smart, General Hausser is about to inspect us!"

They jumped to it and threw on their kit, webbing,

steel helmets, rifles and machine pistols made ready. Voss was hastily running a rag over the half-track to try and wipe off the worst of the mud and snow, I told him to give it up, he was only making it worse. We were called to attention in the middle of the parade ground.

"Soldiers of the Deutschland Regiment, you have fought well for Kharkov and I'm sorry to say that the fight isn't yet won. The Reds are regrouping to make a final push to take the city in its entirety and there's going to be some hard fighting. The Fuhrer has made it clear that we have to hold the city at all costs. That may be so, but I won't lose this Division the way they lost the Sixth Army at Stalingrad. Believe me, if the situation demands it, I will pull you out of the fight until I believe we have a chance of winning. So make sure that you are completely ready to fight and remember, however it goes, if we do have to pull back at all, it will only be to pull the Russians in so that we can counterattack and wipe them out completely. We are going to wipe the Bolsheviks off the face of the earth!" he shouted.

The men cheered lustily. Then his adjutant gave him a box of medals and one by one, he pulled them out to award to officers and men for bravery on the field. I was half-asleep, I must have been, for Mundt nudged me.

"They're calling you forward, Sir."

"Me?"

"Yes, Sir."

I marched forward and saluted smartly, "Heil Hitler".

"Obersturmfuhrer Hoffman, for bravery on the field in single-handedly destroying an enemy tank with a Panzerfaust, an extraordinary feat of arms, you are awarded the Tank Destroyer Badge and the Iron Cross, Second Class."

He pinned the medal on my chest and handed me the badge, my head was dizzy with exhilaration.

"Congratulations, Hoffman." He shook my hand.

"Thank you, Sir."

"You've got a fine career ahead of you, Hoffman. Try and stay alive to enjoy it."

"Yes, Sir."

I stepped back and saluted, "Heil Hitler," turned on my heel and went back to my platoon. The men were cheering and I felt my cheeks bright red with embarrassment.

"Shut up and behave yourselves," was all I could think to say, it had the immediate effect of making them cheer even louder.

Hausser went on about glorious feats of arms performed by the SS, the ambitious plans for Greater Germany, how we would win the war by superior soldiering and weaponry. I wasn't really listening, I had mixed feelings, pride at my awards and dread for the immediate future. Once again, the position was under threat, Kharkov was under threat and that meant Heide was under threat. Even as the General was driving out of camp, I was trying to work out how I could safeguard the future, for Heide, for my platoon and myself, I was definitely not giving up, not yet anyway. In training, we had been told to keep going forward, always go forward, never give the advantage to your enemy. That's exactly what I planned to do. Once I had worked out exactly who my enemy was and who it wasn't, in the snowy steppes of the Eastern Front, I could indeed go forward, but for now, it was by no means clear.

A week later I was just stepping out of the half-track, we had come in from a particularly hard fight and I felt more tired than ever. I'd lost two men, the regiment had been hit especially hard and our casualties were lying on the snow in rows, waiting for medical attention. Suddenly a military ambulance drove into camp with the distinctive red cross on the side. My spirits leapt, could Heide be assigned here? But when the nurses climbed out she wasn't among them. I walked up to ask them about her.

"Heide Thalberg," they looked worried, "didn't you know?" a nurse asked me, she was the suet pudding-faced woman I had met in the hospital at Kharkov.

"Know what, is she hurt, tell me?"

I trembled with fear waiting to hear the worst.

"No, she wasn't hurt. She was arrested three days ago under a Gestapo Schutzhaft."

Von Betternich, or Wiedel, of course! I hadn't realised at the time but they had obviously already targeted her. Their offer made sense now but stupidly I hadn't understood it at the time. 'Join us and we'll leave her alone.'

I suddenly was aware the nurse was speaking to me. "Herr Hoffman, I have a letter for you."

She was thrusting an envelope into my hand, looking around to make sure that no one saw her do it.

"It is from Heide. She said to get it to you if I could."

I tore the letter open and read it with shaking hands.

My Dearest Jurgen,

They are coming here to arrest me, I haven't much time. I have deceived you, my love, but only out of necessity and fear. The truth is I am Jewish. The name you know me as, Heide Thalberg, I took from a girl killed in an air raid. My true name is Rachel Kaufmann, but I had hoped to be able to live my life under an assumed name without fear of arrest and imprisonment. My father, Aaron Kaufmann, was a well-known communist and disappeared into the camps, I have been on the run ever since his arrest. I now realise that it was only a matter of time before the Gestapo caught up with me. They will of course put me in a concentration camp. My love, you should know that these camps are not simply places of imprisonment, they are death camps, it is most likely that I will be dead by the time you read this letter. Jewish prisoners are often executed on arrival.

Do not grieve for me. It is over. I will remember your face until the moment of my death. Find someone else to love and live your life in as much happiness as we shared in the brief time we were together. It was worth a lifetime.

Rachel

I thanked the nurse and walked away, I knew it was of little use enquiring further, no one ever concerned themselves with concentration camp victims. I desperately tried to think of a way to help her, was there anything I could do? But it was beyond me, stories abounded of people disappearing under the Schutzhaft, even high ranking Nazis had been known to vanish into the camps and for Jews it was invariably their only sentence. Despite what Heide said, or Rachel, I didn't care what her real name was, her religion even less, I would try, but I knew it would certainly be hopeless.

I had to force myself to accept that this was to be my war, never knowing on which side the enemy was or where they came from. All I could do was fight to the very limits of my ability and from this moment on, I had to understand that my enemy would not always be wearing a Russian uniform.

THE END

Lightning Source UK Ltd.
Milton Keynes UK
UKOW052307150512

192641UK00004B/12/P